# ZOMBIES
# IN
# NEW YORK
## AND OTHER
## BLOODY JOTTINGS

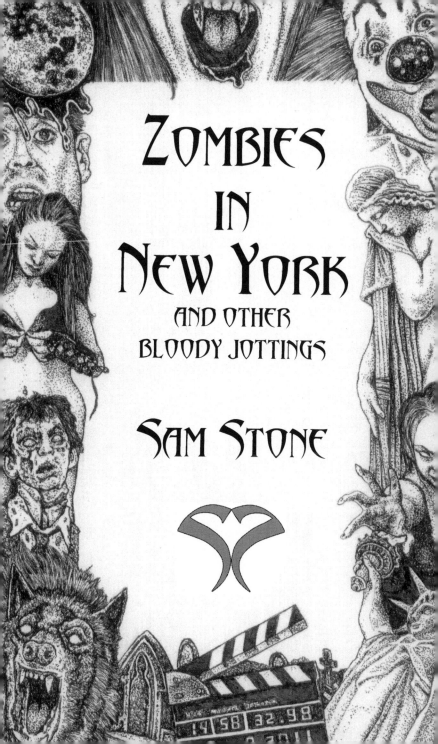

# ZOMBIES IN NEW YORK

## AND OTHER BLOODY JOTTINGS

### SAM STONE

First published in England in 2011 by
Telos Publishing Ltd
17 Pendre Avenue, Prestatyn, Denbighshire, LL19 9SH
www.telos.co.uk

Telos Publishing Ltd values feedback. Please e-mail us with any comments you may have about this book to: feedback@telos.co.uk

ISBN: 978-1-84583-055-7 (paperback)

Editor: David J Howe
Typesetting by Arnold T Blumberg
www.atbpublishing.com
Printed by Good News Press

British Library Cataloguing in Publication Data.
A catalogue record for this book is available from the British Library.

# Contents

# Foreword

## Graham Masterton

There are eight million horror stories in the Naked City … these are just some of them.

Horror and sex are different dialects of the same language. While one talks of pain and suffering and fear, and the other talks of passion and pleasure and excitement, they both speak about taking our physical experiences to the very limit, and surrendering our will to something more powerful than ourselves.

It is not for nothing that the orgasm is also known as 'Le Petit Mort' or 'the little death'. Some women can experience climaxes so intense that they faint, and appear for a few moments to be dead.

Female horror writers are especially literate when it comes to describing the way in which sex and horror are intertwined. They seem less squeamish about visceral detail than their male counterparts, and are able to create monstrosities that are metaphors for some of our darkest, most hideous terrors.

They can not only conceive of Things We Dare Not Even Think About, and gestate them in their minds, they can give birth to them, slippery and kicking and screaming and biting, so vividly brought to life that we can almost *smell* them.

Sam Stone without doubt is a mistress of the grisly

and the glutinous. In every one of the stories in this new collection, she will make you feel that she has not only brought you face to face with your very worst nightmares, she has forced you to touch them and feel them. The thick, malodorous slime; the flaccid skin; the half-broken teeth that snare you like brambles.

Sam Stone writes in blood, rather than ink, as well as sour milk and acid and all kinds of rancorous liquids. She is one of the few horror writers who makes you feel when you have finished her stories that you need to wash your hands. Twice.

One of her secrets is that she is completely up-front about sex and lust and unusual desires. There are none of the euphemisms that a male horror writer might have used to describe (for instance) having intercourse with a bristly red-haired werewolf; or the agony of being fellated by a succubus. When a woman is split open to reveal her internal organs, as well as the unborn baby that she is carrying, Sam describes the scene without flinching.

She never lets us turn our faces away, and never holds back. As she herself says, she deplores the way that women horror writers are almost always associated with horror/romance. When Sam Stone writes horror, she writes horror, and not only her readers but even the characters in her stories are liable to lose their breakfast.

One of the most interesting aspects of this collection is Sam's candid description of how she learned to construct horror stories, which will be extremely useful to anybody setting out to write about the darker side of life (and death). She is remarkably candid in the way that she tells us how each of her stories came to be written, and what they mean to her. Older writers like myself like to keep our stage secrets to ourselves, in locked boxes, and not reveal how we make you shudder, so Sam's openness is very refreshing. Metaphorically speaking, she saws the lady in half and then shows us how she did it: by sawing the lady in half, with all the blood and agony that went with it.

There is no doubt that much of this collection is very horrific and disturbing. My advice: read first, eat later. But it is a fascinating insight into a writing talent at work, and I believe that we can look forward to seeing Sam Stone develop into a major influence in the realm of blood and shadows and things that wake you up, wide-eyed, in the middle of the night.

That, of course, is always supposing that your eyelids haven't been sewn shut.

*Graham Masterton*

# How My Mind Works

When I first considered writing a short story collection my initial thought was that I would write a selection of Lucrezia's stories as a tie-in for my *Vampire Gene* series. By then I'd already written two stories and had ideas for others. These would be based on the missing 200 years that Lucrezia Borgia casually dismisses in *Futile Flame*, the second book in the series. I knew that some of my readers were curious about her and wanted to know more, and I did too. She's a fascinating character with many flaws. That is why the first section in this collection is dedicated to her stories and, as you'll see, they are chronologically ordered to give a little insight into exactly what she was up to during those 'missing' years.

The second part, 'Other Bloody Jottings', is quite different. This contains stories that have come to me in a variety of different ways, through varied forms of inspiration. Some were commissioned, some had loose briefs, and some just *had* to be written. They are also very unique. I decided to focus this collection on a desire to develop my writing in different directions, exploring several genres and styles in the process. Within these pages you will find horror, psychological thriller, fantasy, urban fantasy and crime stories. Some have supernatural events underpinning them, and others are completely explainable in the real world. As well as this I've been flexing my favourite muscle – exploring human

9

and inhuman psychology, examining how different individuals react to addiction, obsession, lust and death.

Writing is not just something I do. It's something I *have* to do. I love it, and want to improve and gain experience along the way. This is why I decided to return to university as a 'mature' student – hate that term – to improve and hone my skills. When I was at university, my screenwriting lecturer, Les Smith, taught me four rules of writing, these rules could be applied in either scripts or prose and it was all about character motivation. The character had to want something specific, that is: love, money, fame, sex, for example.

Character Motivation
1) What the character wants
2) What's the problem
3) What the character does to solve the problem
4) Resolution

Using these four rules was a way of keeping a plot focused; they could help you consider the motivational drive of your character. I don't always take it so literally now – but I do find myself considering constantly if a character's actions are 'worked for', because believability is what makes a story work. You can have the best plot in the world, but if your protagonists aren't created with enough depth, whatever they do won't make the story convincing. Hopefully I have achieved my goal on that score and you will be convinced by the claustrophobic horror filling the streets in *Zombies in New York*; you will tremble with fear as a succubus stalks the Moulin Rouge feeding on wealthy customers in *Ameline*; you may cringe as we explore the secrets hidden within *The Toymaker's House*; perhaps you will laugh in comedic terror at the clownish deaths caused by my *Clown Addict*; or maybe you will enjoy the erotic exploits of Lucrezia as she indulges in bestial lust in *Red*.

Whatever you like, there's something here for you, and I've taken this opportunity to also explain, after each story, where those ideas came from and what motivated me as a writer.

*Sam Stone*
*November 2010*

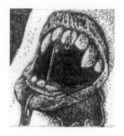

# Lucrezia's Stories

*Futile Flame*, the second novel in my *Vampire Gene* series, is the story of the vampire Lucrezia Borgia. The first section of this short story collection is dedicated to this fascinating *femme fatale*. Never good, but not always bad. Lucrezia's stories explore and explain some of the years that were alluded too, but not explained, in the novel and give an insight into some of what really makes her tick.

You may notice she enjoys a good mystery. If she's feeling really engaged, she might even help the police solve the crime.

But what really motivates Lucrezia? Is it lust, greed, loneliness or just plain selfishness? I'll let you decide …

# AMELINE

Ameline was lying on a bed in one of the back rooms when I arrived.

'What happened?' I asked.

Just one look at her told me that something peculiar had definitely gone down: she was so white she looked like a corpse. Even close up I could barely hear the faint rasp of her weary breath. She looked thinner than the last time I'd seen her, just a week ago, and there was a weird odour emanating from her skin that mingled with the excretions of her last customer. She smelt of sex, sweat and semen – normal smells. But there was something else underneath these heady odours and it hadn't ever been there before. It was a strong, pungent sick smell and it seemed to be reflected in the slightly yellow tinge that coloured her skin.

'I don't know,' said Oller. 'One minute she was fine, the next like this.'

'What's she done this evening?'

'Her usual performance and then a few clients …'

'Who?'

Oller shrugged. 'Mostly regulars. Nothing unusual has happened.'

I pulled her bodyguard, Philippe, in and queried him until he was a nervous wreck. I wasn't sure at all that I believed there had been nothing 'unusual'. Ameline's condition was truly strange.

'Something happened,' I said. 'It's obvious. So why are you lying to me, Philippe?'

'I swear,' said Philippe, 'I was outside the door the whole time. She never called out and the only noises coming from the room were the normal sounds. In fact she …' Philippe paused, looking a little embarrassed, which was odd considering the job he did. '… she was enjoying herself a lot with the last one.'

'What?' That was a surprise.

Part of Ameline's appeal was her innocent appearance. She gave off virginal vibes to all the clients, and mostly all they wanted was for her to play that role. So screams of pleasure wouldn't normally have been on the menu. Actually, Ameline had made a career out of being cold and unresponsive. Mostly she just lay down, opened her legs, and let the client get on with it.

I sent both Oller and Philippe out after they supplied me with a list of Ameline's clients. There was only one creature that could elicit pleasure from a whore as practiced as Ameline. It would have to be another vampire, and I planned to investigate all the names on the list.

I stripped the sheets from Ameline and began to examine her body. Her arms were like thin stalks, the veins prominent but definitely full of blood. I looked in all the usual erotic places, but there was no sign of a bite anywhere. Not that one would have been visible to the naked eye. Vampires know how to cover their tracks. However, since I was one of them I knew I'd recognise the signs.

'I don't know,' I said after throwing a blanket over her naked body. 'There just doesn't seem to be anything obvious at all. She's unconscious at the moment, didn't even wake as I checked her over.'

'We have one of her regulars outside,' said Oller. 'I don't suppose ...'

I glared at him.

'Right. That's what I thought,' he quickly agreed. 'She's on rest now for a day or two?'

'She's on rest until she gets better, Oller,' I said. 'Or we find out what's up with her. One thing is for sure, whatever this ailment is, the affliction was sudden.'

'Maybe it's some kind of influenza,' suggested Philippe.

Oller shrugged. He had no interest in the girls other than their capacity for earning money for him. 'What am I going to do about the aristo outside?'

'Offer him another girl. Chantal is nice.'

It was a wild night, the dancers were doing the Can-Can and the patrons were drinking heavily. I blended with the shadows and watched them move around before I saw a new client coming back out from behind the stage. He'd heard about Ameline but he wasn't too upset when Chantal linked his arm, cosying up to him. She led him through the crowd, then pulled back a curtain that revealed a doorway. I knew this led to another set of private rooms and the dungeons. Some of the patrons enjoyed being restricted while the girl serviced them. Knowing what I knew of men, I realised that this particular fetish helped them shirk any responsibility for their actions.

Joseph Oller had already broken his baby teeth in club management when we met. He owned the Paris Olympia. He started putting money into the building of the Moulin Rouge in 1889 but fell foul of a bad investment. That's when I came into it, offering the money he needed with very little interference. I just wanted some say over the girls. They had to be treated well, given security and kept as clean as possible. It was an offer he couldn't refuse.

I went back into the other corridor behind the stage and into Ameline's room again and found her awake. Someone had brought her a jug of red wine, a platter of cheese and a hunk of bread.

'Lucrezia!' she said and tried to smile.

'My dear girl, how are you feeling?'

'I don't know. Not very well really, and I had the strangest dream …'

'Ameline, do you remember anything peculiar happening tonight?'

Ameline's face was so pale that, but for her dark hair and dark brown eyes, it might have been hard to distinguish her from the crisp white pillow on which she lay. I raised her up and encouraged her to sip some of the wine.

'I don't remember anything about tonight at all,' Ameline said eventually. 'Except coming off stage and there being a client waiting. It was a usual night … I think.'

'Never mind. Your colour is beginning to return to your face. Whatever it is, I'm sure it will pass.'

I helped Ameline sit and passed her a cup of wine. Then I left her, promising to return to check on her health again the next day.

Before the 24 hours had passed, however, Oller sent for me again. Another girl was sick. By the end of the week, almost all of the girls had experienced this strange lethargy.

'I had this dream …' Chantal said. 'It felt like something was sucking the life right from my soul.'

Chantal crossed herself; she was a God-fearing and superstitious girl by nature. Not that it made

17

any difference to her choice of job as a whore. I got a list of Chantal's clients and we cross-checked them with Ameline's for similarities, but there weren't any. None of those that Chantal had serviced had been with Ameline.

'We have our own,' explained Alicia as she lay in her bed looking pale and wan. 'We never try to attract other girls' customers. It's an unspoken rule.'

By now Ameline was feeling better, so I wasn't too concerned. It was as though the girls were just passing around a virus of some sort. Also, that strange smell that had wafted from Ameline's skin, didn't seem to be on the other girls, so whatever it was, they were suffering more minor symptoms.

'It will pass,' I told Oller. 'Just let each one rest until she recovers.'

'And Ameline?'

'She seems fit enough now. Back to work tonight I think, but let's limit the number of clients.'

Oller laughed. 'We always do …'

I stayed at the club that night disguised as one of the dancers. I'd been known to enjoy a client or two when the mood took me, though I usually picked them carefully. No bad-breathed aristocrats with poor body hygiene for me. I preferred the young students who sneaked in. They couldn't pay for the pleasure of having me with money, but I always made them pay with a small amount of blood. Then I'd send each boy home, no longer a virgin. He'd remember his experience with a great deal of fondness but would totally forget that I'd drunk his blood as he fucked me.

There was an aristocrat waiting beside the stage for Ameline. I recognised him as one of the regulars at the club. He was young and good-looking, a rarity among men with money.

'Hello,' I said, appearing beside him; he smelt delicious.

He looked around surprised.

'Hello. I haven't seen you before.'

'Lucrezia,' I told him before he could ask my name. 'I'm new and I'm very exclusive.'

The aristocrat looked me over carefully, 'Your hair is pretty,' he said: I was blonde of course, and that was rare in the club.

'Can I do *anything* for you?' I asked, staring into his eyes until he could barely remember his name.

'*Oui.*'

Of course, he couldn't possibly refuse.

I led him back behind the stage and saw Philippe standing in front of Ameline's door just as the music for the Can-Can started up in earnest. Philippe looked at me with round eyes, but said nothing as he saw me take the man into the room next door. I guess he thought I was interrogating Ameline's clients, and that wasn't too far from the truth. I intended to examine as many as possible before the night was out. If there was something strange happening in the Moulin Rouge, then I was determined to find out what it was.

'Was that Lucrezia?' I heard Oller say as I closed the door.

'*Oui*,' Philippe said. 'She's with Count Du Plessis.'

Oller laughed. 'Not her usual type …'

'Nor she his … He normally only goes with Ameline.'

'I'm sure she knows what she's doing,' Oller said.

Du Plessis was removing his clothing before I even turned around. He couldn't hear the whispers of the two men, unlike me, and so the Count keenly stripped and lay down.

Half an hour later he staggered from my room as though drunk: blood loss makes you feel light-headed and disorientated. I'd taken as much as I dared from him, as his blood was clean and delicious. Then I came out of the room shortly afterwards, leaving it as neat as before. I hadn't spilt a drop, and even the Count's crisp white shirt remained unmarked at the throat as I'd carefully licked his wounds until they closed and disappeared. Of course I'd always be able to see those scars, hidden so subtly under the surface, but they would never be visible to the human eye.

'Having fun?' asked Oller.

I raised an eyebrow at him. Strange how Oller never realised that both he and Philippe were Renfields. It was part of the fun though, making the humans believe they actually had free will to consort with a vampire.

'How's Ameline?'

'On a roll. She seems to be full of energy now. Her act went down well and she's just changing, ready to be visited.'

'Good,' I said. 'Remember, only one or two clients tonight. New ones. At least until I've checked out all of her regulars.

Later, I noticed Ameline among the crowd. Her black hair was flowing around her shoulders like liquid night. Her normal fair skin was vampirically pale. She wore a red satin dress that fell off her shoulders, showing the fine flesh that barely covered her bones. Pale, thin and glowing; you would swear she was one of my kind. *Curious.*

I fell back into the shadows as she chose her client, an overweight banker whom I knew well. He was new to her, though, which meant that Oller, like a good servant, had passed on my instructions to the letter. Despite that, my nerves tingled.

*Something was very wrong with Ameline.*

She took the banker into the back of the club, her black eyes glowing with a feral hunger. The expression of lust on her face was something that could only be described as alien. I followed.

Sending Philippe away, I waited outside her room.

'Take that dress off,' said the banker. 'I've always wanted you. I need to see you naked.'

Ameline complied. 'And you?' she asked. 'Will you take off your clothes too? I like a man with substance.'

They kissed, and I heard Ameline's satin dress fall to the floor with a tiny rustle of expensive fabric. After that the sounds inside seemed normal at first, but then I heard what must have intrigued Philippe the night she fell ill. Ameline was having a lot of fun. I heard their vigorous fucking slamming the headboard back against the wall and smiled. Maybe the whore in her had finally come out, because even with me, Ameline had never shown this much enthusiasm.

'Harder …' she cried, and the banker gave it, his huge bulk clearly not holding him back.

Satisfied that all was well, I began to walk away.

A strange squeal pierced the air. I stopped halfway down the corridor. The sound came again, and I think I'll remember it for all of my immortal life. It was as if a pig was being tortured, and I knew then that the banker was no longer having fun. Not at all.

I tried Ameline's door; found it locked. So I threw myself hard against it. I may look small and fragile, but I am, in actuality, incredibly strong. The door gave quickly and I was faced with the sight of Ameline giving the banker oral sex. You would think that there would be nothing abnormal in that in a brothel, but you'd be very wrong. The banker's face was one of sheer ecstasy, yet the sounds that slipped from his lips were squeals of absolute agony. With every suck and pull from Ameline's mouth, the banker grew thinner. She was ingesting him, taking all of his bulk, his strength; and, I suspected, she was swallowing his soul as well.

'Ameline!' I said and she turned her blank eyes to me.

I stepped back, strangely intimidated by the sight before me, but more by Ameline herself. She was vacant. Soulless. The black pupil had completely consumed the soft brown colour of her irises. Her expression was monstrously cold and so very evil.

There was only one kind of creature I'd ever heard of that was like that, and I had thought such beings were a myth. Just goes to show that even a 400 year old vampire doesn't know all that the world is capable of hiding.

Ameline was a succubus.

She loosened her mouth, releasing the man, and he fell back, flaccid, on the bed. Then Ameline turned to me and opened her jaws. An animal screech emitted from her blackened maw. Her mouth looked like a vile parody of a vagina, only it had rows and rows of rotted points that had previously been perfectly good teeth. It was like the mouth of a sandworm I'd once seen dissected. The gaping hole opened and expanded before my gaze, impossibly wide and definitely not human. Inside the mouth, a tongue that was no longer just a tongue but shaped like a fully engorged penis, protruded between her vulva-like lips. She swished the member around her face. Black semen or some other vile ichor leaked from the tip, and the smell of it was putrid.

I came further into the room, my hand covering my nose.

'Oh, Ameline …'

Ameline shrieked again. There was nothing of her left behind those eyes, not even recognition of me, her one-time lover. But then, perhaps that was why. Ameline *was* empty. Hadn't I always known that? It had taken years of abuse, of lying still, allowing others to use her, and never reacting whatever they did. All that Ameline had ever been had faded away and was lost. It had been leeched out of her. There were two kinds of whores; those who enjoyed what they did and those who survived it. Ameline had always been one of the latter, so why hadn't I seen this coming? All that emptiness had to be filled in some way eventually.

Philippe and Oller ran into the room as Ameline turned her attention back to the banker. Her gentle touch hardened his penis, and Ameline's repugnant lips suckled him once more. The man sobbed as all three of us looked on; it was all he seemed capable of doing while those sharp decaying teeth buried deeper into his flesh.

For the first time in my life, I didn't know what to do.

So, I let her eat him – he was destroyed anyway. It

was the worst thing I'd ever witnessed. Half way through the final stage, when the banker was finally dead, or had at least passed out with shock and pain, Ameline jerked and vomited on him. The fluid she ejected was like acid, it melted the muscles and bones, and then Ameline licked and slurped up the sticky residue until what remained of the banker was swallowed down. There was nothing left of him but a putrefying stench in the room and a revolting stain on the sheets.

Philippe and Oller backed out of the room long before it was done. I heard Philippe heaving outside. Oller fell back against the wall by the door and slid down until his feet splayed out into the corridor. He lay there in shock, listening to the horrible gulping sounds of the banker being ingested.

I stayed with Ameline until the end; I had to see how bad it would get. When she finished, she lay back on the bed and, with a final glance in my direction, slept, looking like an innocent child. The residue of melted fat, blood and skin left a slimy film on her lips and chin. That was the worst thing of all.

The following morning, Ameline appeared normal again. The colour was back in her cheeks, her eyes, mouth, lips were as before. Even her body had filled out a little, looking less gaunt. She remembered nothing of the night before, and if I hadn't seen it with my own eyes I would have found it hard to believe that she had consumed a whole man through her tiny mouth.

But something in her eyes told me her appearance was a lie. Maybe it was the slight flick of her eyelids – there seemed now to be an extra set that came down over her eyes seconds before she blinked. It was weirdly reptilian and I knew that only I could see them. The succubus was in there and it was lying dormant until the next time it needed to feed, but I couldn't let that happen again. I couldn't shake the feeling that had paralysed me as Ameline had turned her blank and horrible face in my direction. It had taken all my willpower not to run into those vile arms and allow that poisonous member to penetrate my soul. I'd seen the dark abyss of death in her gaze and I'd craved it.

So, I took an axe and chopped her up into little pieces.

Those strange lizard eyes stared at me half closed as the first blow fell. Her pale pink lips curved up in a mocking smile as the second cleaved her chest. Her blood sprayed the walls, splattered the sheets on which she lay but she made no sound at all. I knew with each blow that Ameline or whatever was left of her didn't fear death. She was a soulless empty creature.

I felt nothing, only a terrible vacuum.

Philippe helped me burn her remains out on some wasteland. He didn't speak. He was a man of few words anyway, but he and Oller were in shock. I was sure that neither of them would ever forget this horrible night.

Afterwards we returned to the Moulin Rouge.

Lined up in the club, prior to opening for the night, all the girls were quiet and pale. I saw Chantal and the other girls who'd also grown sick and then miraculously recovered and walked the line sniffing and scrutinising them. They smelt normal, but I remained suspicious. I thought it odd that they must have heard the screams of the banker but not one had come to investigate, and their doors had remained closed as Philippe and I passed by with Ameline's remains. Even so, they were showing no signs of changing as Ameline had done. Yet.

'You'll have to keep your eye on them,' I told Philippe and Oller. 'The first sign of anything strange, you know what to do.'

Both men stared at me but I had no doubt that they would carry out my instructions. I passed Philippe the axe. It was still stained with Ameline's blood.

# AUTHOR'S NOTES

*Ameline* is an original story written for this collection. This was a tale that had been working around my brain since my partner, David, and I visited Paris in 2009 and we saw the exterior of the Moulin Rouge. The area of Montmartre is deliberately decadent and we had fun wandering around some of the sex shops looking at PVC and leather clothing of which they had an abundance.

I like my stories to have some basis in reality and so I researched the origins of the Moulin Rouge and discovered Joseph Oller. Anything said about him in the story is completely fictional, however, and I have only used his connection and ownership of the club as a historical foundation.

Exploring the darkness of humanity through the world of the supernatural is a fascination for me. Generally there is more horror in reality. The exploitation of women through the ages gives rise to this, taking such terrible forms as child abuse, enforced prostitution and arranged marriages. (As a modern woman I can't imagine anything worse than being married to someone you neither know nor love.)

So the idea of *Ameline* raised questions. What would it be like to be treated as a commodity your entire life? Perhaps in order to survive you have to stop caring, stop feeling, or wanting something better. What would it be like to be so completely empty and soulless? Would we need to fill the void in order to survive?

Ameline was one such person. She was dead inside and those closest to her didn't notice or just didn't care.

When there's nothing left, an empty shell becomes a living host. What better demon, given her profession, to fill that void, than a succubus.

# FOOL'S GOLD

The blood was what first alerted me to the problem. It just *smelt* wrong. So I dipped my finger in the congealing pool and lifted some to my lips. It tasted like milk with all the cream and goodness sucked out. It was missing something. At that point I wasn't sure what.

I'd been experimenting with blood for years. It was, after all, crucial to my survival. I'd realised that there were several types of blood, and each had a unique flavour. My favourite, and most rare, was later called Rhesus negative. It had a citric bite to it that appealed more to my once-human taste than the sweeter 'O' positive – the common variety. Of course, when I was starving I didn't really care. But once I found Rhesus, it became a luxury I occasionally indulged in.

The dead girl's blood, though, lacked nutrition. All the integrity had been removed. I was hungry, but I knew after one taste, that this thin, watery substance would never sustain me.

'Mmmm. Interesting,' I murmured.

I heard a Peeler's whistle in the distance. Someone had raised the alarm. The girl must have died screaming. Not surprising really since her guts had been ripped out. It was obvious that the throat wound was there to shut her up; I'd have done the same.

I blended into the cold, damp fog and slipped into the shadows hanging around the nearest house as two Bobbies rounded the corner. For a moment their appearance was supernatural. The denseness of the air clung to the uniforms until one of them almost skidded in the rapidly spreading spillage and they came to a halt before the body. I shrank back deeper into the mist: it wouldn't be good for them to find something like me at the scene. They stared at the body for a long moment, as though paralysed, and then one of them turned his head and abruptly vomited on the floor. The other took off his tall hat and rubbed his forehead while wrinkling his nose in disgust at the odour his colleague had created.

'Jeee-zuss, Hobbs,' he said. 'That's a sorry mess if ever I saw one.'

Hobbs dry heaved, his hands on his thighs.

'Pull yourself together.'

The Peeler who'd spoken placed his hat back on his head and pulled out his pocket-watch. He tutted, then began tapping his foot impatiently until his weak-stomached partner pulled himself upright, his trembling hand outstretched to the wall beside him as he steadied himself.

'I'm all right,' Hobbs murmured. 'Just took me by surprise is all …'

'Well you'd better get over here and help me, 'cos I'm not examining her alone,' the other replied.

Shaking, Hobbs wiped his mouth with the back of his hand.

'Yes, Bennett. I'm going to help … like I said, just shock is all.'

Bennett waited impatiently as Hobbs fiddled with his tie, tugged his black jacket down and brushed invisible marks from his uniform while trying to compose himself. He'd already lost face with his senior colleague; he didn't want to lose any more.

'So, what d'you think?' asked Hobbs.

Bennett crouched down; the air billowed around him as he unwittingly mimicked my gesture as he touched a chubby finger to the blood. 'Still warm. He's nearby I reckon. Bet the murdering bastard is watching us even now.'

Hobbs grew pale. Self-consciously I looked around. I hadn't even thought of that and I wondered now if the killer had seen me kneel down and taste his victim's blood. Careless.

'Same bloke?' Hobbs asked, stepping forward with renewed curiosity, all sign of his earlier revulsion dissipated. A sickening gleam came into his eyes as he began to survey the crime scene.

'I think so,' said Bennett, his mouth set into a thin line of distaste as he studied the woman's wounds.

'D'you think the papers will print our names?'

Bennett turned his head and glared at Hobbs for a moment. Hobbs didn't notice as he moved closer to the body.

Her throat was severed by two deep cuts, as though the first strike had failed to silence her. Her blood had dripped down her low-cut dress and over her bosom. It drew a line down to her abdomen where a long, uneven wound ripped through the faded and soiled dress, leaving a gaping, bloody hole. I'd noticed that some of her organs had been removed. The left kidney and a large part of her uterus were missing. The killer must have taken them for some perverse reason of his own.

'This don't look the same as the other one we found,' Hobbs sulked. 'I think it's a different killer.'

'No,' Bennett answered. 'Look. It's the knife wounds on the neck … Bet he was disturbed on the other one, that's why he done this one.'

Bennett turned the woman's head. The left side of her face was slashed. The knife had cut so deep that part of her skull was visible. A clump of hair and flesh was sliced away right down to her eyebrow, where her eye stared sightlessly from its socket. A thick red jell slipped from the eye and down her cheek last a glutinous, bloody tear.

'Fuck!' Bennett gasped, pulling back his hand in

disgust.

Hobbs looked on dumbly as Bennett began to blow his whistle. In response, several running feet could be heard from all sides of Whitechapel, and soon more Peelers poured into Mitre Square.

I pulled a hood over my blonde curls and slipped away into the fog as the police surrounded the dead girl. No-one noticed me, and if they had, all they would have seen was a petite woman in a black cloak – nothing like the killer they were focused on finding. But then, appearances could be deceptive.

'Extra! Extra! Read all about it! "Double Event" as two more killed in Whitechapel.'

I paid the newsboy and tucked the paper under my arm before crossing the busy street to a small park where I sat on my favourite bench. The fog from the previous night had lifted and the late September sun was shining weakly. I placed the paper across my knees and looked around. The park was quiet. It was as though the locals were afraid to be out alone, even in broad daylight. London was in a state of panic.

I shook the paper, straightening out the wrinkles with a small, gloved hand. 'Jack' had struck again. This time they were calling it, 'The Double Event'. There had been two deaths that night. Elizabeth Stride, found in Dutfield's Yard, and apparently the woman I'd found in Mitre Square had been called Catherine Eddowes.

*Jack claims two more in a double event. Four women dead so far …*

The newspaper referred to them as women of 'questionable virtue' as though the common term 'whore' or the slightly subtler 'prostitute' were too offensive for their readers. I looked back at the street again where the newsboy was rapidly selling his stack to passers-by. Humans loved the macabre. This was the most exciting news they'd had in a long time and the virtuous had no need to fear. They could hide at night, peeping through their shuttered windows while the destitute, like Annie Chapman, Jack's second victim, became nothing more than a ghoulish fascination. Perhaps tour guides would soon be touting for the 'Walk of Fear' to New World visitors and morbid locals.

Through the ages, serial killers had never been my concern, but one that could change the composition of blood, that was something else entirely. And so I had returned to the scene, shortly after the police took away Catherine Eddowes' body, and scraped up some of the dried blood that stained the pavement.

Back in my lab I'd mixed the blood with water to create a soft paste and smeared it roughly on a slide. Under the keen lens of the microscope, the blood had revealed some interesting facts. It was decomposing faster than usual because, as I'd expected, the composite had changed. The red blood cells were severely depleted. This was the most severe case of hypochromic anaemia I'd ever seen. One of the main minerals that helped the red blood cells reproduce, iron, was completely absent from Eddowes' blood. This accounted for the thin, tasteless, watery remains. If Eddowes' injuries hadn't killed her, then the iron deficiency would have.

'Miss Collins.'

I looked up from the paper and found my lawyer approaching across the park.

'Good morning, Mr Perry,' I answered smiling.

'Good Lord, you aren't reading that gruesome stuff, are you?'

'One has to keep abreast with the times. Besides it is important to be reminded that the streets of London are no fit place for a woman at night,' I continued, giving him the 'expected' answer.

'What a sensible young woman you are Miss Collins. Really one would believe at times that you held the wisdom of years in your youthful person.'

I smiled politely at his patronising tone.

'Of course, I know that your father was a doctor of some note and I understand he did some pioneering research. I suppose that explains your interest in such things.'

'Indeed, Mr Perry. Blood has long interested me,' I remarked with a slight smile as I stood, leaving the newspaper on the bench.

'May I escort you home?' Perry said, offering his arm.

I glanced down at the paper, which was still open on the story. *Inspector Frederick Abberline said, 'We have many leads and several suspects that are helping us with our enquiries ...'*

Interesting. Now I knew Freddie was involved, I just *had* to shadow the police investigation. It would assuage my curiosity if nothing else, and I'll confess to having felt a little nervous knowing there was a monster in town that was capable of contaminating my food source.

'Miss Collins?'

I looked back at Perry and found him scrutinising me carefully. Obediently I slipped my hand into the crook of his elbow. We walked slowly away from the park.

'Mr Perry, have you any news on the offer I made to purchase the house in Covent Garden?' I asked, quickly changing the subject.

'Why yes. That is precisely why I was so pleased to see you.'

'I don't understand why this is of interest to you,' Frederick Abberline said.

He was sitting behind his desk trying hard to look professional, but I noticed the slight tremble of his tightly-clasped hands as he placed them before him. Oh yes, Freddie would tell me everything I needed to know. I smiled.

'Freddie, you know I've always been curious about your work. Do you really have suspects?'

'Miss Collins … Lucy. I can't discuss police matters with you. That would be highly inappropriate.'

Frederick kept his face serious; it was part of his appeal. When he was angry with me he always took on the austere countenance of a bank manager, and he had good cause to be annoyed. I hadn't been near him for months.

'Freddie …' I moved closer, touched his arm.

'Oh my God, Lucy,' he cried as his composure broke.

His hands reached for me as he tried to rise from his chair to take me in his arms.

I stayed him with one hand on his shoulder, pressing him firmly back into his seat.

'No.'

'When? When will you take from me again?' he begged.

I'd fed from Freddie several times over the years. We'd met on the streets before his promotion to Inspector. He'd mistaken me for one of the local whores until I bit him and drew his sweet nectar into my mouth for the first time. Frederick was the walking blood bank of my favourite brand. My luxury. My Rhesus donor. Though I'd made the mistake of revisiting him too often and now he was somewhat addicted to my bite; he craved it, and unlike my other donors, he always remembered it.

'Soon, Freddie. But you know it can't be too often,' I soothed.

'Tonight, please …'

I looked into his eyes, knowing if I wanted to I could take every little bit of information about the case directly from his mind. But that wouldn't be much fun and I was starving; I hadn't eaten in days.

'All right. You help me and I will help you.'

He pulled me to him and I let him kiss me. I didn't remind him about Emma, his wife. That would have been too cruel, even for me.

I walked the streets of Whitechapel every night for more than a month, but all remained quiet. It seemed that Jack's frantic killings had ceased and it wasn't long before the whores of the city fell into a false sense of security once more. Even so, many had ceased doing trade out in the open. As I searched the city, I rarely saw the frantic rutting in the back alleys and corners of quiet streets anymore. The girls were taking clients back to their tiny hovels now. The occasional drunk and the Bobby on the beat were the only midnight occupants of the mausoleum streets.

'What are you doing out on your own, Miss?'

The Peeler was standing under a gaslight watching me quietly. He looked jaded. He was holding a small lump of rock, which he turned over and over in his fingers in a subconscious gesture to allay his boredom. The light hit the rock as it moved; it had the shine of precious metal.

'Nice respectable lady like you shouldn't be out here with that monster on the loose,' he continued.

'I'm not afraid of monsters,' I answered quietly.

'Here. Where you from? That's a nice little accent you got there. French are you?'

'Italian.' I smiled walking towards him. I was suddenly very hungry.

'Long ways from home then?'

'Yes.'

He continued to play with the rock as I approached him. I reached out and held his hand briefly, taking the stone from his compliant fingers. His mouth opened and froze in an 'O' shape as he met my gaze. I knew the gaslight would make the green in my eyes seem like cool fire.

'What is this?' I asked, opening my hand to gaze down at the rock.

His paralysis broke.

'Fool's gold,' he smiled. 'There are bits of the stuff scattered all over the city.'

The rock gleamed. It was hard, with shiny brass-yellow crystals peppering its surface. It looked and felt like a gold nugget.

'It's iron see,' continued the Bobby. 'Something happens to it to make it look like gold. Then a "fool" might believe it's the real thing.'

I knew what fool's gold was, but I let him speak.

'… and you're no fool are you?' I flirted. 'You say there have been many of these found around the city?'

'Yes. The Chief says it's because of the meteor shower we had a few months ago. D'you remember that, Miss?'

I nodded. I remembered the night well. It was in mid May, I was out hunting when the sky lit up and tiny balls of flame flew across London. I knew instantly that a small meteor had entered the Earth's atmosphere and was breaking up. It was quite a display, reminding me of the fireworks on Queen Victoria's coronation day.

'Reckon we are only just finding the remains of it now,' he continued. 'Keep it if you like.'

I looked at the Bobby. He wasn't very old, maybe 25. I sniffed the foggy, damp air around him. Despite the freezing, autumn weather, his body smelt warm in his big coat. I could feel the rush of blood in his veins as he noticed my scrutiny. I dropped the hood of my cloak back off my golden hair and felt the gaslight touch my scalp.

'You're a very pretty lady,' he said quietly. 'If you don't mind me saying.'

'I find you very appealing too.' I was famished and the pull of his blood made tiny hairs stand up on the back of my neck.

I stepped back out of the halo of the gaslight into the shadows as my teeth began to lengthen. The Bobby followed me meekly. I slipped the nugget of fool's gold into a pocket inside my cloak and took his hand. His body began to shudder as he felt the waves of blood-lust trickle into his skin. I pulled him into a nearby alley and pressed him against the wall, rubbing my body against him in a desperate gesture as I sniffed at his throat again. His blood smelt clean. One had to be so careful these days. His hands were inside my cloak and all over my body. I let him touch; it meant nothing to me as long as I fulfilled my needs. I felt his hand lifting my skirt, and he spun us around so that I was now against the wall. With one hand, he reached down and unbuttoned himself, then yanked roughly at my undergarments until they fell around my ankles. He knelt then, helping me disentangle one leg from my pantaloons. He obviously used the whores on a regular basis and knew just what to do.

He lifted my legs, bracing me against the wall, and wrapped them around his waist, pushing inside me as hard and fast as he could. I let him rut for a moment, while I licked his throat. He shuddered at my touch. His sweat tasted of salt. I could feel the blood rushing beneath the skin, throbbing there. I listened to its call until I couldn't bear it any more. When I grew bored of having my back pounded into the hard wall, I sank my fangs deep into his straining neck. I sighed with pleasure. He went flaccid immediately and his member slipped uselessly from me. He slumped against me. I was powerfully excited, and I gripped my legs hard around him as I swallowed the blood I needed until I felt the strength leave his limbs. Then I put one leg down to steady us as he weakened. His eyes fluttered closed, and his mouth smiled in pleasure, as I gently licked at his throat. My saliva closed the puncture marks and stilled the flow of blood.

I propped him up against the wall and kneeled

between his legs, buttoning him up before I left him. He'd wake with a headache and the vague memory of having been with a whore in the alley – nothing more. There wouldn't be any marks by morning.

I pulled my cloak tight around me as I walked away and I felt the fool's gold bounce against my leg. I took the rock from my pocket. Smelt it. Licked it. Iron: one of the flavours I liked most in blood, and, let's be honest, after 300 years of living on it; I am a bit of a connoisseur. I knew there had to be a link. Iron was missing from the victim's blood and fool's gold was being found around the city. But what did it mean?

I'd persuaded Freddie Abberline to let me see the body of the other victim, Elizabeth Stride. There had been a distinct lack of iron in her blood too, but not as much as Catherine Eddowes, which confirmed the police assumption that the killer had been disturbed while working on the first one. But I couldn't explain to Freddie what I knew, even though I wanted to help him solve the crime. The thing was, if this person – and I suspected it wasn't human at all – was able to drain one of the most important nutrients from blood, then its very existence was a threat to my future. I had every intention of finding him or her before the police did. There was only room for one monster in London and that was going to be me.

'There was another one last night,' Freddie said, as we lay naked in the large double bed of my suite at the Waldorf.

'It was the worst I've yet seen.'

'Mutilated?' I asked licking his throat gently. The bite wounds in his neck healed and faded until two pale pink scars remained.

'Yes,' Freddie sighed, as he snuggled deeper into my arms, 'and … he'd slit her throat until he'd almost cut her head clean off.'

'I see.'

On 9 November, 'Jack' had struck again. It was Saturday afternoon when I heard the news of Mary Jane Kelly's brutal murder at Miller's Court. Freddie told me how the girl's abdomen was emptied of most of her vital organs.

'The killer even took the heart this time,' he continued.

'It seems more frantic, more desperate.'

'Yes. That's what we think. I'm dreading the next one. But how much more can he possibly do to them?'

'It's interesting how you say "he",' I murmured. 'Couldn't the killer be of any gender?'

Freddie stared at me, horrified.

'No, I can't even bear to think that. To consider a man capable of such brutality is one thing. I couldn't even contemplate that kind of sickness in a female!'

If only Freddie knew. A monster can appear in any guise. I was a classic example. I supposed he thought my penchant for drinking blood was a sexual perversity, but I hadn't always allowed my victims to live. Humans have such a selective grasp on reality.

That evening I went to Miller's Court and surveyed the crime scene. A policeman had been posted outside, presumably to keep the curious away, but I waited until he left his post for a hot toddy at the nearby tavern, and slipped in unseen.

The room was tiny. Mary Kelly had lived a solitary life in a single room with little more furniture than a bed, a small sideboard and a tiny table with one chair. Near the open fire was a small pot that she used to cook her meagre meals. Kelly had been all but destitute, like most women on the streets, but she at least had a dry place to sleep.

There was a strong odour in the room. Metallic. I touched the blood-soaked mattress of the bed. The blood was in the same condition as that of the other victims I'd seen, thin and depleted. I bent and sniffed the bed, detecting the iron deficiency, and then something glittering caught my eye. I turned to look at the fireplace. Among the ashes of the now dead fire, something gleamed. I walked to the fireplace and looked down. *All that glitters is not gold* ... A large lump of fool's gold, oddly shaped like a human heart, blinked in the soot as light from the street filtered in through the slightly parted curtains on the window. I scooped it up and rubbed the ash away on the corner of my skirt. Black blood oozed over my fingers. I looked closely. So this was Mary Kelly's heart, oxidised and transformed, half iron, half human flesh. I dropped the mutated flesh back into the ashes and knelt to light the fire. I wanted to burn this monstrosity.

The fireplace was big and the chimney wide and sprawling. I heard the wind howling across the top and felt a breeze filter down into the room as I reached for the half-open box of matches on the hearth. I lit a taper and glanced up into the chimney but could only see as far as the first bend. It had been newly swept, but a tiny glittering fragment could be seen perched on the corner. And then there was another gleam of light there.

I frowned. Something moved. I heard a shifting deep inside the chimney and a fine dusting fell on my upturned face.

Then, golden eyes opened to stare down the chimney.

I fell back seconds before a knife-like iron claw swung at my face leaving a trail of rust particles in the air in its wake. The creature crawled down towards me, its imposing, impossibly stiff, wormlike body clattering down. Bits of iron pyrite broke off into the fireplace as it emerged with a mournful cry.

I backed away, and in the shadow of the room I could barely make out the creature before the front part of its body reared up before me. The head almost touched the ceiling. The torso was a deformed mess. I could see human organs, partially absorbed, protruding from its body. The fallopian tubes of a female uterus, ripped and jaggedly unattached, were sprouting from the arm of the creature, and I realised that the monster had been digesting the organs somehow. A claw swung again. I dived to the left, rolling across the room. The arm smashed into the wall, shattering the sharp blade at the end of the appendage. The monster roared in rage and pain. Howling, it rolled and thrashed on the floor, smashing its snake-like body into the furniture. This made the being cry all the louder. I stepped back and pressed myself against the door, narrowly avoiding the claw that reached for me. This time its arm smashed against the window, breaking a pane of glass while ripping the curtains from the wall. Gaslight poured in through the exposed window with a rush of cold, foggy air. The being groaned and writhed as the damp air swirled around it. Swivelling and writhing, the creature tried to drag its damaged body back to the fireplace.

It all began to make sense. Fog *stung* the alien body like acid; corroding and rotting the metallic limbs even as I watched. Every particle of the iron-based composition was rusting away. The smog and damp of the London atmosphere was poison and, I speculated, this was just the final stages of a deterioration that had been occurring with frequent exposure: this explained the insatiable need to replenish iron and the fool's gold deposits all over the city. On instinct, I edged to the window, twisted the catch and threw the window as wide open as I could.

A gust of wind rushed into and through the room.

The monster thrashed and doubled over. A damp miasma poured in, as though drawn to the creature like a magnet. The smog settled over the head and torso, eliciting a cry so sorrowful that my heart could not help but respond to the agonised sob. The creature tried to nurse broken and decaying limbs against a collapsing body. The fool's gold glint gradually dulled to brown rust as the metal oxidised. The pained cries ceased. Golden eyes glared in fury from a bulbous, deformed head as the carcass shrivelled. I sank to the floor below the window and watched.

An hour or more passed. No-one came despite the commotion and I reasoned that they must have been too afraid, or that the lure of the tavern was too great on a cold night. The being had shrunk dramatically and now resembled a large, half-human foetus. The stolen human vital organs fell away as it rusted. I looked into a gaze that cried out to me. The monster wanted to live. In a flash of empathy, I realised that this was nothing more than an alien child, probably stranded during the recent meteor shower.

Hunger and the will to survive drove even humans to animalistic instincts. I understood that more than most. The deaths of the women were borne of desperation. 'Jack the Ripper' was a starving baby, who wanted only to be fed the basic nutrients it needed in order to endure.

The creature's eyes dimmed as its body oxidised. The damp, misty air from the chimney and window continued to blow around the body. The alien's chest cavity crumpled inwards, a burst of red dust puffing up into the atmosphere as its final breath huffed from the open torso. The being's slash-shaped maw gaped in a final silent cry and the fool's gold light went out from the pitiful gaze. With a shudder, the corpse disintegrated into a pile of red-brown rust.

I looked closely at the remains. A breeze picked up outside and a rush of air came down the chimney. I glanced back up the flue. I could only surmise that the creature had sought heat and warmth where it could, even as the damp, London fog had slowly oxidized its alien flesh until it rotted away to nothing. The agony of the alien child's death reverberated in my mind. A confusion of inarticulate screams left my body aching as I shook my head in a subconscious gesture. I wanted to wipe away all that I'd heard in those last few moments, but the memory stayed with me long into the night.

Opening the door, I let in more of the London fog. On the floor the rust stirred and dispersed. Swirling like fallen leaves in the strong autumn breeze, the dust scattered, leaving no trace of the monster that had once been.

Leaving Kelly's house I headed into the fog. In the tavern I could see the Bobby, who'd tired of guarding the crime scene, enjoying a drink in the company of several women of the night. 'Jack' was no more, and yet no-one in this world but me would ever know who or what he had been.

I felt no remorse.

There really is room for only one monster in the city.

# AUTHOR'S NOTES

*Fool's Gold* was first published by NewCon Press in their anthology *The Bitten Word*, which was launched at World Horror Con in Brighton in March 2010.

I'm particularly proud of this story, which was written to order in some respects. Ian Whates was talking to me at a BFS open night in London. He mentioned the anthology and asked me if I wanted to submit a story. When I heard of the line-up, including such greats as Tanith Lee, Storm Constantine, Simon Clark, Kelley Armstrong and many more, I just had to be in it.

The brief was simple: A vampire story with a difference. It could be traditional, because Ian wanted both period and modern pieces in it. So I decided to merge the genres – as I rather enjoy doing that. As we talked, a picture of Victorian London emerged in my head. That was when the idea to put my vampire in the world of Jack the Ripper was first formulated. But of course, the Ripper couldn't be any of the usual suspects, it had to be something new and original, so why not an alien baby? This is a horror story, but it also has foundation in science fiction and fantasy.

# LEAD POISONING

The year had been a whirlwind of success, so it wasn't surprising that I noticed her. She reminded me of that black and white film actress Fay Wray. You know the one: that monster King Kong had the hots for her. Blonde, waif-like; she had that certain something, a vulnerability that all good actresses had in Hollywood at that time. As Karolina De Vere walked down the staircase she was illuminated as if in stop motion, as camera flashes marked her progress. For a moment she was blinded, her beautiful eyes blinked and reflected sparks of energy back at the crowd. She stopped and posed, ever the professional, while waiting for the right moment to discourage the paparazzi nicely. She smiled, posed again to a myriad sparks of light, and then drifted down the remaining steps and into the protection of the gathered throng before being ushered into the dining room.

A few moments later she was sitting with Gerard

Hampshire at the banquet, waiting for the awards to be announced. She was nominated for 'Best Newcomer' and the film was the usual type, boy meets girl, monster wants girl, monster dies trying to kidnap girl … I couldn't remember the name of it: it didn't matter. The only thing that mattered was that she was so magnificent that all I wanted to do was scoop her up and steal her away.

But then, I am the archetypal monster, and sometimes we have to behave as expected of us.

Karolina deserved immortality like no other movie star I'd met, but there was one major flaw in this whole daydream of mine. Gerard Hampshire. I suspected she didn't love him, despite the rumours that peppered the newspapers. I saw no passion in her eyes as they talked. When he touched her, she stiffened, ever so slightly, and her lips trembled. Ever the consummate actress, Karolina gave none of this away to the casual eye. All of Hollywood was talking of her affair with Hampshire – a relationship that was, apparently, made in heaven. Hollywood, however, didn't have my vision. I saw through the façade. Karolina could barely stomach Hampshire, and that was because he was an abusive moron. She only put up with him because he was good for her career.

Hampshire had his quirks too. He was known to be an obsessive clean-freak, always washing his hands like some wannabe Howard Hughes. That night he was wearing white gloves, the type men wore a century ago: they were a little out of place in 1975. Even so, this was an era where affectation was a must in Hollywood and partly because fashion was in something of a quandary.

It was Samhain, so I left the awards ceremony soon after Karolina's category was read and she had won, as I knew she would. I'd known that she was going to be a huge success and she would earn her immortality on screen, just as Marilyn Monroe had before her. That night I had better fish to fry, and Halloween was always a good feasting time as there were so many innocents abroad, looking for candy.

I flew out into the city and fed on a glorious young couple. She was wearing the archetypal witch costume with luminous green make-up and he was Dracula. I left them swooning in a park just off the street they'd been 'trick or treating'. Clearly they didn't realise that there really are monsters in the city, and part of me wanted to leave them with the memory. I toyed with the idea for a while, then let them be. It was safer for me and for them if they didn't recall a thing.

All this time I didn't know that cameras were once again illuminating Karolina's face and flawless complexion. This time a police photographer took her picture as she lay in the centre of an obvious crime scene. Her beautiful eyes were dark and vacant. That's when I stepped into her story in the real world, foregoing my shadowy, voyeuristic ways, and no longer observing her from a distance.

I was working in the morgue in LA, in a hospital in

Hollywood. It was a job that suited me as I have an … affinity … with the dead you might say. Many aspects of working in the coroner's office appealed to me. But nothing could have prepared me for Karolina's body being wheeled into the morgue around midnight.

She lay still and frozen, deathly pale – and that's not a cliché, it's a statement of fact. Karolina was exceptionally white, except for a slight tinge of blue around her mouth. I examined her quickly, looking for a visible cause, but nothing was evident. There were bruises though, on her arms, torso and legs. Places they wouldn't have been seen under ordinary circumstances, and mostly yellowing, so a few days old. Perhaps cyanosis, caused by poor oxygen circulation through her lungs … but why?

I lifted my head and concentrated, scanning the hospital. Hampshire was on the premises, I could smell him. I knew he'd done this to her and I wanted to beat the shit out of him.

'Hey, Lucy,' said Vance entering the morgue, all smiles and *bonhomie*. He looked at the body on the slab. 'Oh my God! Is that Karolina De Vere?'

I nodded.

'What killed her?'

'I don't know. Yet. Will you do her bloods for me?'

Vance got to work, drawing out several samples for analysis, while I began the autopsy. I hated desecrating her perfect body but it had to be done if I was to find the cause.

'What you got?' asked Detective Morgan later.

'Nothing,' I said. 'But there are still a few more tests to do and not all the blood tests are back yet.'

'She can't have died of nothing.'

'I know. But all her organs were functioning and intact, which is really strange considering the signs of cyanosis … We're just checking for drugs. Have you interviewed Gerard Hampshire?' I asked.

Morgan gave me a long look. He didn't *get* me. He was very curious as to why a woman like me would want to spend all my time in a morgue cutting up dead bodies. 'Yeah. The man's devastated.'

'Really? She was covered in bruises … maybe you should ask him to explain that …'

Morgan's mouth opened but he thought better of saying anything more. He turned and left my office. He was a good cop, wanted to find out the truth, but sometimes his type can miss the obvious. All he needed was a little nudge in the right direction. That, of course, didn't solve my immediate problem of finding the cause of death.

'Look at this,' Vance said, entering the office and handing me the results.

I glanced down at the file, but couldn't quite believe what I was seeing. 'This doesn't make sense.'

'I know.'

'Lead? Lead *poisoning*. Vance, is this a joke?'

Vance shook his head.

I read the sheet again. 'Her entire blood stream was filled with minute lead particles. But, there was absolutely no sign of them in her organs? This amount would have caused major heart failure, seizures. So it would seem to be what killed her.'

'I know,' said Vance. 'But the cops say Hampshire found her dead in the living room. The only symptom was that she'd complained of stomach cramps earlier.'

'Let's X-ray the body – I want to see her bones, that should tell us how long this has been going on.'

Lance made a call and then wheeled the body away, down to X-ray. I sat and waited, running all manner of possibilities through my mind. Lead was extremely dangerous, we knew that, but usually there were symptoms before the poisoning became so severe that it caused death.

Lance returned sometime later with a large brown envelope lying on top of the white sheet. I picked up the envelope as he stowed Karolina in the fridge. Then I flicked on the viewing light, clipping up the large negative.

The X-ray showed no lead on her bones. They were clear and perfect. The contamination had been in her blood stream only. This meant that Karolina's contact with lead was recent. I examined her body again, looking for needle tracks. If the lead was only in her blood stream, then perhaps it had been injected directly, but I couldn't find any trace of an entry point.

'We need to test Hampshire too,' I said. 'If it's something

in their home, old pipes that have gone unnoticed … But none of this makes sense, Vance. If it had been ingested it would show up in the stomach as well as her other vital organs. This would seem to be a sudden influx of the poison into her blood.'

Vance nodded, and rubbed his chin, looking at my face as if searching for the answer there. Then he headed off to get the blood tests from Hampshire.

I gazed at the X-rays again. Maybe I had missed something.

'Anything new?' Morgan had appeared behind me. I glanced back. I had known he was there of course. No-one could sneak up on me without me knowing.

'Vance said something about lead traces …' he continued.

'Did you speak to Hampshire?' I asked.

'Look, Lucy, you do your job and I'll do mine.'

I turned to face him, and he made the mistake of looking into my eyes. A moment later, he began to tell me everything I wanted to know.

'He admitted that sometimes their role-play gets a little rough … He said Karolina liked it.'

'If only bodies could talk,' I muttered. Perhaps they could.

I went to the fridge and retrieved Karolina's body.

Already I could see decay appearing in tiny cracks, invisible to the human eye. Her flawless beauty was rapidly fading and there was nothing I could do now to help her. Or was there? Hampshire knew more than he was saying; I was sure of it.

'Bring him in here,' I ordered.

'What?' Morgan said. My glamour was wearing off.

'You want the truth? I'll get it for you.'

'Look, lady, you're not without charm, I'll give you that, but what makes you think he's gonna spill his guts to you like that?'

'He'll spill,' I said, meeting Morgan's eyes again. I gave his mind a little push; not enough to hurt, but enough to make him think the suggestion was his idea. His eyes clouded and then cleared.

'What if I bring Hampshire in here?' he asked. 'Confronted with the body he might just give something away.'

'Good plan detective.' I smiled as Morgan went off to get Karolina's erstwhile beau.

Hampshire fidgeted with his cufflinks when Morgan brought him into the morgue. I'm good at reading body language and it was clear that he was upset, but whether that was from guilt or just because he really did love Karolina I wasn't sure. Earlier Vance had given me a note that said that Hampshire's blood was clear of any signs of lead, which convinced me that the deposits in Karolina's body weren't accidental. I had to get to the bottom of what had happened.

'You loved Karolina?' I asked.

'Sure,' Hampshire said. 'She was gonna be the next

big thing.'

I was taken aback by his honesty and so was Morgan.

'You loved her because she was going to be a star?' Morgan asked.

'I make stars. That's what I do. Karolina … she was going to be huge. Now look, a young death, and barely any films in the can. The public will forget she ever existed inside a year. What a waste.' Hampshire was clearly gutted, and for all the wrong reasons.

'I agree. Her death was a waste. Awful. That's why I want to get to the bottom of it, Mr Hampshire.' I said.

'Yeah. But it won't bring back all the time and money I invested in her, will it?'

I fought the urge to slap Gerard Hampshire across the face and for a moment I fantasised about sending his toned, tanned body flying across the room, crashing into the glass instrument cabinet while I towered over him, all fangs, rage and destiny. I shook myself mentally, and felt my gums stop itching. A good sign.

'Okay. So it's about money and fame in your world, not real love.'

Hampshire's eyes narrowed with confusion, he clearly didn't get my irony.

'What happened tonight?' I asked bluntly, tired of going around the houses with him.

'She won the award; she was going to be a star.'

'I know. When you left the awards, where did you go?'

I looked into Hampshire's mind and I saw the evening unroll as if I was him.

*… liked her. She was a sweet kid deep down, but he made her hide any vulnerability behind the starlet façade. She was going to be his crowning glory, his major success. When she had a few films under her belt he'd marry her and they'd have a kid. It would be a beautiful, public story. That was what Gerard had planned for Karolina. But the best laid plans don't always come true.*

*Karolina sat in the chair opposite him. She was sipping sherry and she was excited, but a new coldness was there that he hadn't seen before.*

*'This is how it's going to be,' she was saying. 'For the public we'll pretend we're together. When I finish the next film, there will be a natural parting of ways.'*

*'What are you talking about, kid?' he said laughing. 'We're going all the way and the fans are going to love it.'*

*'No.' Karolina stood up, pulling her fox fur wrap around her shoulders. 'Send for the car.'*

*'I let the driver off, thought we'd be celebrating together for the evening,' Gerard said.*

*'No. I don't want to. Haven't you figured it out yet? I don't like you, Gerard. Everything I've done has been for the things you can do for me.'*

*Gerard was surprised, not by what she said, because he had always known this was true, but that she had indeed voiced it. He'd thought they'd play this love game longer.*

*After all, being with the most beautiful starlet of all time wasn't going to hurt his career either. He liked her too, he really did, and that was the closest he'd ever come to love before.*

*'You're tired,' he said. 'Perhaps even a little overwhelmed. We'll talk again in the morning.'*

*'No. I don't want to see you again, Gerard. I signed a contract today. Fox. A five film deal. I'm on my way up and I don't need you now.'*

*Karolina turned to pick up her bag and Gerard grabbed her.*

*'You're not walking out on me you bitch! I made you.'*

*Karolina laughed. 'I made myself, Gerard, and if you think by digging your fingers in my arm you're going to make me change my mind, then you can think again.'*

*Gerard let go, giving her a push that sent her sprawling back into the chair she'd just left.*

*'I do like it when you get all macho, Gerard,' Karolina said smiling. 'Maybe we could have one last night ... I don't mind that.'*

*She stood and wrapped her arms around his stiff body. He was angry, but she knew exactly what to do to get her own way.*

*'You're such a bitch.'*

*'I know.'*

*'You're always playing games.'*

*'I'm an actress. You, of all people, should know that's what I do.'*

62

*She laughed, kissing him passionately. They went to bed. It was hotter and more exciting than it had ever been. Karolina enjoyed her games. Telling him it was over was just one of them, Gerard knew that. By the end of the evening she was curled up in his arms and sleeping like a virgin. As he watched her sleep he knew then they would get married, she'd be his and their future success was assured. He felt incredibly …*

I pulled away from his mind, surprised by the information that I'd retrieved. I'd been wrong about Karolina and Hampshire. He really did love her, he just hadn't known it.

Morgan turned his head to look at Hampshire, then me and back again. I quickly sent him a thought that poured into his mind all of the information that I'd taken from Hampshire, making him think that this was what Hampshire had just told us at the same time.

'So that's your story?' Morgan said. 'Games. You two play games with each other. That doesn't explain why she's lying with a shit-load of lead in her blood stream.'

Hampshire shook his head. He was trying to figure out what he had just said himself – having someone else root about in your memories can do that to a person. Often though, they just capitulate and decide that what is now known must be what was just said … how else could it be known?

'It's all I know. I woke up and she wasn't there. I thought

it was another diversion! I went looking for her and she was lying on the floor with that fox fur wrap around her and nothing else.' At that moment Gerard Hampshire's voice broke. 'I've just realised, I'm never going to see her again.'

He looked from me to Morgan and back again as tears welled up in his eyes. There was nothing we could do to comfort him though. Morgan was a hard-nosed cop, and I was ... well, let's say that comforting the bereaved was not in my job description.

'There's something weird going on here,' Morgan said as Vance led the sobbing Hampshire from the morgue. 'He knows something, he's just not telling us.'

'I think maybe he has seen something, but it doesn't make sense to him and so he's dismissed it from his mind,' I said, and waded once more through the memories I'd taken.

Morgan left with a promise to look further into Karolina's past. All we knew about her was the public biography, and most of those were made up by some studio executive whose job it was to make his stars look good.

I replaced Karolina in the fridge and headed out of the hospital. It was almost dawn and I wanted to swing by Hampshire's house and sniff around before all of his employees trampled whatever evidence might remain.

The lounge was cordoned off with yellow tape pasted across the doorway in a huge 'X'. I slipped through one of the gaps, leaving the tape intact. The room was exactly as I'd seen it in Hampshire's mind. The chair that Karolina had sat in was slightly askew and there was white tape on the floor where the body was found. I imagined the paramedics pushing Karolina onto her back as they attempted to revive her.

A sherry glass stood half empty on the renaissance table beside Karolina's chair. I bent down, careful not to touch it, and sniffed at the contents, half expecting that deep, dark poisonous lead smell to be merged with the sherry. But the amber liquid smelt of dry, strong alcohol, nothing more.

I walked the room looking for some clue, some sign of how Karolina had died. Above the fireplace, an impressive open mantle made of marble, was a painting of a smart, almost beautiful woman wearing a fox fur. The name, *Mae Hampshire*, was carved into a bronze plaque underneath the painting with the dates, *1918-1965*. I assumed it was Hampshire's mother; there was something about the eyes that reminded me of him, but other than that she barely resembled him at all.

I turned away and then back again to the picture. Something about Mae Hampshire disturbed me, a distant memory. I'd seen her before somewhere.

I swept through the house, checking as much as I could, but turned up nothing of interest. My eyes kept being drawn to the picture though … there was something nagging in my mind.

As soon as I could, I headed to the public library and looked her up. 'Here you go,' said the librarian as he placed a stack of old newspapers down beside me.

He was cute, so I took him into the private stock area and drank from him before I began my search.

As I waded through old newspapers and microfiche, the scandal that had followed Mae Hampshire emerged and I remembered why I knew her. I found the first piece in the *Chicago Tribune*.

She had been a notorious gangster's moll, albeit briefly. Some years before Gerard was born, Mae, then known as Mae Gelders, had a very public affair with a known associate of Al Capone. There were few pictures of her, in most of which she tried to hide her face, but there was one really stunning photo and in it she was wearing a long flowing white silk dress, with a fox fur wrap around her shoulders. The pose reminded me of Karolina's stance the night before, as she stood on the stairs for the cameras.

All this only served to satisfy that irritating memory I'd had of Mae Gelders, though, and it didn't give me any more information on what had caused Karolina's death. I went and checked on the librarian. He was recovering nicely from my bite, and he was up and working before I left. If there'd been time I might have tried him out another way – he was very cute indeed – but it was just too risky in broad daylight and I didn't want him to lose his job.

I went back to the morgue. Karolina was tucked in the freezer and I stared at her notes and test results for a long time, trying to discern anything that might give me a clue as to what had happened. Nothing was forthcoming.

'I'm beginning to think you can't stay away from me,' I said as Morgan came into my office later.

'I brought these.' He placed a large see-through plastic bag on my desk. 'Karolina's possessions. I thought you might be able to run some tests.'

'Interesting. I assumed your own forensics would do that.'

'They did. They came back with zilch. Lucy, let's not beat around the bush, you and I both know you have a talent for these things. I don't know how you know what you do, but sometimes you're very insightful.'

'Why, thank you, detective. But you don't need to flatter me. I'll look at these and see what I can do.'

I signed Morgan's evidence receipt to say I'd take care of them and took them into my lab. Inside the bag was the long, red satin dress Karolina had worn the night before; long red matching gloves; her purse containing a powder compact, red lipstick and her underwear. I carefully lifted the dress, sniffed it and swabbed anywhere that showed traces of any stains or marks.

A few hours later, after examining all of her possessions and finding nothing, I headed to the coffee machine. I didn't really need the coffee, even though I like it, but getting away from the lab for a few minutes felt like a good idea. The nearest coffee machine was in the waiting room for A & E. I pumped money into the slot and cast my eyes around the room. It was unusually quiet in there with the exception of a small child, who was crying gently in his mother's arms, his hand clasped against his chest.

Karolina De Vere's golden smile greeted me from the pages of a newspaper that had been left open on one of the chairs. I went over, picked it up and found myself looking at the fox fur wrapped around her shoulders. It was weirdly familiar, but not because I'd seen her in it on the night of the awards.. I realised that it was, or looked identical to, the one that Mae Hampshire had been wearing in the picture above Hampshire's fireplace. But then these things always looked the same to me.

I left the coffee in the machine and rushed out. It was night time and I didn't go looking for my car, instead I went straight up into the air and headed for Hampshire's house. I wanted an informal entry; a car parking in the drive would have notified the occupants that I was there.

Oddly, as I flew over the house, only the kitchen and the master bedroom were lit. Hampshire was still tearful, and as I entered the house I could hear his soft sniffing as he prepared for bed. In the kitchen the house-keeper was clearing away the crockery from the evening meal that had gone untouched. I heard her soft muttering as she scraped the food into the bin.

I made my way to the darkened lounge and slipped once more through the tape. It hadn't been removed yet as Forensics clearly weren't satisfied that they had examined the room thoroughly enough. The drapes were open and the light from the security lights poured in, illuminating the furniture with a yellow glow. Mae Hampshire stared down sternly from her painting, the fox fur wrap slung casually over her shoulders.

'I'm so stupid,' I murmured.

'How did you get in here?'

I turned to see Gerard Hampshire staring through the taped barriers.

'Mr Hampshire, you know I'm working with the police on Karolina's death. I didn't want to upset you by coming here so late. So please forgive me for sneaking in unobserved.'

'What do you want?' he asked.

'The truth.'

'We all want that. I loved her, you know.'

I nodded, 'Yes. I do know. I'm sorry for your loss. But you could help me get to the bottom of this.'

'How?'

I turned and looked up at the painting of Mae Hampshire. Hampshire slipped into the room, carefully climbing through the tape as I had.

'This is your mother,' I said. Hampshire nodded. 'She died quiet young. What happened to her?'

Gerard shrugged. 'Murdered.'

'Mr Hampshire, I remember the scandal surrounding your mother some years ago. She was seen with Sonny Capelione wasn't she?'

Hampshire sat down in the chair that Karolina had so recently occupied.

'My mother was a wild one in her day. But then she met my father and settled down. They lived many happy years together. I didn't know anything about Sonny Capelione until after she died.'

'I see. How *did* she die?'

'It just happened that my parents were eating out in a restaurant, when some crazy decided to rob the till. They were killed in the cross-fire.'

'Shot?'

'Yes.'

'I'm sorry.'

It was no use; I couldn't see any connection between Karolina and Mae now. The only similarity was the fox fur, and they were ten-a-penny among starlets. I looked up at the painting once more and I still couldn't shake this annoying feeling that the fur *was* the connection.

'My mother loved that fur,' Hampshire was saying. 'She wore it everywhere. I know some guys would have given their girlfriend their mother's jewellery, but it was the fur that meant so much to her, and, strange as it seems, I really took pleasure in seeing Karolina wear it.'

'It's the *same* fur?'

'Capelione bought my mother that fur,' Hampshire

said. 'But I only learnt about him when I was sorting through her things after the funeral.'

Capelione had been incarcerated long after Capone. They didn't have as much on him, so he wasn't imprisoned at Alcatraz. They suspected he was a henchman for Capone, even though most of the accusations were never proven. After that, Mae decided she wasn't going to wait for him to serve his time. Hampshire learnt all of this from the letters Capelione sent to Mae. Capelione felt betrayed, and he was insanely jealous when Mae married Gerard Hampshire Senior. Mae and her new husband moved from Chicago to Hollywood, but somehow Capelione's letters still found their way to her.

Hampshire gave me the shoe box he'd kept that contained the letters.

'I don't know why I kept them,' he said. 'I just thought that maybe one day it would be important.'

'What happened to the fur, Gerard?' I asked gently.

For a moment he looked confused, 'Karolina was wearing it when I ...found her.' He stared at the tape marked floor.

'It wasn't with her possessions.'

'I think,' said Hampshire, 'I put it back into the wardrobe. I don't know why, it was like a reflex. My mother would have hated it to be strewn on the floor like that. Yes. That's what I did. I pulled it away and I threw my robe over Karolina while I waited for the ambulance.'

I went back to the lab with the fox fur and the box

of letters. I swabbed the letters, opening each envelope until I found a small pile of unopened ones, tied with a single blue ribbon. Mae Hampshire had, at some time in the year before she died, stopped reading the letters Capelione sent, yet still kept them. I scrutinised them all.

The first envelope in the pile contained minute traces of lead. Suddenly the whole thing came together.

Morgan was in his office when I turned up at his precinct. It was dark and gloomy in there, all mahogany and leather, but worn and ugly, lacking imagination, flare and comfort. On his desk I saw a photograph of a woman with a baby.

'Your wife?' I asked, and Morgan looked up, surprised to find me so quietly standing before his desk. You see *I* can sneak up on *him*.

'Yes. I'm surprised to see you here, but I guess that means you have something for me.'

I nodded, 'May I?' I said, pointing to the seat opposite him.

'Sure.'

I sat down and took a breath. I wasn't really sure how to tell him what I'd learnt. I placed the evidence bag before him and the box containing the letters.

'What do you know of a criminal called Sonny Capelione?' I asked.

Morgan sat back in his chair, 'Capelione? He died

about ten years ago.'

'Yes,' I said. 'He died a few days before Mae Hampshire and her husband Gerard Hampshire Senior were accidentally killed in cross-fire when a thug tried to hold up a restaurant they were dining in.'

Morgan nodded. 'I remember that too. Sad business. Hey, of course, that's Gerard Hampshire's parents.'

'Do you know what Capelione died of?' I asked.

'As a matter of fact I do. He had some kind of bone-wasting disease.'

'Before I came over here, I took the liberty of checking the medical records. Fortunately for me, Capelione was treated in Hollywood because his final place of incarceration was here.'

'And?'

'He died of *Colica Pictonum*.' I smiled. I can't resist showing off sometimes. 'I suspect he was exposed while handling the stuff when he made his own, untraceable rounds. I'm sure your recall the expression used for mafia murders? They die of "lead poisoning". Or are "shot full of lead". It was ironic really that Capone's arch henchman died of actual lead poisoning.'

'Really? I didn't know that. But what has this got to do with this case?'

'Karolina De Vere was murdered by Sonny Capelione.'

'What?'

'The fox fur she was wearing contained dangerous

traces of lead, all buried in the fox's claws and coating the fur. The eyes weren't the traditional glass; they were lead bullets painted to look like eyes. Very artistically painted I might add. I didn't notice it at all at first.'

Then I explained to Morgan how Sonny had given Mae the fur, years before. At the time the lead wasn't dangerous; the claws and eyes were coated in a glossy resin that made them shine and gleam, and the fur had been treated with a moth repellent that similarly acted as a barrier. But as the years had passed, this valuable fox fur had worn. The protective barriers had decayed, and the lead had become exposed while it was left hanging in Mae's wardrobe.

'Hampshire gave Karolina the fur in good faith. He wanted her to have something that his mother loved. He never knew the history.' I explained.

'Technically her death was an accident,' Morgan said.

'Well no. Not really. That's where these letters come in. But you need to wear some surgical gloves before you touch them, they're covered with lead deposits. I don't know if you realise it, but lead is extremely dangerous, even in small doses, and some people are more susceptible than others.' I handed over a pair I'd specifically brought for Morgan to use.

Sonny was obsessed with Mae. There was an element of 'owning' her and he felt his possession had been stolen. After serving years in prison for crimes linked with Al Capone, Sonny hadn't let it go. And it was clear, even on his death-bed, that he resented Mae's abandonment.

*I'm dying*, he told her in his last letter, never knowing that it would remain unopened until ten years later. *The doctors say there's nothing they can do for me. But I curse you and that goddamn fur, which you love so much. Something bad will happen if ever you wear it again. I'm taking this to my grave. I swear to God I'll never forgive you.*

Sonny died that night, leaving behind his curse in an envelope that Mae received, but never opened. It went into the box with the others; she'd stopped listening to his feeble threats. Capelione was nothing without Capone to back him up. On her death, Gerard Junior had glanced through a few of the letters, but hadn't read on as he wanted to remember his mother as the happy person he'd known. He, also, never knew of the curse.

'I gave Karolina the fur on the night of the awards,' Hampshire told me. 'She knew how much it meant to me and I wanted to show her, in my own stupid, stumbling way, by giving her my mother's favourite fur, that I loved her.'

'So, why wasn't Hampshire poisoned?' Morgan asked.

'He was wearing gloves. He has an obsessive-compulsive disorder that makes him constantly wash his hands. The way he avoids drawing attention to that is by wearing gloves. Hampshire took the fur from Karolina's body on the night she died, automatically hanging it back up in the wardrobe. Then, he immediately washed his hands. He can't help himself. That's why he had no traces and why the lead didn't have time to poison him.'

'Good. Because I don't believe in curses,' Morgan said.

'Fortunately you don't have to, because what happened is actually explainable.'

But deep down I wondered. Mae Hampshire technically died of 'lead poisoning' when she was gunned down in the restaurant the last time she ever wore the fox fur wrap. And Karolina De Vere, beautiful, talented and innocent, died the very first night she wore it.

After the inquest, Gerard Hampshire asked for Karolina's possessions to be returned. He particularly wanted his mother's fox fur wrap, but strangely it had disappeared from the evidence vault.

It was never to be seen again.

## AUTHOR'S NOTES

When Carolyn from the website Book Chick City (www.bookchickcity.com) e-mailed me and asked if I'd like to contribute to their Halloween Special I immediately said yes. Book Chick City is a great website, full of interesting reviews and information on all the books I enjoy. I had originally planned to write some kind of Halloween chiller – so much for the best laid plans. I was in the middle of writing stories for my collection and already had some character names and plotlines going through my head, but I didn't bargain on *Lead Poisoning* taking on a life of its own.

*Lead Poisoning* is a mystery that slowly unravels to reveal the cause of death of the starlet Karolina De Vere. There are lots of real-life influences that went into writing this. I originally wanted to set it in 1920s Hollywood, and my movie star was going to be the star of black and white silent films, which have always had a fascinating appeal. Then I realised that actually the 1970s was when it *should* be set.

My main character in the story is, of course, my vampire Lucrezia, in one of her guises as a doctor in 1975 LA. Lucrezia likes and enjoys mysteries, often solving them for her own purposes. So, in *Lead Poisoning* I have her research into the life of Al Capone. Because the title, as you might guess, is a bit of a giveaway. I've always loved the old expression, or mafia in-joke, for shooting someone: 'Filling them full of lead,' or explaining that someone died of 'lead poisoning'. Clearly I just had to play with that …

# Zombies in New York

A multitude of alien eyes looked down over Central Park. Rocco could feel the intense pressure of their gaze as he lay on one of the scenic rocks overlooking the ball court. His eyes flew open and he looked up at the sky, noting, as always, how the pure blue was marred by the grotesque towers as they loomed above the trees. Not for the first time Rocco wondered whether anyone else noticed the city's dominance or whether it was a particular quirk of his alone. He supposed that most people would probably think it 'quaint'. It was part of the experience of New York City, and many a visitor had been delightfully overwhelmed by the towering landscape.

Normally he felt safe in the park, but this day was different. Every time Rocco closed his eyes his vivid imagination wouldn't leave him alone. He felt some imagined threat lurking around the corners of blackness. Panic tightened his chest but he forced his eyes to remain shut. He wasn't given to flights of fancy and he wouldn't let this silly paranoia affect his routine. Not even the eerie quiet of the park.

New York City had a reputation; it wasn't the safest place to live. You had to know where to go and where not to go, particularly at night. However, Central Park was usually secure in the daytime, which was why Rocco's fears were so irrational. There were always cop cars cruising around and a steady stream of tourists wandering through, looking up at the trees and the buildings around them.

Rocco had always thought that nature never really managed to keep back the city for long: this was 'the city that never sleeps', after all. Normally, day or night, he could hear the steady hum of traffic noise, the bizarre beeping of horns – despite the penalty of $350 the driver would pay if caught honking – and the loud blur of sound that was a combination of club music and people talking loudly. But not that day: yes, the buildings lurked as always, but the city was quiet. It was the silence that was so terrifying.

At the Shadow Club, the night before, it had been an unusually noisy start. The assistant manager had taken over at two but there was a problem with one of the waitresses. She came in acting weird, appeared drunk or stoned, and had this awful streaming cold. Naturally Rocco stayed a little longer to see how Daryl handled her. He was always aware that the final responsibility lay on him, and if things became screwed up, or if a customer complained, then it would be he that would have to answer to his business partner Lucrezia.

'What's up, Roxie?' Daryl asked the waitress.

'Nothin', I just got a cold.'

'Don't you think you oughta go home and rest up then?'

Roxie stared at Daryl and her face showed a variety of confused expressions; one minute anger, the next resignation.

'I can't afford to be off sick. I got a kid to feed, and do you think that lazy bum I married will ever get a job? He's too happy sitting at home watching cable and drinking the beer I pay for.'

Daryl backed off from her. He didn't like to become involved with the staff and their personal issues. So he let her go out and take orders, even ignoring it when she sneezed into the beer of a regular customer. The guy didn't see anyway, and to make an issue of it meant throwing away a perfectly good beer.

At three Rocco left; all was okay and he really needed his sleep. Running the club had taken up so much of his time since Lucrezia had left town on some obscure business trip. Everything now fell to him as joint-owner, and if it hadn't been for the money she'd injected a few years earlier then the place would have long since closed down. Rocco would have lost everything. Having her around made life easier too. It wasn't all his responsibility anymore, and she spent half of the week or more there, giving him much more free time: until now of course. Her absence made Rocco realise just how good it had been recently. Plus she was really popular with the wealthy clientele. Senators, actors and even businessmen frequented the club. The rich and the beautiful liked it there, and Lucrezia had a way of making them want to come back again.

As he climbed into his car, not for the first time, Rocco wished Lucrezia was back in town.

Back at his apartment, Rocco threw himself down on his black leather sofa and switched on the flat-screen TV that was sunk into the wall. He lived alone and liked it. There was no-one to complain if he put the TV on at 4.00 am, or object to his unsociable working schedule. He planned to catch up on his soaps and then crash, but the news channel was on and the scrolling headline was intriguing.

*Riot in Times Square as hundreds lapse into drunken brawl.*

'Insanity wreaked havoc in Times Square earlier this evening,' said the reporter. 'The following footage was filmed from the safety of the news truck.'

A warning flashed up on the screen. *Scenes of a violent nature.*

Rocco, brought up in the toughest part of New York, was shocked as he saw tourists of all ages fighting and attacking each other using anything they could: bags, chairs from a local café or just their hands. Two men were rolling around on the floor, snarling and snapping at each other like rabid dogs. An elderly couple beat each other with their walking sticks, and a woman took off her stiletto heels and jabbed the sharp tips at the eyes of a man as he stood frozen with horror. At the last minute the man lifted his arm to defend his face and the stiletto was stabbed fiercely into the soft flesh of his forearm. Blood splattered the woman as she pulled back her makeshift weapon and jabbed it once more at her terrified victim. Bedlam ensued. It was so horrible it was almost funny, and for a moment Rocco thought it was a television stunt, just like that radio show from years ago that sparked panic when everyone thought that the aliens were really invading.

The footage *wasn't* a joke though, and the carnage was very real.

Rocco switched off the screen as he saw armoured police arrive to beat down the rioters. The world was going to shit and he didn't really want those images in his head before he slept. He'd never seen anything like it in all his years in the city.

What was even freakier was that he'd been in Times Square earlier that day. In fact he'd had some fun with a cute little English tourist. So much so that he'd gone back to her hotel room for a while. They'd drunk some beers, had sex and Rocco had given her a special present before he left. He wondered if she was okay, and hoped she was still in her room sleeping off the booze, just as she was when he'd left her.

That night he was glad he lived on the outskirts of Manhattan, away from the worst of it. He was also glad for the security in his apartment. The self-locking doors and key-controlled lift gave him a sense of protection that might have otherwise been lacking. He thought of calling the club, but realised that the drama was already over so there was no point in warning everyone to avoid Times Square.

Later, in bed, the news report kept flashing before his eyes. He couldn't get his head around the insanity. Plus the city was screaming. The sounds of police cars and ambulances merged with the cry of a fire truck as it made its way through the streets. Even the double glazing was failing to keep the sounds at bay. Rocco found it impossible to sleep so he got up again.

Switching the TV back on, Rocco found that things had deteriorated still further.

'... although police managed to contain the brawl, there were several serious injuries and two fires were started on Broadway. An investigation is underway into this mysterious outbreak of violence ...'

*It's like Zombie City in New York*, Rocco thought, shaking his head. *Mindless violence, ordinary people attacking other people. Whatever next?*

In Central Park, taking his daily constitutional, Rocco went for a breakfast burger at the usual stand.

'Hey Hank, did you see the news last night?'

Hank nodded. 'Yeah there sure were some crazies out.'

'What do you think it was?'

'Probably drugs. It's always about drugs.'

A woman jogged by, stopping briefly to take a swig of water from a water fountain near the path. Rocco admired her figure as she bent over to re-tie her laces.

'Quiet today though,' observed Rocco.

'Yeah. Riots are bad for business,' Hank muttered as he flipped the burger over and moved the onions around on the griddle. 'I guess everyone is still freaking out over the news stories. The police did recommend staying home as much as possible. Like they care about what that does to my business.'

'Really? I didn't know that.'

Hank pressed the burger down and flipped it into a bun, added some onions and passed it to Rocco. Rocco helped himself to a plastic cup of coffee from the jug stewing on the counter.

Rocco sat at a small table. He couldn't shake his unease. He wasn't really sure why, but as he looked up at the sky everything felt wrong. Hank came out from behind the stand and wiped the table over for him.

'You can't be too careful,' said Hank. 'There's probably vermin all over these during the night.'

Rocco nodded as he chewed the first mouthful of his burger. It was good, as always, which was why he came here in the mornings instead of going to one of the local cafés. Hank's stand was clean, the food hot and fresh, and sometimes those things were hard to find in the same place.

The park began to fill up a little and Rocco's anxiety slowly slipped away as he sipped his coffee. He was tired; the lack of sleep the previous night was already taking its toll, and he had a full day to get through.

When he finished he swept the crumbs to the ground for the birds, and slipped Hank a special tip. Worth it not to have your burger spat in or reheated from the previous day's left-overs.

Rocco left Central and caught a cab down to Battery Park and the Staten Island ferry station. The next ferry was in 20 minutes. He had business over on the island: Lucrezia's lawyers were dealing with the purchase of a house for her and he had to oversee the details in her absence. His work with her stretched into all areas these days, not just the club.

Rocco bought a newspaper at the kiosk and sat down on one of the cold marble seats to read it.

'Heated Arguments in Heated Streets' read the front page. Rocco glanced down to take in the story.

'People descended into animalistic behaviour as an extreme heat wave hit New York City last night. The temperature rose to over 100 degrees, coinciding with a rise in irritability. Several fights erupted in Times Square causing major injuries. The Fire and Ambulance services were inundated with emergency calls as the evening erupted into a riot …'

'Man, it's hot.'

Rocco looked up as an attractive young black woman sat down beside him. She was wearing a thin vest top and her pert breasts protruded through the fabric, belying her words even as she fanned herself with a magazine. Her top was damp with sweat. Through the corner of his eye, Rocco noticed her pulling the fabric away from her skin. He tried to focus on his paper, but found it difficult when the woman stood again. As she bent to search for something in her canvas bag, Rocco noticed a tramp-stamp tattoo on her back, proclaiming her 'Harlem's Finest'.

Rocco stood up and walked to the closed ferry doors before she could talk to him again. He wasn't interested in finding out if she was indeed 'Harlem's Finest'. He'd seen her sort before and he never messed with it.

The ferry was making its way into the dock. Rocco was tired. Mindlessly he watched the ferry bump the wooden sides of the dock as it was guided in. The station was full now, so more people came over to the large doors to wait for the arriving passengers to disembark. The ferry stopped. The bridges were lowered, doors opened and the first people tumbled forward as though in a panic to be on dry land again.

Something was wrong with them though, and there was a collective hush behind the glass doors as the passengers watched the stumbling gait of those disembarking. One woman was sneezing incessantly, and her eyes glared with fury as her mouth became covered with streaming snot, which she wiped over her face with her hands. She staggered forward, almost blind with her own secretions, and stumbled into a man to the side of her. He turned around and, without warning, punched her savagely in the face. Amazingly she stayed upright, but her nose exploded with the blow, sending blood and mucus out into the crowd. Rocco watched her stagger blindly forward, arms outstretched, but all of the other disembarking passengers were giving her a wide birth.

A giant of a man, wearing a security uniform, stepped forward to tackle the woman's attacker.

Rocco saw him mouth 'What the fuck's wrong with you?', but when the man turned to face him, he stepped back afraid. Rocco looked on as the violent man took a further step towards the security guard. Mucus was seeping from his mouth, and his eyes seemed *wrong* and unfocused.

'What's going on?' asked 'Harlem's Finest' as she appeared suddenly beside him. Her voice was breathy with fear.

Rocco couldn't answer; he didn't know, but he had a theory. He watched the crowd shamble away, wondering where he'd seen the woman with the streaming cold before. Rocco felt sick. She reminded him of the English girl in Times Square, the same mousy hair and slight figure.

'The world's going nuts. It's the heat,' said an elderly woman behind Rocco.

The remaining ferry passengers exited without further incident, but over half of those waiting to board backed away from the gate doors as they opened to allow them through. Rocco stepped forward and boarded, but he was careful not to touch any of the railings. He was beginning to think there was something more going on in New York City, and it looked contagious.

On board the ferry he found a seat on one of the outside platforms but kept his hands in his lap. 'Harlem's Finest' sat down beside him. There was no-one else there, so she put her hand on his leg. Rocco sighed. Why did they always hit on you when you're not in the mood? He ended up giving her something special to get rid of her; he didn't want a scene.


'Quiet tonight,' Rocco said as Daryl turned up for his usual shift a few nights later.

Daryl didn't look well and half the other staff had called in sick, but it didn't matter that much, because the usual clientele was also down by half. Everything was too quiet.

Rocco looked at the takings figures for the week and knew Lucrezia would be dismayed by his efforts. He really didn't want to disappoint her.

'Maybe we need to get some flyers printed and send some of the girls out into the streets to promo the club –

half-price drinks, anything as long as we get some bodies back in here.'

Daryl shrugged; he was unusually surly.

'Whatever you say, boss,' he said, rolling his eyes. 'Things will be all right again when the lady boss gets back.'

Rocco felt a momentary annoyance as Daryl's comments made him feel he was to blame for everything.

'I think the riots scared the tourists away,' he said, then bit his lip as he realised he was making excuses to a subordinate.

'Yeah,' said Daryl.

Rocco looked out over the club through the two-way mirror in his office, which was positioned on a platform above the dance floor. From his vantage point he could see what was happening pretty much everywhere, and he'd become expert in assessing body language.

'What's happening there?' he asked, and Daryl came over.

'Roxie?'

'Yes.'

Down below there was a commotion. The customer that Roxie was serving didn't look happy. Daryl went down to try to resolve the issue, and even though his shift was over, Rocco followed.

'Is everything okay, sir?' asked Rocco.

'I ordered Southern Comfort on the rocks and this

stupid bitch brought me Scotch malt,' complained the customer, a suited man whom Rocco recognised as a regular. Rocco couldn't place his name, because his brain just didn't seem to be working well today.

'He's a lying little shit,' Roxie butted in. 'He ordered the malt, he just don't wanna give me a tip.'

'That's it!' said the man. 'This place has now lost my considerable custom.'

'Go in the back!' Daryl ordered Roxie. 'I'll deal with you later.'

Rocco apologised to the man and sent another waitress to get him a Southern Comfort. A free meal and some special attention from the girls meant that he would be happy enough by the end of the evening.

'What the hell is up with you?' he asked Roxie later. 'You don't like this job or something? You can't go around calling the customers liars. And he may well be a jumped up little shit, but you sure don't call him one to his face.'

They were in the kitchen. Rocco always spoke to staff, especially female ones, in a public area. That way he couldn't be accused of anything. Around them the cooks, also short-handed, were working flat out to produce food. A stream of new customers had just poured in after the theatre, hungry and thirsty.

One of the juniors was chopping peppers on a board behind Roxie. Roxie cast him an annoyed glance and then turned back to Rocco.

'He lied!' she insisted.

'I don't give a shit. The customer is always right. We're short tonight, so you're lucky I'm not throwing your bony ass outta here.'

Daryl came in. 'Jeez is she still here? I thought this dumb bitch would be finished at last.'

The junior cook placed his knife down beside his chopping board and tipped the chopped peppers into a bowl. He ignored the row between the bosses and Roxie, even though he'd always liked her. He didn't want to lose his job by interfering. He turned away as Roxie glanced once more over her shoulder.

Daryl hadn't finished with her though. Her blasé attitude annoyed him. If Rocco wouldn't fire her ass then he would wind her up until he had to. Not for the first time he wondered if Roxie had something on Rocco, but a glance at his boss told him nothing other than that he too was frustrated with her.

'What the fuck's up with you?' continued Daryl. 'How many chances do you think you deserve?'

'I deserve to be treated with respect,' Roxie said.

'Respect? You're just some stupid …'

'Don't call me stupid! I ain't stupid.' Roxie stood upright, all sign of indifference gone, her eyes blazing. Rocco saw a thin stream of liquid emerge from her nose.

'You're not stupid?' goaded Daryl. 'You are so fucking stupid. Only some stupid whore would throw away all the chances she's been given. You're that dumb you …'

The cooks all stopped work and turned to watch as they felt something in the air ignite. The head chef came across to Rocco. 'Boss?' said the chef. He did not appreciate this sort of argument taking place in his kitchen. 'Can we take this elsewhere?

'I said don't call me stupid!' Roxie yelled.

At that moment Roxie reached behind her and grabbed the knife from the worktop, bringing it round in one sweep and slashing into Daryl's throat before either he or Rocco could react.

As her arm flew back for another blow, the kitchen staff dived on her. The knife was knocked out of her hand and skittered across the polished tiles before coming to rest under one of the counters.

Rocco caught Daryl as he fell to the floor.

'Someone call 911,' he yelled, 'and keep a hold of that crazy bitch!'

Roxie struggled, kicking and screaming. Her teeth gnashed together as she turned her head, snapping at her captures. White foam collected at the corners of her mouth. She was insane. Rabid.

As Daryl bled to death on the floor, Rocco stood and punched Roxie in the face, knocking her out.

'Stick her in the meat locker 'til the cops get here,' he ordered.

The chef and his kitchen staff did as they were told. They were quiet and shocked by what had happened. The chef locked the door, leaving Roxie on ice.

'You shouldn't have hit her, boss,' the chef said quietly to Rocco.

'Yeah. I know. But someone had to do something to stop her …'

The kitchen reeked of blood, sweat and sickness.

'She gonna be all right in there?' asked the junior chef.

Rocco looked at his fist. One of Roxie's teeth was buried in his knuckle and it hurt like hell.

'Get me the first-aider,' he ordered. 'We need someone here to help Daryl.'

The first-aider was a waitress called Marlene. Marlene rushed in with the junior chef behind her, but hadn't been briefed. She stopped dead when she saw Daryl and the blood that was rapidly spreading out over the usually spotless floor.

'Fuck!'

'Get your ass down here,' said Rocco as he kneeled beside Daryl. 'What should we do?'

'It doesn't matter,' said Marlene.

'What the fuck are you talking about?'

'He's dead.' Marlene's eyes were as empty as the corpse of Daryl that Rocco was now cradling.

'He's got a wife and kids …' Rocco said.


When the paramedics and cops arrived, they couldn't do anything more for Daryl, and the club was closed, all customers sent home. Rocco's staff answered their questions in the same dull, shocked voices. They couldn't believe how Roxie had lost it, or that Rocco had lost it when he punched her in the face.

'He had no choice,' said the junior chef to a female officer. 'She was crazed. Insane.'

He was the boss and no-one would have said a word against him anyhow, but deep down they all knew that Rocco had really had no choice but to stop Roxie. The sight of her wild eyes and demented expression would remain with them for many years to come.

Rocco held a glass of Jack Daniels in his undamaged hand, but raised the other to his face. The paramedics gave him a tetanus shot after pulling out the crumbling remains of Roxie's tooth. Then they patched him up. His knuckle was broken; the tooth had penetrated right to the bone. His hand throbbed. It felt twice the normal size and the huge bandage wrapped around it didn't help. His arm ached too, but worse yet was how he felt inside. It felt as though Roxie had bitten right into his soul.

*I'm being stupid,* he thought. *The last few days have been completely weird and they've freaked me out.*

Rocco downed the whisky and slammed the glass down onto the bar. The staff had all gone, only he remained, and the quiet was peculiar. He even missed the loud music, often not his thing, blaring out of the speakers. He realised he'd rarely been in this place without other people buzzing around: cleaners, staff or patrons. Even the week before, when it had been his turn to lock up after everyone else left, he hadn't really been alone, because Roxie had still been here until he closed. She'd been fine then. It was all so fucked up.

After he locked up, Rocco went downstairs to the basement garage to get his car. The quiet made him feel unhinged. It was 3.00 am. He switched the light on in the basement, and fumbled with the lock in his car. He felt woozy; probably a combination of the shots he'd been given by the medics and the booze he'd consumed since.

*It'll be just my luck to get pulled for driving under the influence*, he thought as he yanked the seatbelt around himself.

Driving through the streets, Rocco's unease increased. He saw abandoned cars and taxis on the roadside. Bars and clubs that were normally open were deathly quiet. The city felt like a graveyard. Then he began to notice the bodies. There was a man and woman splayed out like crumpled dolls on the sidewalk. In the middle of the street he swerved to avoid the hunched body of a man kneeling in the road. He was twitching and jerking. As Rocco passed him, he glanced at the man. In the gloom; he looked like a melting wax figure. Rocco's heart lurched. He slowed down and pulled aside as another man threw himself out from behind a truck. His car stalled. For a moment he considered getting out, but one glance in his rear-view mirror made him realise that it would be a bad idea. The man who'd almost thrown himself in front of his car was shambling towards him, his fists up, covered in what could only be blood. It reminded him of Roxie and the way she'd charged at the cops when they'd opened the meat locker, kicking and screaming in profound rage until they'd knocked her down and cuffed her. It was terrible to see anyone behaving like that, let alone a woman.

Rocco locked his doors and restarted his engine, speeding away just as the man reached his side door. He felt and heard the hard thud as the man smashed his fist into the rear door, and as he looked in his mirror again, he saw the man violently thumping his fists, then his head, into the side of an abandoned truck. It was almost as if he didn't feel any pain. Up ahead the cars were more randomly scattered, some even blocking the road, and so in order to get out of the city, Rocco drove the wrong way down a one-way street. Driving like this, it still took him more than an hour to get out of the centre and head for home.

*Something's really wrong*, Rocco's mind chanted.

Rocco experienced a brief respite from his anxiety as he turned into the car park under his complex and reached for his remote, but some ass-hole had left the gate open again.

'Goddamn it! This place is supposed to be kept locked.'

There'd been a lot of vandalism lately, kids from surrounding territories getting in, stealing or damaging the expensive cars. Rocco drove in, pressing the remote as he passed through the gate, and heard the doors shut behind him. Once parked, he couldn't shake his feeling of unease, so he hurried quickly through the lot to the lifts.

As he waited, Rocco turned and looked out into the dark pools of the car park. Every sound and creak dragged anxiety from him. He couldn't wait to be in the safety of his own home. When the lift finally arrived he hurried inside, pushing the button and inserting his key before pressing himself to the back wall and looking anxiously out through the doors. He felt like a thousand sinister eyes were watching him, and he kept having this crazy thought that any moment someone would come running out of the darkness and throw themselves inside with him. It was a relief when the doors slid closed and nothing happened.

When the lift arrived at his floor, Rocco paused a moment before exiting, just in case there were some crazy people waiting for him there. The hallway was empty and silent. There was, however, a splash of red on the beige carpet outside the lift.

Paranoia engulfed Rocco. He hurried down the corridor, his head turning left and right as though he expected the doors to the other apartments to fly open. But there wasn't a sound coming from any of the rooms. His whole body was trembling so much as he reached his apartment that he could barely place the key in the door. Down the corridor he heard the lift door open again, and thought he heard someone emerge onto the floor.

Rocco steadied the key with his injured hand and threw his door open, almost falling inside as he yanked his keys back from the lock. He slammed the door shut, resting with his back on the wood as though he expected an immediate attack. His heart was pounding, blood rushed in his ears so hard that he couldn't trust his hearing. He thought he heard someone outside in the corridor, but now inside his place, he wasn't sure if the whole evening's insanity had just temporarily unhinged him. After all, what had he seen that night that couldn't be explained as New York's usual populace of drunks and druggies?

He forced his breathing back, swallowed the anxious gasps that choked his throat. Calmer, he listened at the door.

Nothing moved. All was quiet. But the terrible silence was the worst of it. It stretched out beyond his flat, further than the corridor outside and out into the streets around him. Not even the distant cry of a police car or ambulance. The absence of noise spoke to him. It called to all his senses, demanding to be heard.

Rocco moved into his apartment. Sat down on his sofa and reached for the remote. He had to know what was on the news. He had to find out what was really going on.

Something slammed against his front door. It rattled and shook. Rocco jumped up from his seat and ran back into his hallway. The door was hit again. He stared at it, sickness and fear paralysing his heart and lungs until he had to force himself to breathe. He crept forward, afraid the assailant would hear his movements, and cautiously opened the security peep-hole.

For a moment he couldn't understand what he saw. The reception security guard was holding a fire extinguisher.

'Thank God!' Rocco gasped, reaching for the lock.

At that moment the security guard slammed the extinguisher into his door.

'What the fuck!'

The security guard was enraged. Insanity inflamed his bloodshot eyes. The peep-hole magnified his vile leer as the guard realised he was being watched.

'Little pig, little pig … let me come in,' the guard laughed.

Rocco felt sick. The guard's white teeth dripped saliva. The magnification of the peep-hole lens elongated his nose, and Rocco felt that the man was indeed the Big Bad Wolf. There was no way he would let him in here.

'I'm calling the cops!' Rocco said.

'G'head. But I'll be in there before you get to your phone, ass-hole,' replied the guard.

He was over six foot, an ex-boxer, and he kept himself in prime shape. Rocco was five ten, 20 or 30 pounds overweight; he knew he had no chance against the guard.

'Why are you doing this?' he yelled as the guard slammed the extinguisher once more against his door.

The guard laughed, then began to choke. He coughed

and spluttered, spraying blood and mucus over the peep-hole.

Rocco used those moments to draw the security bolts across the door and ran into his apartment looking for anything that could be used as a weapon. He looked at his prized designer ornaments, heavy, ugly and male; he'd been proud of the bachelor feel it gave to his place. But he shook his head: *that'll be no good against the brute strength of the guard.* In the kitchen he rummaged through the drawers until he pulled free the carving knife his brother had bought him one Christmas. He'd never used it: he didn't cook, so it was pristine and sharp.

The guard was still coughing outside and hadn't resumed his assault on the door. Rocco tried to see what was happening, but all he could make out was a distorted image swaying in front of the door. But as if he knew Rocco was there, the guard slammed against the door once more and renewed his attack with more vigour.

'You bastard!' yelled the guard. 'I always fucking hated your smarmy attitude. You think the world owes you everything, like all the others did …'

'What are you talking about?' Rocco said, trying to keep the panic from showing in his voice.

'I killed 'em. I killed 'em all! They didn't even see it coming.'

'Why for God's sake?'

''Cos I could. And they all treated me like shit, just like you.'

Rocco couldn't believe what he was hearing. The man outside didn't sound like the security guard he knew. He'd exchanged many pleasantries with the man. It was hard to believe he'd become psychotic like this. He'd even given the man a special drink a few days ago and thought that had ensured a casual friendship.

'Look … er …' but what was his name? 'If I offended you, I'm sorry. But I thought we kinda got along.'

The security guard threw his entire body against the door, and the bolts and hinges groaned and creaked as they became compromised by the constant attack. Rocco knew that the next one would probably be the last and the guard would break through. He stood back and waited, holding the knife at his side. He wanted to use it only as a last resort; he was still hoping he could talk the man down.

The door screamed as the assailant barged through holding the extinguisher high above his head. Rocco looked the guard in the eye and recognised nothing human there. He didn't hesitate. He ran forward to meet him, throwing his own weight behind the knife as he raised it between them.

There was a sickening crunch as the blade skimmed the guard's breast bone. Rocco pulled back on reflex when he felt the resistance. The guard was incensed, even though he didn't seem to feel anything in his rage.

Rocco stepped back just in time to avoid having his skull crushed by the extinguisher. He ducked down under the guard's arm, skirted around the back of him and waited as the guard swivelled. Rocco saw his chance, and this time thought better about his aim. He stepped into the guard's arms with the knife at his side and then, as hard as he could, he thrust upwards.

Fabric and flesh tore as the carving knife slid into the man's body. Rocco felt it scrape against the ribs as the knife juddered in his grasp. It was a horrible sensation, a combination of carving fresh meat but killing it at the same time. Instinct made him throw himself forward, putting all his strength behind the lunge. He felt a moment's triumph as the blade hit home. The guard let out a surprised, angry sigh and Rocco stepped back, pulling the knife with him.

The guard stared at him for a moment before the strength finally went out of his arms and he dropped the extinguisher between them. Blood poured from the man's eyes and mouth, but Rocco doubted that it had anything to do with his injuries. There had been something wrong with him anyway; otherwise he wouldn't have been coughing up blood and phlegm.

The guard took a step forward, but Rocco was pumped with adrenaline now, and despite the nausea that rolled in his stomach as he glanced down at the blood-covered knife, he plunged it into the man again, this time twisting and turning all the way in. The guard fell to his knees and Rocco jumped back as he tumbled forward, dead.

Rocco stared at the body. Blood was seeping from

underneath it onto his laminate floor. He turned away, falling against the door frame even as his stomach dry heaved. The knife was still in his grasp and his mind replayed the feeling of resistance, and the sound, smells and sensation of the blade slipping into the guard. Rocco thought he would never feel the same again. *I've killed someone,* he thought. But it had been self defence, surely?

He looked at the body again, and for the first time noticed the deterioration of the man's flesh. He was newly dead but looked like a month-old corpse. Skin was dripping from his fingers like vile mucus. His face was all but melting into the floor. The corpse was already rotting.

*It's a fucking zombie! Everyone's a fucking zombie*, his mind screamed, but still Rocco fought to find another explanation for all that he saw, because the idea of zombies was just too insane.

Outside, the landing was quiet once more. He wondered if the guard had told the truth and the other occupants were indeed dead. He wasn't sure and didn't want to investigate. Once the adrenaline in his body dropped, he felt scared and exhausted. And with the door compromised, he had never felt so unsafe in his life.

He left the body of the guard and, still clinging to the knife, made his way down the hall and back into the lift. In the basement he hurried back to his car. There was only one place he could go that was safe and secure: he headed back to the Shadow Club.

The drive back was eventful. Rocco saw a house burning unchecked, a car rammed into the front of a 7-11, a rabid child tearing the throat out of a terrified woman who had been caught on the streets. By the time he got back to the club, Rocco had seen sights he never wanted to see again. He saw a tramp eating a dog alive, even as the dog snapped and bit back, and a mother choking her own baby to death, holding it around the throat at arm's length in the middle of Broadway, while a man, presumably the baby's father, laughed hysterically, shouting out, 'That'll shut the little bastard up!'

Rocco drove swiftly by all of them, but they barely glanced in his direction as his car once again weaved in and out of the streets of Manhattan.

Rocco felt more dead than alive by the time he opened the club entrance. All he wanted to do was lie down and sleep on one of the couches in there. When he got to the main door however, he found the grille unlocked. He wasn't expecting to find anyone else inside, and only he had the keys since Daryl was dead, so he figured he must have left it unlocked in his confusion earlier.

The main door was locked and so he inserted his key, turned it and pulled open the door.

'What the fuck is going on?' asked Lucrezia as Rocco closed the main door behind him.

She stood half in the doorway of the bar. The light behind her made her more shadow than person.

Rocco raised his knife and pointed it at her, his hand trembling.

'There's blood all over the kitchen, Rocky. I expected to find this place open, instead I get here, it's locked up tight and there's fucking crazies outside killing each other.'

Lucrezia stepped forward into the light and Rocco saw that she looked normal. At least, that is, normal for a vampire. In fact she was a sight for sore eyes. She looked stunning with her long blonde hair cascading and curling over her shoulder.

'How'd you get in here?' he asked, lowering the knife.

'I do have keys ...' she pointed out.

Rocco turned and carefully locked and bolted the door behind him.

'I don't know what the fuck is going on ...' he said.

'Jeez, Rocky. You look like shit.'

Rocco walked towards her and noticed something in her eyes he'd never seen. She was wary and suspicious of him. Not surprising really, he was covered in blood, holding a large carving knife and had that evening punched a woman in the face and then killed his apartment security guard. He stared down at his hands, realising for the first time that somehow he'd lost the bandage, but he couldn't remember when that was.

'Rough night?' Lucrezia said as though she'd read his thoughts.

'You could say that. And there's fucking zombies in

New York City.'

'That's impossible. Zombies don't exist. Believe me, I'd have heard of them before now if they did.'

'Yeah? Well tell that to those fucking walking corpses out there.'

'You're in shock,' she said. 'Get in here; I'll pour you a drink.'

Rocco came into the bar, the couch beckoned and he stumbled over to it, lying down before the urge to fall down overcame him.

'You won't believe what I've been through,' he said.

Rocco lay back, closing his eyes as Lucrezia put a neat whisky down on the table beside him. With her here he felt safe. Now she was back, the world would right itself again, life would return to normal. Rocco drifted to sleep, leaving his glass untouched. Just before he fell into unconsciousness it occurred to him to wonder about Lucrezia's strange clothing. She was wearing some kind of silver jumpsuit. Not her usual style at all.

'He's here,' Lucrezia said. 'Sleeping like a baby.'

'Thanks for the tip,' the man from HazMat said through the speaker in his clear visor. 'How did you know he was the carrier?'

'I have some experience in these things,' Lucrezia said. 'Speak to your colleague, Dr Norton. He'll vouch for my credentials.'

'You didn't touch him?'

'Would you?' Lucrezia said, turning to look at Rocco as he slept on the couch. She too was wearing a visor and a HazMat suit.

'Hell, no!'

Rocco looked awful; his skin was dripping from him like warm butter. His eyes, nose and mouth were weeping pus and blood mingled with drool. To the casual eye he looked as bad as one of the 'zombies' outside.

'Take him away,' said the man from HazMat. 'We'll have to decontaminate the place.'

'Of course,' Lucrezia said.

Rocco woke as they were strapping him to the stretcher. He could barely open his eyes, his lids looked like melted wax and the sides of his mouth drooped as his face dissolved.

'Waz zappening?' he slurred.

'Please do not struggle, sir. We're here to help you.' A woman said from behind her hazard suit.

'Loucreesha?'

'It's all for the best,' she told him as they wheeled him away and out into the waiting unmarked truck.

Rocco didn't struggle, as there was no strength left in his disintegrating muscles.

After they'd gone, Lucrezia removed her suit and packed it in her holdall. She left the club and locked the door behind her, pulling closed the heavy grille to secure it. The HazMat team would return to decontaminate, but she would be long gone. She had to be before they spoke to Dr Norton and learned that he had never actually heard of her.

She felt a momentary angst at having to leave behind everything that she had worked for, all because of a silly error in judgement.

It'd started with the phone calls after she'd left New York on her trip. Rocco's insecurity had poured down the phone almost as soon as she landed in Los Angeles.

'How long are you going to be? I'm missing you.'

She'd made him her Renfield some years before, fed off him and given him some of her blood. It tied him to her for life; she knew that, and it was intentional. That way it made Rocco hers to control, he became her public and business face, helping her avoid all those nasty questions and curiosity. And it had worked well, until now.

Leaving him for so long had an impact she wasn't expecting. Usually she never left her Renfields, except when she no longer had use for them. Then she dealt with them permanently before departing.

'You've been gone for a week now. I need you,' he'd sobbed down the phone. But even then she hadn't realised the extent of the problem.

'It will do you good to be away from me a while, Rocky.'

'I'm lonely.'

And of course he would be. She was the centre of

his universe, even though he didn't realise it. She had him completely under her thrall. That of course was the mistake. If she had left him even an ounce of his own will Rocco would have coped better with her absence. But over the years she'd drained it all away.

*I've always been a control freak*, she thought.

As the days stretched to weeks it got worse for Rocco. He didn't know what he was doing of course. A touch here, a stroke there. He was only passing on what she'd given him.

Roxie was the first; he kept her back after work. They had sex in his office and afterwards Rocco fed her some of his blood. It was all downhill from there. The infection spread in body fluids, became airborne in a sneeze. In a city as dirty and germ-filled as New York it didn't take much for it all to breed and spread. It was somehow ironic that Roxie had brought the virus back to Rocco and infected him when her tooth penetrated his knuckle.

*I should have realised that he'd try to create a bond elsewhere to help fill the void,* Lucrezia thought.

Of course if it had been just Roxie, it would have been easier to contain and the damage might not have been so severe. There'd been the English girl Rocco picked up in Times Square of course, and finally, out of desperation, the security guard. Each time Rocco forgot the blood exchange as soon as it happened. He'd been programmed to do that. But feeding others his contaminated blood was something he'd decided to do on his own.

Lucrezia found Rocco's car in the club parking lot. There was the dead body of a girl dissolving on the back seat. She was face down, and Lucrezia could barely make out a flamboyant tattoo on her lower back.

*Things really did get out of hand.*

She left the parking lot, looking out on the street as it began to come alive again. HazMat vans were everywhere cleaning up the mess. The zombies were too weak now to put up a struggle. She merged with the shadows, scaling the wall of a building until she stood on the top, 30 storeys up.

Lucrezia surveyed the chaos. *Death by a strain of Ebola, which affects the brain of the infected.* That would be the official story; after all, the reality would never even be considered. Breathing in the sounds and smells of human misery and woe. It was disastrous, a mistake she wouldn't soon repeat, but the horror of it was glorious.

## AUTHOR'S NOTES

I wanted to write a zombie story for this collection because zombies are the only monster that actually frighten me. They've been portrayed in many ways. Hammer horror films have shown them as helpless victims of a voodoo priest. There have been mechanical shuffling creatures capable of sudden attack, usually cannibal (*Zombie Flesh Eaters*). They've also been shown in a humorous light, 'Send more paramedics …' (*Return of the Living Dead*). But it is the sheer mindlessness of them as well as the cannibalistic urges that I have always found so terrifying.

Visiting New York recently I was struck by the sheer gothic element of the city. The first morning, David and I walked around Central Park and I observed the imposing nature of the buildings around the park. It was unusual that every time I looked up at the skyline, in the middle of this vast park, all I could see were these ugly buildings. Maybe it was the jetlag, but I found them overwhelming. They looked like they were stalking the park, ready to pounce. It was really quite creepy. So, what better place to set my zombies free?

The idea for this story developed further with a trip on the Staten Island ferry. We were joking about the reaction of the people on the other side of the glass gates, if zombies emerged from the ferry towards them.

Later I had a horrible nightmare where my home was attacked by terrorists and I fought one off with a knife, burying it in his chest before he could kill me. I woke up feeling like I was going to be sick. I vividly remembered the horrible sensation of resistance, the vile gore, the actual death of the person. It had been so clear. All of these elements have been used to create some of the imagery within this story, as you can see.

That is how my strange mind works and how ideas for stories and novels form. Sometimes dreams and bits of real life experiences are mingled to create the fiction. As with most of my stories, I use a combination of realism and supernatural. The normal occurrences emphasise the weird and exaggerate the terror by the juxtaposition.

I was also attempting to up the ante in this story by building on Rocco's fears as he moved from one place to another. Fear often makes situations seem more intense, and judgement can be impaired. This is why Rocco is torn by what he sees and what he imagines is going to happen – as the imagined horror is usually worse than the reality.

Obviously I was looking for a different cause or angle. I was a little bored with the apocalyptic stories, but played with the ideas anyway, hinting at a contagion. I'm not sure, but I don't think zombies were ever created by a vampire's Renfield before, so that in itself should be different. My 'zombies' talk, don't feel pain, don't necessarily eat people but may bite in rage. They melt and rot away as the infection becomes advanced, find stress difficult to cope with and often resort to violence, displaying a complete lack of judgement and inhibition as their brains deteriorate. They aren't dead first and then rise, they disintegrate into the condition.

So, although Rocco calls them 'zombies', I'll leave it up to you to decide if my creatures really do fit that genre.

# TAR

There was a noise down the hall, a subtle scraping, like dogs' claws scratching against the tiled floor. I raised my head and looked towards my office door; the secure lab was down the hallway. The subtle sound continued. I listened for a moment then shrugged. *Dental pick on fossil bone.* Mystery solved. I glanced at the clock: it was late. The other scientists often worked long hours. My colleagues were a dedicated crew. It was hard to imagine how they managed to have a social life outside of the Pits. For me it didn't matter, I had no-one to go home to. I chose my life to suit myself.

There was a buzz around La Brea Museum. It had been there for several months, ever since Michael and I found the fossils. They were like nothing we'd ever seen before. Tomorrow was the big reveal, but was the world ready for an eighth wonder? I wasn't sure. And if I'd found the fossils alone, I'm certain I wouldn't have even shown them to Michael.

'This is far bigger than any wolf's head we've recovered so far.' Michael had said, at first only vaguely curious. But it was the semi-human skeleton with it that sparked the first excitement.

I watched him rubbing his eyes, as though he couldn't trust his own vision when we found the pelvis. After that the pieces came together like a jigsaw. The excavation was a complete success, and all because of one tiny little bubble of tar breaking up from a newly-mown lawn. The area hadn't even belonged to the Museum. It was a small garden at the back of a little café close by. Once the right sum of money changed hands, the old *barista*, able to retire, happily turned over the keys to his shop.

'This *is* twice the size of the usual wolves,' I commented, picking up the skull carefully from the box and turning it around in my gloved hands to scrutinise the prominent snout.

Solid black tar covered the bone. The fossil would need painstaking, specialist cleaning before we could properly examine it.

'Wolves' heads are ten-a-penny,' Michael replied.

The jaw was missing. The top canines snarled, lipless. I began a mental reconstruction; though it was not a talent but merely experience that enabled me to mentally recreate a fossil. The skin filled out before my eyes, sinew and muscle, interlinked with veins and blood vessels. The lips plumped up; hair sprouted from the face, head, chin. The eyes were the last; they bulged with intelligence, a calculating and feral anger flooded the veins. The jaw began to open in my palm.

I blinked, sending the illusion away.

'Lucy? You okay?' Michael stared at me.

'Fine. I was just …'

Michael took the skull from my trembling fingers.

'It *is* much bigger,' he said.

We had spent most of the week excavating the site, painstakingly cutting through stinking, damp and clingy tar, thoroughly examining and trying to identify all the bones we found. Then Michael found the pelvis.

'My God! That appears almost human, but it can't be.' He placed the fossil with the others in the rapidly filling box.

'Well, we haven't managed to find the missing link,' I laughed. 'Who's to say it isn't a wolf, and not a monkey we evolved from?'

Michael's laughter echoed around the garden of the former café.

I opened my door to find Bella, my assistant, standing nervously outside.

'What's wrong?' I asked.

'Oh, Lucy! I didn't realise you were still here.'

Bella had been acting peculiar for weeks. I stared at her long and hard. Down the corridor the echo of feet breathed silently to my sensitive ears. Bella's eyes darted away from mine when I tried to make eye contact.

Sensible girl. Although she had no idea I was a 16th Century vampire, one look in my eyes and I would know everything there was to know about her. But I had to be careful. Working in pathology, with blood and criminals, suited me just fine, and with the decades … well … centuries actually … of experience behind me, I was the best in the world. Which is why I'd ended up working in LA at the tar pits in La Brea. They needed an expert in fossil reconstruction, with specialism in bone structure and wolves, and among the many things I'd studied over the years was exactly that.

'I'm just leaving actually,' I told her and took careful note of the perspiration beading her top lip, the dilation of her averted pupils. 'You should go home too.'

'I am. I just have one final piece of work to do before tomorrow.'

I took my jacket from the hook at the back of my office door and looked around for my handbag. The office was bland, tidy and characterless and that was just how I liked it. I shut down my computer; the wolf screensaver blinked before the monitor clicked off. I straightened the post-it pad and my paperweight of Fool's Gold then turned to leave. When I reopened the door to the corridor, Bella was gone.

I walked through the museum, glancing briefly into the glass laboratory that faced out into the visitors' area. The remains would be displayed in there tomorrow. They were all set out on a large surgical trolley, which would be wheeled in from the secure lab in the morning. I didn't like working in the glass lab; being scrutinised by the patrons made me feel like an animal on display at the zoo. The lab was empty now, and so I looked into the dark, where I could vaguely see the remains of the latest Mammoth find, spread out in a semblance of order on the huge table.

I made my way through to the employees' exit.

'Good night, Dr Collins,' the security guard nodded.

'Night, Hank.'

I sneaked back in through the roof window a few minutes later. This was my favourite trick; I didn't like anyone to become suspicious of how late I liked to stay. Most nights I didn't go home at all.

I blended into the darkness in the way that my kind have a particular knack of doing. Unseen and undetected. In the dark of the corridor, Bella scurried along to the secure lab, no doubt hoping that I had not become suspicious of her strange behaviour. She was an odd girl. I often thought she must be taking some form of addictive substance, though I'd never smelt anything on her. Bella's behaviour was always nervous, twitchy and strange. Tonight though, she was worse.

She checked each room along the corridor, from the janitor's closet to the glass lab. It was as though she wanted to make sure that no-one else was on the premises. Perhaps she was just making a last check on the exhibit.

But no. She was wearing a red cardigan.

I'd never seen her in anything other than pastel shades. Pale pink and girly powder blue dresses, skirts and high necked blouses. I watched the sway of her flowing black dress; it swept the floor. No wonder she was nervous. Why hadn't I noticed she was wearing something so salacious? She glanced around, but I merged with the shadows so that she couldn't see me observing her. The dress gaped open at the neckline. Interesting. Clearly my mousy assistant had a rendezvous, but which of my married colleagues was it with?

Bella slipped into the lab and swiftly closed the door. Within seconds I pressed my ear against the wood and listened.

'You came!'

'Of course I did,' Bella giggled.

I heard kissing, hot and passionate, but I couldn't recognise the other voice. It was deeper and harsher than that of any of my cultured colleagues.

I thought about intervening. I was annoyed that Bella had brought in an outsider, particularly into the secure lab. The remains of the large wolf were in there.

I hadn't allowed many people access to the latest find either and here was Bella, a shoddy undergrad, letting in her boyfriend. But then, I shouldn't be here either, and how would I explain to the security guard that I had sneaked back in without him seeing me?

The chanting started while I was having a mental debate with myself.

A cold, raw sound. It was mimicry of a psalm but without the reverence. I shuddered. I didn't care much for churches or religion, for obvious reasons. St Peter's church flashed before my eyes. It had been a long time since I had been in Rome, and the Vatican held a lot of painful memories. I shook myself. I could smell candles and incense in the air.

I've always preferred discretion when dealing with humans who overstep the mark. I knew the best way to handle this was to get security to throw them out, but an angry vampire doesn't always see reason. I took a step back from the door, saw the candlelight flickering underneath. Put two and two together and made four – some kind of kinky satanic rite was occurring in my lab! And boy was I pissed.

The chanting increased in volume; the sound echoed round the room and out into the corridor. There were many voices and they were praying as though they were raising the anti-Christ.

I opened the door with practised discretion and slipped inside the narrow gap before closing it again.

Nothing could have prepared me for the sight that greeted me, and I thought I'd seen it all.

Thirteen candles created a large circle around Bella and her lover, and 13 robed figures held them. Bella was naked, spread out like a whore. Her arms and legs seemed to be held down by an invisible force. She looked scared, and I could see why.

Her lover was changing. He was a beautiful, semi-naked black athlete. His ebony skin shone in the candlelight. But the skin, already toned and muscular, rippled and warped as his torso stretched. His face changed, jaw bone cracking agonisingly as his face expanded and distorted into a muzzle. I shrank back into the shadows.

The enormity of my discovery began to make sense as the frame of the man became bestial. His spine curved as the bones reformed. He fell to his knees, back arching, hands and fingers cracking and growing into claws. Bone and sinew reformed. He stood up on his hind legs, his front paws reaching up to the ceiling, and his male member grew larger and more erect as he towered over Bella. She was unable or too afraid to move, but her mouth gaped and her eyes grew wide until the whites consumed them. Her head fell back as her body grew tense against her invisible bonds. White foam burst from her lips and dribbled down her chin as her head turned from side to side. My guess was she had not known her lover was a werewolf.

The chanting continued.

Within the circle lay the fossil bones of my exhibit. I'd known it was a half human, half wolf creature but the transformation of this man put it into perspective. The bones lay in the gap between Bella's parted legs and I fought with myself to hold back and remain unobserved, even though I was afraid the fossils would be crushed under the weight of the black werewolf.

The ritual change seemed almost complete. I remained hidden from the worshippers, too mesmerised to intervene as the wolf stalked around Bella. His grinning maw appeared to be smiling in that lecherous way some men have. A shudder ran down my spine. Even I, a monster in my own right, felt the horror of that hungry expression, which suggested a craving for neither lust nor blood, but for both. He knelt between her legs and ran his vicious clawed hands over her breasts, but did not break the skin. It seemed more of a threat or warning, in case she protested. Bella was beyond rational thought. He lifted her body up. She was like a doll in his paws as he turned her, forcing her on her knees, on all fours. She complied, body shaking beneath him.

Bella, a seemingly homely girl, had been led astray by the beauty of a man. Possibly she wanted excitement, maybe even romance. Bella had definitely received more than she bargained for.

She screamed as he took her. Blood poured down

her legs, over the fossils, and I became galvanized into action. She was human; how could she possibly take this animal and not be irreparably destroyed inside?

'Stop it!' I yelled.

Rushing forward, I threw aside the chanting followers like paper dolls until I reached the wolf. But too late. He was sated and Bella was unconscious, her body limp and bleeding on the cold floor.

'You broke the circle!' a woman screamed, and I turned to see that the worshippers were surrounding me. They were all female.

'You're insane,' I yelled.

The women fell to their knees, shuddering as the wolf reared up before me. I guess they weren't so crazy after all. They'd seen the treatment one woman received; maybe they didn't want to be next on the wolf's rape list. Or perhaps they did …

'Woman! Stupid woman! You don't know what you've done,' a gruff half human, half animal scraping sound came from his strangely muffled throat.

His paw swiped at me and I pulled back seconds before his sharp claws could rake my face. With this and the overpowering smell of blood, my fangs burst from my gums in response to the challenge.

'Oh dear doggie,' I said. 'You just made your biggest mistake yet.'

Werewolves are fast, but vampires are faster.

The 13 girls were sliced and diced as incidental

casualties. The wolf went wild, tearing up the lab in frustration, but every time he tried to reach me, he was sadly disappointed. He was like a crazed dog chasing his tail, so it was very unfortunate that Bella decided to wake up and start screaming. The wolf's paw swung, his claws half-severed her head and she crumpled once more, her life's blood spilling on the lab floor.

All thought of my fossil find was gone. Never piss off a vampire by invading her personal space; we are an unforgiving race. I charged the wolf in a rush of air, knocking him flat against the examination table in the corner. There was a metallic crash as cleaning instruments fell to the tiled floor. I watched a dental pick skid on the damp red surface and skitter under one of the cupboards. A glass measuring jug fell and smashed at my feet.

I jumped back, narrowly escaping the furious wolf, but leapt back into his space the minute he raised his paw and smashed him full in the snout, bloodying his nose. He howled. As his front paws reared, I ducked down and kicked him firmly in the groin – that works for animals as well as men – and he doubled over.

I've never seen an animal vomit before. It was strangely therapeutic. The wolf shuddered and groaned. Losing his grip on the animal inside him, he slowly began to change back to a man.

Clutching his bruised groin, the man looked up at me with watery eyes.

'Look at the mess you made in here,' I told him, hands on hips. 'You really should have done your homework. How many rules do you think have been broken by your careless invasion of my territory?'

'W … wh … at *are* you?'

I sighed. He really was just some stupid animal when it all came down to it.

'Well, let's put it this way … I'm your death.'

I finished him as viciously as he had finished his dumb female followers; slashing his throat with elongated claws. I was very careful not to ingest any of his blood, because it smelt very different from human haemoglobin. I didn't know if it would have a bad effect on me. But I wasn't hungry anyway. Witnessing bestial rape has a way of dulling your appetite.

I looked around the lab, wondering how I was going to explain all this and why the security guard hadn't shown up at the first sign of trouble. After all, there had been a lot of noise.

Something else was wrong.

The lab was liberally splashed with the blood of 14 women and a werewolf, so I'm not sure how I first noticed that the fossil bones were missing. But from where they had been there was a blood trail. I looked around, following it with my eyes. A path scraped through the blood and entrails that led to the now-open door. Maybe one of the women had managed to get out.

I followed the trail. A unique odour permeated the air, pungent, mixed with the many varieties of blood. It smelt like wet dog.

The museum was unnaturally quiet.

I felt like I was in some sorry B movie as I crept into the main exhibit area. I couldn't believe I was looking around in the dark for a crazed and wounded werewolf worshipper, but if I had any hope of salvaging the museum, the exhibition and my continued anonymity then I had to find that other girl before she did any more damage.

The blood trail ended where I found the body. She obviously hadn't brought herself this far either. She was a mess. It was as though someone had stuck her into a meat grinder, waist first. Her stomach and entrails were shredded and gnawed.

'That's done it,' I muttered. 'Looks like I have to find a new life. Fucking monsters, screwing up my life – again!'

Well, maybe I'd outstayed my welcome in LA anyway.

A deep-throated growl drew my attention to the Mammoth exhibit. The wolf I'd initially mistaken for one of the many life-size and realistic models that populated the museum began to move slowly in my direction. Stupid. I'd been so intent on finding the girl, I hadn't noticed the creature standing there in plain sight. Living among humans had dulled my senses.

The large wolf moved forward, padding towards me on all fours. Light from the laboratory area fell on his shiny coat, and I hadn't been prepared for the colour of his fur. In the half light it appeared the colour of the blood that had covered the remains of my fossil.

He reared up on hind legs; he was ten feet tall or more. There was a wary intelligence in his eyes. He sniffed the air in my direction, but didn't move closer. Merely halted and looked at me with curiosity. His eyes were blue.

It was impossible, but I knew it was true. My fossil bones had been revived, had absorbed the blood, and perhaps the followers had indeed known some magic to raise this monster from the dead. The whole thing had been planned. Maybe Bella had leaked the information to the werewolf and his harem, but now there was no way of ever knowing.

*Fenrir*. The name floated behind my eyes, echoed in my ears. Yes, my research into wolves had revealed many interesting things. I'd looked into the mythology of lycanthropy when I'd first found the skeleton, but had laughed off the possibility. Such is the arrogance of immortals.

'A wolf god.'

He nodded his snout as though he understood my words and thoughts.

'You're beautiful,' I breathed.

His head tilted to one side and then he fell forward

127

onto all fours and howled. It was the most magnificent sound I'd ever heard.

He paused before the large glass window. A shaft of moonlight from outside fell on him and the change took him by surprise. He rolled over on his back like a dog in mud and cried in pain as his body restructured itself. Animal limbs shrank, but not by much. The red pelt sank into his skin, leaving luscious white flesh, as pale as a newborn baby's. His snout retracted, leaving a strong, well proportioned chin, nose and curved, sensuous mouth. The red hair remained on his head. Long and rich, it wrapped around his shoulders as he curled up like a foetus, shivering in agony. The black wolf had made the transformation seem painless in comparison.

I went to him. All thoughts of murder gone.

'Do you have a name?' I asked, but his pleading blue eyes just looked at me.

A wolf god out of his time. How exactly would that feel? I took his arm, helped him stand. He was tall, perhaps six foot four or five. He seemed weakened by his change. *I should kill him now, before he revives.*

'I usually kill monsters who invade my territory …' I said.

Maybe I was getting soft in my old age, or maybe I understood the isolation and confusion I saw in his eyes. Whatever the reason, I used my strength to support him as we staggered back through the museum. After all, this was the discovery of the century. How on earth would I explain the missing bones? The corpses in the lab? My raped and murdered assistant? And a bloody trail dragged all through the exhibition room?

There was only one thing to do, get out of Dodge, and I was taking the *Fenrir* with me. I'd worry about what to do with him later. But first there were bodies to dispose of and blood to sluice. I've always liked the tar pits; they hold the mysteries of the past and they are a great place to hide the secrets of the present.

## AUTHOR'S NOTES

Following our first trip together to the Gallifrey One convention, in LA in February 2009, David and I spent the rest of the holiday with our friend, actor Frazer Hines, and our publicist Emily Danyel.

During the trip we'd done some of the usual tourist things but preferred instead to randomly go shopping or walk on the odd beach, eat out, drink cocktails and wine and generally chill. Halfway through the week, Frazer suggested that we go and meet his friend, actor Roy Dotrice, for lunch on Hollywood Boulevard.

Roy is a lovely man, a really traditional actor, now in his eighties. You'll remember him for his starring roles in *Beauty and the Beast* on television, *Hellboy II* and many more. He is also a real gentleman. We had a lovely lunch and talked about where we'd been and what we'd seen during the visit. Roy suggested we visit the La Brea Museum, because only that week it had been publicised that they had unearthed new mammoth remains. We decided to head off there and Roy said he'd come with us.

Once there I soon became fascinated with the large number of skulls they had on display. All wolves. David and I began to discuss the possibility of what can be found or lost in the tar and how interesting it would be to raise an ancient evil from its dark and poisonous pits. Mmmm. You see where this ended up then.

As we walked around the museum I took careful note of the working environment, especially as we could see the technicians cleaning the remains in a large glass-covered lab. It must have been like working in a fish tank for them, but generally they just ignored us and carried on.

Afterwards we left the museum with some leaflets and information and Roy bought two toy mammoths: one for Emily and one for me. Mine has taken up residence in the kitchen and I call it 'Roy' to remind us of the great day we spent. I hope he won't mind!

After I finished writing *Tar*, David wasn't as

impressed with the ending as I was. He felt that I should kill the wolf off. But I liked Red and you'll see, as you read on, that I had other plans for him ...

# Red

'Lucy, what do you think of this?' Red said.

My *Fenrir* was all naked and hard. Just the way I liked him. His blood red hair was draped over his shoulders. He was so gorgeous he was almost pretty, but there was nothing feminine about this powerful creature.

'I like it,' I said. 'A lot.'

Red looked down at his hard-on and laughed.

'Not that. It's a full moon tonight and that's kind of instinctual. Although you know I find your charms somewhat addictive. I mean this.'

He held up a note pad and I saw the large scrawling writing of a five year old child.

'That's great!' I told him, 'Your handwriting is really improving; it's legible now.'

Since his revival from the tar-covered remains we had found at La Brea I had been teaching him all kinds of new tricks, reading and writing being some of the more obvious. The learning, however, was a two-way street. For his part, Red had fucked me every which way from Sunday; especially doggy-style, which he seemed to like a lot: horny little wolf that he is.

At first I hadn't known what to do with him at all. I couldn't just leave him in the carnage for the authorities to find. Realistically that could have led them to me, after all. I'm nothing if not careful. Even though it wasn't my fault – and believe me I was still furious about that cult of Weres invading my lab and raising their God up from my fossils – but I digress. As you can imagine, I didn't make a habit of taking strays home, that just wasn't my style, but Red was intriguing.

At least he wasn't human and would probably have a little longevity. He certainly had stamina. Even when I bit him – which didn't happen often, because generally he didn't appreciate me feeding from him; that Alpha male thing, I guess – very exciting things occurred. First, he turned half-wolf. Second, he got a hard-on that lasted all night. I never knew how exhilarating it could be to be pounded, until you beg for mercy, by a horny werewolf. Third, and most important of all, Red's blood was gorgeous. Velvet in liquid form: nectar from a god. Red was, after all, a wolf god, and his blood gave me a rush I hadn't felt since my human days. I suspect it was like cocaine or heroin. Not that I'd tried drugs: wine and sex were my vices in 16th Century Italy; but you get the picture? It was the biggest buzz I'd ever experienced.

# RED

Red was certainly a force to reckon with. He didn't need the moon to change; he could do that anytime, and frequently did when it was most inconvenient in the early days. I'd lost count of the number of times when I was out with him and had to pretend he was just a huge dog that had slipped his leash. Then, I had to teach him to talk, as well as observe proprieties like keeping your clothes on. His world had been one of packs hunting for food. Howls and barks were the only speech required, though Red did have another language and he tried to communicate with me in his own words at first. It was a combination of basic sounds, grunts and gestures. Although none of the words he spoke sounded like any language I'd ever heard before, he'd obviously had to deal with humans at sometime or other. Luckily for me he was a fast learner and he took to the English language naturally. In fact he spoke it too perfectly. At times his speech was a little clipped and formal, and there wasn't a trace of accent in there, unlike the Italian inflection that occasionally still slipped into my vowels.

Sometimes, though, I couldn't help but wonder why I even cared. He was just an exciting toy to me, wasn't he? Or was I just kidding myself? Red turned me on to the world in more ways than just the physical. Also, the experience of teaching him was fun. I hadn't had anyone relying on me, hadn't wanted it in fact, for years. Red needed me; that was why, and maybe I'm making excuses here, he ended up becoming so much a part of my life in a very short space of time. So much so, that I couldn't imagine life without him.

Following our swift flight from La Brea, we'd obtained new identities. My cover was fucked over, and although I'd done my best to destroy evidence and clean up the mess, the werewolf and his ladies had trashed my lab. There was no way to repair the damage to all that. Furthermore, the precious bones we'd excavated had disappeared, and how was I going to explain to the authorities that actually they hadn't, they'd merely come alive after my assistant had been sacrificed over them? It would be a very difficult interview and one I wasn't willing to have, especially with the FBI. So, we ran. Or rather I did, dragging my sexy wolf-boy along for the ride.

Now we were in the south of France, new names, new lives, and for the first time in ages I was having a great deal of fun.

'Don't you remember anything from your life before?' I asked Red as we drove towards the beach.

'No.'

'I keep thinking the memories will come flooding back one day and that you'll be able to tell me of your life. I'd find the history fascinating, you know that.'

'Yes. I do.'

'So you'll tell me if anything comes back? Anything at all?'

'Of course.'

I ran my hand over his leg as I negotiated the windy

road down the hillside towards the coast, while Red gazed off into the distance. I found myself wondering, not for the first time, if he really would tell me what was going on in his head.

I was covered in sunblock. Although the sun doesn't kill me, it sure as hell itches if I don't have protection. Red, on the other hand, despite his blood red hair, tanned beautifully, and his lovely, sleek and firm body was like polished gold. Red, as you can tell by my description, was utterly delicious in every way, and I just wanted to stand on the beach and oil him up, just for the hell of it. (I'm sure some of you will think this description is clichéd, but give me a break; I'm a vampire, not a fucking writer. How else do you describe perfection, except to say it is just that?) He was wearing shorts and a vest T-shirt and these really nice canvas designer shoes I'd bought him. Not that they would stay on his feet for long. Shoes were the one thing he really struggled to get used to.

We parked the car and I let him do the man thing and get the icebox from the back of the boot. It had a little picnic in there for Red, although I'd eat some as well, just to please him. Even so, I just wanted to snack on his neck and hang pretence. At least he was now behaving like a human instead of a huge doggy. He'd also gotten over all that 'I'm God and you're my slave, now bend over' stuff too; and although I really went for that in private, it was very inconvenient in public.

'Lucy?'

I turned to see Red pointing to the sunbeds closest to the sea. He loved the water, but I had to watch that he didn't turn all puppy and start running in and out, snapping at the waves. Last time he did that I had to explain to a frightened tourist that he was my brother and he had 'issues' but our mother thought he was her very 'special' boy.

'Looks good to me,' I said and followed him over to the beds.

As soon as we were settled, the beach attendant, a tasty 20-year-old life-guard with blond hair, blue eyes and a tan so dark he could have been black, came over to be paid.

'That will be 20 Euros,' he said.

'I'd like a parasol,' I told him, 'and, you're not charging extra for it.'

I looked the boy in the eye and raped his brain for a while. There wasn't much going on in there really, but he ended up thinking I was a 'supermodel' even though I was a little on the 'short side', which was funny. I sent him away believing I'd let him oil up my breasts and that he'd been paid double the fee as well.

Red sat on the edge of his bed trying to rub in sun cream and making a real mess of it.

'Silly boy! You know I love doing that. Lie on your back.'

I began oiling up his chest, deliberately teasing his nipples, and Red's shorts began to rise up at the front, like that weird party trick that some people think is so amusing: a napkin and a knife.

'Mmmm …'

'Lucy!' Red gasped, sitting up and pulling me to him.

'Down boy.'

'Too public?' Red asked looking around at the mostly empty beach. 'There is hardly anyone here.'

Oh, and did I tell you, he always states the obvious?

I lay back on the sunbed as the attendant returned.

'Over me,' I said, giving the boy a look that said, *on me and in me now, big boy.*

The boy smiled with a full set of pure whites offset against his amazing tan, and then he set up the parasol so that I was completely in the shade. Bliss.

Red slipped off his shorts, down to the black thong I'd bought him, and then he ran towards the sea. I sat up under the parasol watching him, and that's when I began to feel it for the first time. At first I thought I was horny, because desire for blood, food and sex is the only thing that ever gets a rise out of me these days. I had been inspired as a doctor, and found excitement in investigating the past at La Brea, but since meeting Red all of that had become unimportant. He was my experiment now. As he ran in and out of the water, child-like in his pleasure, I felt this strange pain in my chest. It was a tightening; a rush of anxiety hurried through my veins, speeding up my heartbeat. I'd been a doctor long enough in this lifetime and in many others to be able to recognise the signs. I was having a panic attack.

I took a breath and began to analyse myself. I am immortal, I'm a vampire. I have nothing to fear because I am invulnerable. I need no-one. My eyes flashed to Red and I felt that pain again mingled with longing.

Not for the first time I wondered about Red's mortality. On the surface he was human but under that perfect, muscular skin hid the wolf. Red was so much more than human or wolf alone. He was a *Fenrir*, the God of werewolves, and his bones had been swallowed in tar, perfectly preserved until his followers raised him. That made him immortal, didn't it? So my fears were irrational. If he died, all I needed to do was get the blood of a virgin – God, that was so clichéd, and yet it had worked the first time – and throw it over his remains.

A small dog ran into the water and began leaping and cavorting over the waves with Red. The owner, an elderly French woman, stood at the water's edge looking uncertainly at them. I could tell what she was thinking. She thought he was retarded or something. It was hard to imagine anyone normal being so free and excited by the common sea. That is unless they've never seen it before, as Red hadn't until recently.

I got off the sunbed and walked towards the water, hoping that Red wouldn't decide to change and play chase with the dog before I got there.

'Red!' I shouted. 'I need some oil rubbing on my back. Will you come here please?'

Red galloped out of the water, the dog at his heel, and then the dog noticed me and stopped short. I met the animal's eyes and he yelped and ran back to his owner.

'Come on,' I said. 'I just can't take you anywhere.'

'I was fine. I wasn't going to change, I remembered what you said.'

'Okay. But I still need you to oil me.'

'Lucy, you're under a parasol all the time.'

'I have very sensitive skin …'

Red laughed and I took his hand. To everyone on the beach we must have looked just like any other couple in the world. I glanced back at the little dog. He cowered down as my gaze fell on him, and his owner couldn't coax him until I looked away.

'Can we have a dog?' Red asked as he opened the sunblock and began to apply it to my snowy skin.

'I think having one untrained puppy around the house is enough, don't you? Besides, they don't like me very much.'

'That's because they don't know you like I do.'

I said nothing more as Red massaged my back and undid my bikini top. His fingers slipped around to the front, brushing the bulge of breast that mashed down against the sunbed.

'I like these,' he said, and I chuckled.

His hands slid down to my lower back and over the back of my thighs. 'I love your shape.'

'It's a human shape. Do you miss female wolf?'

'I don't know. I can't remember it. But you aren't human.'

'True,' I agreed, and I thought how strange it was that he'd realised that from the start.

Later, back in the villa, I pushed Red back onto the bed and rode him until he howled. I wanted his blood and this was the best way to get it. By then I'd stopped feeding from humans altogether. *Why have water when you can have wine?* I wanted Red's wine, more than anything else. I ran my nails over his chest, drawing blood, and bent to kiss the rivulets as they poured, then healed. Red didn't notice. He was insatiable. It was, after all, the full moon. I bit into his breast and he bucked against me, growing still harder and bigger. The half-change came on him, and I felt his cock, already substantial as a man, grow and thicken to painful proportions inside me. I laughed. Then gasped. I opened my eyes to see his face had changed too, the snout was half formed. The usually smooth body was covered in short, coarse, red, beast hair. His fingers had elongated and the normally trim nails had grown and sharpened to long, thin claws.

He lifted me off him effortlessly and I shuddered with excitement as he flipped me over. How many times had I used sex for my own reasons? It was a means to an end, and I'd thought nothing about spreading my legs to achieve that objective. Sexual pleasure had occurred in rare moments. But this half-wolf, rearing up behind me, looking like a monster from your worst nightmare, had the ability to make me enjoy sex more than I had for years.

He penetrated me and I screamed. I felt his huge member pull back and thrust over and over, until I sobbed into the pillow. It was agonising taking him like this, so big, so animal, and yet the pain made it all the more exciting. I wouldn't have stopped him fucking me, even if I could.

He shot his hot wolf seed into me, howling at the moon, and then he fell away onto his back as I collapsed forward, still spasming with my own orgasm. At least in our little villa, in the middle of two acres of land, I wasn't that worried about the neighbours overhearing us. The howls would have been very difficult to explain.

He was quiet and spent, so I fed on him as he slept. The werewolf blood rushed around my veins, pumping life and strength into me until I was high on him. I pulled away, watching the fang marks heal, and I rolled over onto my back.

'Ouch!' Sex with Red left me battered and bruised on the full moon, but his blood speeded up the healing process, and I felt the soreness between my legs slowly fade away as I listened to his breathing.

Once I could stand again, I went into the bathroom and showered. I was revived and ready for a night on the town, but it wouldn't be safe to take Red out anywhere tonight or for the next two nights. As I washed away blood and semen I felt that pang of anxiety once more. Red was controllable, for now, but once he knew all he needed to about the world, would he then want to leave me and go and explore on his own? What if in the end my physical form, although able to repair itself, was no longer enough for him? What if Red woke one day, realising he needed his own pack?

I had never been so insecure in my life.

I returned to the bed, watching Red sleep. The taste of his blood was still in my mouth and I loved it, craved it in a way that made me feel like I wasn't in control of my own urges. I was over 500 years old, yet around Red I felt like a fledgling vampire, always wanting my next fix. It was insane, and the idea that I *needed* Red in much the same way formed in the back of my independent female monster brain. I didn't like the thought one little bit. Since when had I ever needed anyone?

The answer came to me in short sharp images. Red almost running back into the tar; me holding my hands out to him. Surely not? No. Not then. I didn't believe in love and I believed even less in love at first sight.

I'd fallen for him the first time I'd taken his blood, not before. I'd been so fascinated with the idea of fucking the wolf, I guess it was just something I hadn't tried, and in those early days Red was such an animal. He was always playing by his instincts: he woke, he wanted sex, and then he needed food. At first I kept him at arm's length and then, one night, he was in that half-turn state and he was up so hard that I just had to try it. So I stripped and

Red howled, dropping to all fours, and I let him come and nuzzle up to me. His big tongue started licking my breasts and it was so, so sensual. I stroked and patted him, feeling the coarseness of the hair, and as I pressed against his huge wolf bulk, feeling that hair against my skin, I felt hopelessly aroused. That's why I lay on my back and let that long, sensual, slightly rough wolf tongue lap all the way down.

It was soft and sensitive. His snout nuzzled and suckled and the movement was so right and so erotic that I bucked under him, coming on his tongue until all strength left my body.

I've never been scared of anything, but I was a little afraid of doing the wolf, and it was almost like he knew. As the thought occurred to me, he slowly slipped back into human form, and then he slid back up my body. I wouldn't have stopped him if I could, but I found myself opening up to him eagerly as his lips pressed against mine. He tasted of me.

We made love as though we were just a man and woman. Then I had to get too excited and go and stick my fangs in him, didn't I?

The first bite had sent me into a frenzy. His blood was so unique and the nutrients in it made me feel stronger than ever. I wanted to guzzle him dry in one greedy feast, but Red turned beast and threw me off. We fought. I was desperate to have my teeth in him and have him back inside me; I wasn't sure which urge was the more insistent. Stupidly I tried to wrestle him to the ground, only to discover that he was stronger than me. He turned me over and fucked me until I submitted. The fight had aroused him, and in the end he probably needed a little relief after being buried in the tar. What was most surprising was how sexy I found it too; though as first I thought it was the headiness of the blood. After that, Red in human form, half wolf or all wolf turned me on so much I was willing to give it to him whenever he asked. Also, during the full moon, when he was less in control, I got my regular fix of blood, because he didn't seem to mind it too much then. Perhaps he even got a kick out of it.

Turning over in bed I pushed aside the fears and phobias. I had enough excess baggage to last me a lifetime without creating more. Red would want to stay with me. After all, a wolf couldn't give him more than I could, except maybe offspring.

I squeezed my eyes shut, blanking my mind, and slept until late morning when the smell of frying bacon woke me.

I pushed aside the covers to discover Red was gone but I could hear him moving around in the kitchen.

Naked, I walked through the house and found him making a bacon sandwich. He'd learnt how to do this by watching me, and his capacity for independence never failed to surprise me.

'You bit me,' he said.

'You fucked me until I was sore,' I answered. 'Besides, the bite obviously does it for you or you wouldn't go all bad-boy and wolfy on me.'

'Do you want some bacon?' he asked, biting into a huge sandwich filled with crispy bits and brown sauce.

'No.'

I had fed well the night before, and real food rarely interested me these days. In fact, the smell was making me feel nauseous, so I left Red and went to the bathroom to brush my teeth.

As I spread the toothpaste on my brush I glanced up at my reflection and found a shocking sight. Large blue circles were under my eyes and my hand shook. I actually didn't feel well. Dizzy and sick, I clung onto the sink until my blurred eyes began to refocus. Maybe I hadn't fed enough from Red? I looked at the door as though expecting to see him there and wondered if he would let me have a little more of his blood, but knew the chances of that were pretty slim.

I glanced at my reflection again and saw the blueness recede and disappear. Whatever it was, my body was healing again. I shook my head. The faint feeling had fled and I was more myself again.

When I returned to the kitchen Red was gone and he'd left the mess for me to clean up.

'Domestic bliss,' I muttered under my breath. 'This is what happens when you let a man in your life. That and they pee on the toilet seat.'

I went into the conservatory and saw that Red was outside, in the pool, swimming several lengths as he usually did in the morning.

I cleaned up the kitchen, but for all my cursing I loved having him around and knowing he was there. It was interesting how easy I found it after years of living alone.

Later we drove into the local town and did some clothing shopping, stopping at a small coffee shop for lunch. As we sat down at the table outside the shop, I noticed Red scrutinising a woman as she passed by. She was a sophisticated French woman, with long, dark hair that was scraped back into a low ponytail. She was covered in designer clothing; a white fitted skirt and chiffon sleeveless top. Over her shoulder she carried a white jacket. Her style went as far as a matching Gucci bag and stiletto shoes, which made her look taller and emphasised her slim ankles. She was attractive and tanned, with bright red lipstick that set off her brown skin well. Red was usually the one being admired, but he sat forward and stared at her intently and then did the strangest thing. He began to sniff the air.

'What is it?' I asked, placing my hand possessively on his arm.

'Nothing,' he said. 'What does the menu say? It's too confusing.'

I read him the food choices and he decided what he wanted to eat. Reading was the one thing he was finding it difficult to master. Sometimes it depended on the lettering style used.

'It may take years,' I said, consciously pointing out that he still needed me. 'But I'm sure you'll be able to do it eventually and you know I'll always help you.'

Red said nothing but guzzled his wine when the waiter brought it. I ordered us rare steaks. I really felt a need for the bloody animal protein all of a sudden and Red always loved meat, it was his nature after all. We fell into our usual and companionable chatter as Red asked questions about all he saw with unfailing child-like curiosity.

After lunch we walked along the main high street and browsed the shops until Red stopped suddenly before a doorway. He sniffed the air again. I glanced through the shop window and saw the woman he'd noticed earlier. She was sitting alone drinking coffee, and she looked up at the door as though she could sense our scrutiny.

'She's not human,' I said.

'No.'

'What is she?'

'Wolf.'

Then that strange anomaly occurred once more and my heart palpitated as anxiety and fear flooded my face.

Red took my hand and walked away. I didn't look back at the shop but I felt, rather than saw, the eyes of the wolf woman as she hurried to the door to watch us leave.

For days I didn't want us to go anywhere, and the craving

for Red's blood began to intensify, which was strange as usually one dose a month was enough.

The air was hot, the sun high in the sky, and everything should have been happy and glorious, but the atmosphere around us had become tense. Red prowled the villa like a caged animal. I couldn't help but be paranoid. He'd been quiet and distant since our trip, and even the swimming pool had lost its appeal.

I rubbed my hand down his chest and lower to the top of his shorts.

'Come to bed, or the sofa or, hey, what about the pool?' I suggested. 'That could be sexy; we haven't done it there yet.'

I stood on my toes and kissed him, but for once Red didn't respond. Instead he became impatient and pushed me aside as though I was an insect that was annoying him.

I found myself blinking rapidly. I was so unused to rejection, and how could this gorgeous, highly sexed creature even want to refuse? But the image of the woman leapt behind my eyes and I thought once more of her glamour, her style and her wolf heritage. Fear gripped me and I slid closer to Red, trying once more to distract him and make him remember to love me.

'Not now, Lucy,' he said, but this time he put me aside a little more kindly than before.

'Please, Red … I need …' I sat down on the sofa feeling deflated and embarrassed: I'd never begged for attention in the whole of my immortal life and I wasn't going to start now.

'I'm remembering something,' he said.

'Remembering? The time before the tar?'

'Yes.'

'Tell me.'

I was relieved that his distance wasn't down to me after all. His memory was returning. That was a good thing, wasn't it?

'I was running with the pack, we were being chased by … I guess they were humans … although I didn't really understand that at the time. I knew they were different but there was no name for it.'

'What happened?'

'I'd been living among them, as one of them. I even took a wife.'

A pained expression flittered across his face as the memories flooded back.

'Her name was Leela, and after some time I gave her a child. But when it was born, it was not as their children were and so … so she took a rock and dashed my son's brains out.'

'It was the way of the times,' I said gently. 'If the baby wouldn't survive, they deemed it kinder to kill it.'

'There was nothing wrong with him, except that he was half wolf, like me.'

'I'm so sorry.'

Red ran a hand over his face, rubbing his eyes as

though he fought with tears that would burst from him at anytime.

'I took that same rock and killed my wife. I can't tell you the rage that came upon me. I'd wanted the child, craved it. Perhaps more than any of the others did, as this meagre race of people barely cared about each other. They lived in their caves together to provide safety, herding with little more than instinct as other animals do. Their language too was basic, nothing as complex as the speech you have taught me, and other than a few words, mostly they made themselves understood by grunts and gestures. I left the caves and I turned full wolf, hiding in plain sight amongst the feral packs that the humans sought to avoid. That way I observed them, and I went back from time to time to watch the women. I wanted my own offspring and so, one night, I returned to the village and picked one of the young girls. Her name was Usula. I had seen her around helping her mother and I knew she was as yet untaken. I stole her away and brought her to a sheltered cave near the favourite hunting ground of the pack.

At first, Usula was afraid of me, and I never showed her my wolf-self, but she knew I wasn't human. There had been rumours among the people about the deformed child, and when I'd killed Leela for murdering my son, it had raised suspicion that I was in fact some demon living among them. Usula submitted to me but cried as I took her, and always washed in the river immediately afterwards. I was unused to this behaviour, as my wife,

Leela, had enjoyed our sex. So I tried to be kind, but Usula was only young, and maybe she didn't want to be the mother of the race I wished to create.'

'Did you mate with the female wolves in the pack?' I asked, and Red was surprised by the question.

'No. They were only animals, not the evolved creature that I was, but they made good minions. In fact, it never even occurred to me that I might create children that way.'

Red told me that eventually Usula had conceived.

'As her stomach grew, I stopped bothering her for sex. After that she was happier and we had a kind of domesticity that became a wary friendship. I had achieved what I'd wanted, so I felt no desire to hurt her anymore. When she had the child I made sure I helped her with the birth. I didn't want another son murdered. But Usula shocked us both and gave birth to twins. Both of whom looked completely human. One boy, one girl.

She was a good mother to them and they were healthy, but not long after their birth, Usula's tribe found us.

I don't think it was intentional, they hadn't deliberately tracked us, and even though Usula's father was among the warriors, as I said earlier, they didn't care about each other that way. The tribe had moved outwards with the changing weather; a lack of food had made them track beasts further afield than usual.'

Red paused as though looking for words to explain his old world in modern language.

'You can't explain the animals or describe the beast you ate?'

He shook his head. 'No. The situation, too, is hard to explain in your so many words.'

'It's all right, just do your best.'

'The warriors were afraid when they saw me. I was tracking food in my half-wolf state.'

'I'm not surprised they were afraid. After all, they probably still recognised you.'

'They did, and that's why they attacked me.'

Red described how the warriors had thrown spears in fear and instinct.

'At first I changed back to full human, hoping they would start to understand that I meant them no harm, but then Usula's father threw a spear. It pierced me here …' he said, indicating his side. 'There was so much pain, so the wolf came out in full change and I attacked. Ripping and shredding all but two men, who, realising they couldn't win, turned and fled.

'I went back to my cave, wounded but rapidly healing. Usula was feeding our young, holding one child on each breast. When she saw the blood she began to chatter and gesture in panic, but her eyes grew wide with fear as she stared at the rapidly disappearing scar.

'After that it was only a matter of time before she ran away back to the tribe, never realising that there was more danger in going back than in staying with me. I would never have hurt her; she had given me the children

I wanted, and that meant I would have guarded her just as I did them.'

'I'm a little confused,' I said, interrupting. 'Red, you know how I found you?'

He nodded.

'And you understand how you were revived?'

'Yes, Lucy. You explained it very well.'

'The thing is, I had your bones carbon dated; that's a kind of laboratory testing to see how old they were.'

'I understand,' said Red, and so I continued.

'The bones dated back to two point eight million years ago. That fell in towards the end of the Pliocene Epoch. I know that these terms mean nothing to you, and to be fair, I had thought all this out before, but was unable to explore it with you due to your lack of memory. However, what you're saying means that there were human life forms, evolved enough to hunt in packs and make spears.'

'Yes,' he agreed.

'But that's impossible. Humanity wasn't even around then, or at least science says it wasn't.'

'But it was, Lucy, and science is wrong.'

I fell silent, shocked by this intriguing revelation, and the scientist in me was powerfully aroused by the implications of Red's very existence. I had thought him a fluke, a freak of nature. I had even considered that his bones had been nothing more than those of a large wolf until the cult had intervened with their ritual magic and my assistant's blood. This new information, though, left little doubt that all of that was just naïve on my part. From what Red said, he was an evolved species of his own, before he joined the tribe.

'Where did you come from? Before you joined the tribe?'

'I …' Red frowned. 'I don't know. I can't remember that at all.'

I didn't know what to say, and so I encouraged him to continue his story.

'Usula left?' I prompted.

'I came back from a hunt the next day to find the twins crying: she'd abandoned them. They were going to starve to death, so I called to the pack and pulled in a she-wolf, who lay down. As I fed my children from her teats, the change came over them for the first time. After that they stayed wolf and followed the She everywhere.'

'It might have been some form of defence mechanism,' I said, 'and it could explain where you came from. Maybe you were submerged in a pack until you came upon the tribe.'

'Possibly. But I really don't remember.'

'What happened then?'

'Sometime later the warriors returned. This time they were better armed, and in greater numbers. They carried with them Usula's head on a spike, and I was attacked.

'Of course the wolves came out in force to defend me and we beat them back, but I knew the tribe was afraid. Fear and an instinct for survival were the codes they lived by, which meant that they would return, and return until they killed what they saw as the threat: me. So I led the pack away from the tribe, and that ultimately was our downfall. As we crossed the open planes, we knew nothing of the danger hidden beneath the surface, and when a herd of …' Red stopped, gesturing and half-describing a kind of large animal.

'Mammoth,' I ventured, and he tried the word on his tongue.

'Mammoth. The word suits them.'

It seems the mammoth herd stampeded. Red and his pack were caught in the cross-fire, and it was a matter of run or be trampled, and so they ran; right into the tar.

That was all he remembered, but his revelation was so huge that it took my mind away completely from my momentary insecurity and I forgot the chic, coffee-sipping she-wolf. Red's distance was easily explained, so I felt safe once more. But my security was false and short-lived.

With the return of his memories, Red became more confident. He began to go out more alone. At first this made me anxious. I was uncertain if he could control himself in all situations.

'You don't know enough about this world,' I said.

'Lucy, you need to trust me. I've been with you a long time, you have taught me well, and I know now who and what I am.'

Now he remembered his past, he was no longer the childish clean slate that he had been, so I couldn't use his lack of control as an excuse any longer.

'I'm far safer in the present than I ever was in the past.'

When every excuse had become exhausted I let Red leave, and he went for a walk. This became a regular occurrence and I began to understand that the wolf in him had to have some freedom. Occasional walks became whole days, and soon he stayed out overnight too. Red, inevitably, came back after each excursion, but soon they became longer and I began to realise that I was losing him to some obscure part of his wolf's nature.

Red let me feed more and more from him. It was like a trade-off. I didn't query his trips and he let me drink his blood. It was an unspoken rule. Whenever he returned, we had sex, I fed and for that time I was happy. The only problem was, the more I fed from him, the more I needed to, and if the gaps between became too long, I started to develop symptoms of sickness. When Red disappeared for a week, the longest time ever, I was frantic and starved by the fourth day. My stomach hurt, I began to dry-heave, and that tired and ugly blueness appeared once more around my eyes. By the sixth day I could hardly get out of bed; I even began to hallucinate.

When Red returned the next day to find me in this state, he immediately gave me blood.

'What is wrong with you?' he asked later, as I was

157

sitting, shuddering on the sofa in the lounge.

'You were away so long. I needed you.'

'No. I mean why didn't you go to find blood elsewhere, like you used to?'

I stared at Red as though he was insane. Didn't he realise that after him, no human could ever taste the same?

'I … wanted your blood.'

'This is wrong, Lucy. This isn't healthy.'

'I need more,' I said.

'No. You've had enough for now.'

I threw a tantrum, smashing all of the ornaments in the room, until Red caught hold of me and held me down.

'I think you need to stop drinking from me.'

'No!'

'I think my blood is hurting you. Look at yourself.'

Red pulled me up and dragged me struggling across the room to a mirror that hung above the fireplace. I stared into dull, hollow eyes and took in the gaunt cheeks before I realised that I was looking at myself. I pulled away, shocked, and threw myself across the room as far from the mirror as I could get. I had never looked ill or old since my rebirth, and even when I'd been unable to eat, the only bad effects had been severe cramps. Starving had never affected my looks before.

'It's your fault,' I yelled. 'You should have been here.'

Red stared at me, his hands by his sides, as I crawled

across the floor towards him.

'I need some more, Red. Then I'll get well again. Then I'll regenerate.'

He shook his head. 'I think that's a bad idea.'

Red turned away, and left the villa. I collapsed on the floor and fell into a stupor. He had finally left me. I believed at that moment that I, like David Bowie in *The Hunger*, was aging and dying: my time as an active immortal was up.

A few hours later, Red returned. I heard him enter but struggled to pull myself round. Through film-covered eyes I saw him place something down before me. It took a moment for the shapes to make sense, and then I realised that he had brought me food. A woman lay, unconscious, on the sofa.

'Come, Lucy,' he said. 'Drink this.'

My fangs were out long before I reached my gift, and I tore at her throat. The blood from her jugular pumped out over the furniture before my mouth closed fully over it. I remembered thinking briefly that it was just as well the furniture was black leather, and then I lost all thought as I fed deeply from her.

She was dead before I could drink my fill, and as Red lifted the body and removed her, I rolled over onto my back on the floor and slipped away into oblivion.

'Here's the deal,' said Red a little later on. I looked at him and felt like a parent hearing her own words coming from her child's lips. 'I'm no good for you. Or at least my blood isn't.'

'What are you talking about?' I asked.

I felt wonderful. The human blood was pumping through my heart once more and Red was looking gorgeous. I wanted him, and so I reached for him.

'No!'

'Oh, stop it, silly! I'm fine now. It must have been that I hadn't fed enough from you. Clever boy bringing me a snack.'

I stood up and caught sight of my reflection. The young and beautiful me was back in full force. In fact I had never felt better.

'Okay, if you must go away so much I will at least feed from humans in between. But you mustn't deny me your gorgeous body. You know I crave it.'

Red sighed.

'Lucy, when I'm sure you are better, I'm going away again. Maybe you don't realise how you've been behaving lately, so I'll explain things to you. You're … I think the word is, *addicted*.'

I laughed, throwing back my head in denial at the absurdity of the suggestion.

'Don't be ridiculous.'

'I've been rebuilding my pack,' he said. 'I wasn't going to tell you. I thought we could still have fun together though; fidelity is not something that wolves really care about, and my mate, Talia, is not jealous or insecure. I feel you are, and that creates a problem. Plus I can no longer give you my blood now that I've realised it has been poisoning you.'

'What are you talking about?' It felt as though Red was talking a foreign language.

He was the only man I'd ever wanted, ever needed, in all my immortal life, and now he was dumping me! My mind refused to understand him, even though my heart felt like it splintered in two. That huge pain filled my chest and my breathing came in sharp gasps. And yes, I knew I was panicking, but there was nothing I could do to stop it.

When Red left, I thought about following him and ran scenarios in my head of me chasing him down the drive, begging and pleading. The thought was not the slightest bit dignified or appealing. I stayed on the sofa staring at the spot where the woman had bled and wondering if Red had taken the body to feed to his new pack.

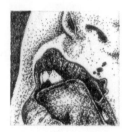

# Author's Notes

*Red* is an urban fantasy story written exclusively for this collection. The idea came from the 'what if?' element at the end of the previous story, *Tar*, but it took two years for *Red* to be written. I always knew I had to see what happened to him and investigate Lucrezia's immediate fascination with him, but the time to write the tale seemed to slip away from me, until now.

I wanted to toy with Lucrezia's weaknesses a little. Explore whether she was always as in control as she seemed. Vampires by their nature are victims of their own addiction to blood, but what if the blood source is poisonous to the vampire, yet so hopelessly compulsive that it means certain destruction to keep indulging? Just like a junkie, Lucrezia would ultimately have to be saved from herself.

Other human fetishes and obsessions were also in my mind as I planned and wrote *Red*. Although the idea of a werewolf mating with a human has bestiality stamped all over it, can it be said that such is the case with a werewolf and a vampire? Both are supernatural creatures, but clearly are not the same species. This also is relevant to the consumption of Red's blood. He isn't human and therefore he is not the right food source. Just as Lucy is not the right mate to satisfy the wolf ultimately, and he has to take a mate of his own kind in order to rebuild his pack.

Eroticism was a must for this one too. The whole idea of having a god-like wolf boy hanging around with a drop-dead gorgeous and sex-hungry vampire was way too charged to resist, and I just had to indulge the two of them and let them get down and dirty. Sometimes you just have to let your characters have their fun, don't you?

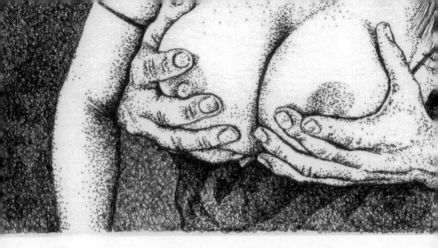

# Angels Love Vampires

He was standing under a street light looking all casual and incredibly sexy in a crisp white suit. Even though I knew he wasn't human, I didn't immediately recognise what he was. After all, why would I? I'd never seen anything like him before. In fact, I would have told you, quite categorically, that they don't exist, and that an angel was the last thing I expected to see.

'What are you?' I asked, walking up to him, bold as anything.

'What are you?' he mimicked.

I folded my arms and glared at him, 'No, seriously. What *are* you?'

'No, seriously. What are *you*?'

Bollocks to that. I turned to walk away. I had no time for games. He might be all hot and steamy in some dark sultry way, but he was obviously a moron. It was lucky for him I wasn't feeling hungry or I might have just snacked on his neck for a while. Food was about all he seemed fit for, but I wasn't in the mood for that either, so I took flight.

Serenely soaring over the brightly-lit city, I quickly forgot all about the retard in the white suit until I realised he was there beside me, matching me.

Now don't go getting any ideas that angels really have wings – I mean, that would have been a dead giveaway, wouldn't it? He travelled through the air as I did, in a kind of controlled, but fast, floating. His arms were forward (a little like the classic Superman pose if I'm honest, but I was doing that long before Christopher Reeve donned his blue tights), and he looked for all the world like he was having a really great time.

'What the fuck …?'

He grimaced at my expletive and I turned back towards the ground, floating downwards slowly. I hit the concrete pavement with barely a tap and then turned towards him as he landed beside me.

The whole thing was a little weird, but since I can't be killed and I can repair any wound, I was more aroused than scared. This being was a little intriguing even if he wasn't too smart.

'So, are you going to talk properly to me now?' I said once his feet were back on the ground.

'I *was* talking properly to you,' he answered. 'Your structure is very strange. What are *you*?'

'Oh! You mean … you *weren't* taking the piss?'

He looked confused, frowning slightly as his eyes went blank. It was the kind of expression that humans adopt when they are trying to recall something.

'You thought I was mimicking you?' he said.

'Yes.'

'I wasn't. I was merely asking you the same question as you asked me.'

I laughed. 'Okay, let's be grown up about this. My name is Lucrezia. I am a vampire. And you are …?'

'A vampire …?'

'You're a vampire too? You don't *feel* like one,' I said.

'No. I mean it as a question … *you're* a vampire? I'm a little surprised. I didn't think they existed. How intriguing.'

'Yes. They do exist and I am one,' I was starting to lose my cool. 'Now what the fuck are you?'

'Simeon,' he said. 'I'm an angel.'

And that was it. I'd heard of angels, of course. You can't be a supernatural being living in a world of humans without tapping into the panoply of belief that they have built up over the years. Some of the things they believe in don't exist, of course. Others do. And some of the things that they don't believe in are as real as my hand … Strange things, humans.

But an angel … obviously I just *had* to corrupt him.

I was staying at this time in the Radisson Blu Strand, near the waterfront. It was old enough to appeal to my sense of history, but contemporary renovation made the place irresistible to my obsession with the modern world. I took Simeon's hand.

'Come on.'

'Where to?' he asked.

'Back to my room.'

He didn't take any persuading at all. And foolishly I didn't realise that this was the start of the problem.

We floated back into the air hand in hand, and Simeon concentrated less on the flight and more on my hand in his. He seemed fascinated by it.

'This feels nice ...' he said as we landed on my balcony.

I pulled him inside the room and then let go of his hand. He stared at his fingers for a moment, then looked around the room with vague curiosity. It was like he'd never seen the inside of a building before.

I sat down on the bed and watched him wander around, touching and examining my personal effects.

'You've made a life for yourself, and yet you are not really part of this world,' he observed.

'Of course I am part of the world.'

'How so? You are different, not one of them.'

'That doesn't mean I can't live among them. Humans don't know I'm different. At least not until I decide to bite them.'

Simeon grew quiet. He picked up my hair brush from the dresser and pulled a stray strand from the bristles. He sniffed it. It was vaguely pervy, so I decided to change the subject.

'So, if there are angels … is there like, a God and stuff?'

'Interesting question. But since you're immortal the answer is irrelevant,' he said.

Simeon, I soon learned, was expert at telling you everything while telling you absolutely nothing, and since I wasn't given to philosophy, I just couldn't be bothered pondering the depths and breadths of his answers. It was enough of an eye-opener that angels even existed – assuming of course that he was telling the truth – but I wasn't given to flights of fancy, or to worrying about what else could be out there. I just wanted to get him out of that perfect white suit. I am a very naughty girl at times.

'I suppose you have to avoid sin then?'

'It depends.'

'What do you mean?'

'Maybe sin is one's calling,' Simeon answered ambiguously.

I pulled him down beside me on the bed and began to unbutton his perfect shirt. He watched my hands move but said nothing. When it came to taking off his trousers, I wondered for a moment what I might find. Would he be smooth and sexless there? Or would an angel have the equipment to satisfy a human woman … Simeon, I discovered, was very much a man.

Once I had him naked I felt a little awkward. Well you would, wouldn't you? I was about to fuck an angel, and although I'd long believed that God had deserted me, if indeed he really existed anyway, part of me wondered if a thunderbolt was going to suddenly strike me dead at any moment.

'Have you ever done this?' I asked.

'No. But I like the feel of the air on my skin.'

*That's all I need. A naturist virgin angel.* There was something very biblical about his affinity to being bare though.

I left him sitting on the bed and went to the window. My balcony overlooked the water and I admired the stillness of the night, the clear black sky and the vivid stars as they looked down on us.

'Maybe we're being watched,' I said, looking back at Simeon, who was lying back on the bed.

He looked gorgeous. Perfect. He was utterly at home in his nakedness. He reminded me a little of that actor, John Philip Law, who played the angel Pygar in *Barbarella*. And so, I did what any full-blooded female vampire does when faced with a beautiful, naked man: I stripped my clothing off, climbed on the bed, straddled him, and placed his hands on my bare breasts just to see what he would do.

I looked into his eyes as his cock grew hard against my stomach. Even if this was his first time he was a very fast learner and his hands explored my body with a mixture of curiosity and excitement.

'Your skin feels so good to me,' he said. 'It sends a sensation through my body.'

'It's called lust.'

I lifted myself up and positioned my body over him, rubbing against him till he gasped. Then I showed him what to do to ease the pain and he was away with the fairies in seconds.

I got bored with this game a lot quicker than he did, and it wasn't because it was exhausting; it was thrilling and wonderful in fact. We made love in a variety of positions; he was inventive and exciting, using his fingers and lips and tongue as well as his lovely cock to pleasure me. After a few hours I learnt that Simeon was insatiable. This was a first for me. It was a long time since I'd had so much sex that I'd actually had enough – even Red hadn't been able to do that to me. It all added to the fascination, and after several days in the hotel, I finally admitted defeat and let him have his way with me completely.

I didn't mind his companionship at first, but after several weeks I began to feel somewhat suffocated by his constant presence. You've got to realise that I'm pretty much a loner these days, and if the truth be known I gave up on love after Red left. Simeon was nothing more than a distraction to me. Unfortunately though, I was more than that to him.

'Look, it isn't really healthy to be with me *all* the time. I mean, don't you have a purpose?' I prompted one day, trying to hint that I needed some space.

'Purpose?'

'Yes. What were you doing when we met, for example? You must have been in Stockholm for a reason.'

Simeon blinked at me, his eyes glazing a little as his mind went away to his life before meeting me. He shook his head.

'Before doesn't matter,' he said. 'Only the now. And my purpose is to be here with you.'

It wasn't the answer I was looking for but I left the conversation there.

At times I went out in search of blood, but even then the angel followed, always staying at a distance: I could feel his presence. I thought that he was merely curious about my habits, but soon realised it was more than that. Simeon was as obsessed with me as any mortal man might have been, and in the same unhealthy way that I had been addicted to Red. He couldn't be apart from me for long. The privacy and solitude I'd always enjoyed disappeared. I didn't like it. But it was all my own doing and I realised that I was out of my depth. Getting rid of him certainly wouldn't be as easy as ridding myself of a mortal. I just kept hoping that eventually he would get bored. Months went by, though, and Simeon's intensity grew.

'What's the meaning of life?' I asked him, hoping

he'd remember his main objective and also perhaps to trick him into revealing his purpose here.

'To exist and be happy,' he replied.

'But surely there are rules. What about your job?'

Simeon insisted he didn't have a job.

'Vocation then. What is it you're meant to do?'

'Like you, Lucrezia, I am meant to exist and learn about life. Make mistakes perhaps, but try to find a level of contentment. Then I have done all that I am meant to do.'

'You mean,' I said, 'that's the sole purpose of humanity? To learn contentment? Be happy?'

'Of course. But humans aren't very good at it. They keep choosing to be miserable and unsatisfied instead.'

At this point my brain began to ache. I didn't want to think these deep and philosophical notions: it just isn't my way. I admit it, I'm selfish. Always have been. My only agenda is to make myself happy, not anyone else. So, I related totally to what he said – but humans being the same way? All of them? It just didn't seem possible.

'We are only responsible for our own happiness,' said Simeon. 'Humans, however, constantly worry about everyone else.'

Humanity was a bit of a bleeding heart these days to the point of annoyance, I had to admit. They were always worried about political correctness, abandoned animals or starving people in third world countries. In the Machiavellian world of my birth era, life had been far less complicated on that score. Those with money had everything while the poor were left to rot. Simple. The trick was just making sure that you had money. If you couldn't steal it, inherit it, marry it, win it or be given it, then life was pretty shit. Luckily as a vampire I had several tricks up my sleeve that meant that men were only too happy to give me their wealth in exchange for the forever-unfulfilled promise of eternal life. That wasn't what Simeon meant, of course. He was referring to the pagan sentiment of 'do as you like, but hurt none', and of course I was as familiar with this faith as I was any other.

'Not a particularly Christian view, though,' I pointed out.

'Religion has nothing to do with it really,' Simeon said.

I waited for him to go on, but as usual he ended his commentary there.

'I suppose all I'm going to get from you is ambiguity,' I said. 'I'm tired now, Simeon. Go home. I need a few days alone.'

'Home?'

'Yes. Or wherever it is you came from.'

Simeon seemed completely confused. I reminded him again of when we met, pointed out he must have had an objective.

'Everything that happened before doesn't matter,' he

answered. 'I'm happy here with you. So I will stay with you.'

'No. I want you to go.'

'Why?'

'Because … I'm used to time alone. I need it.'

Simeon's usual happy expression changed. He looked hurt, angry. 'Leaving you does not make me happy. I will stay.'

'According to your philosophy, I'm only responsible for *my* happiness, so I don't care if it makes you unhappy.'

'I don't understand why my being here does not make you happy.'

'That's exactly my point, Simeon,' I said. 'You don't understand. Now. I'm going out. You stay here. I will go hunting. Alone.'

Simeon was confused but couldn't argue further. I took a quick exit and flew from the window, heading out quickly over the sea.

I flew far enough away to be alone, and for once Simeon didn't follow. I hunted in Salem – a tiny place situated between Södertälje and Botkyrka, just south-west of Stockholm – taking down a teenage boy. I ripped his throat out, then drank from his cooling corpse. Normally I'd feed from a current lover, usually ending the relationship by draining them completely once I grew tired of them. Simeon was different, however.

I wasn't sure if it would be a good idea to drink from another supernatural being, especially after Red's blood had poisoned me so badly. It had taken months to shake off the effects of that addiction.

I shivered as the thought of drinking from Simeon floated through my mind. I didn't know how powerful he was, or what he could do. All I knew was he said he was an angel. Anything more he kept to himself.

Now I was away from him I felt free of his claustrophobic obsession. I began to understand how difficult it had been for Red and knew that his leaving me had ultimately been the right thing to do. I didn't want to go back to the hotel. I couldn't face Simeon once I realised it was definitely time to bale. So I flew towards the coast and jumped onto a ship that was leaving from the harbour.

It didn't matter to me that I was leaving everything behind. I had houses all over the world and places where I knew at any time I could retrieve passports and money. I'd run or walked away from things my whole life; leaving was easy. What was important at that moment was to regain my freedom, and as the ship pulled out to sea, the fresh cool air swept away all of the feelings of suffocation. I didn't look back, instantly forgetting Simeon.

A few days later I was walking around the deck and I found Simeon leaning against the railing looking out at sea.

'What are you doing here?'

'I missed you,' he said. 'Don't leave me again.'

I stared at him for a moment, then took flight, leaving the ship and heading across the sea towards Britain. Simeon, I knew, was following, but he kept his distance.

Hours later I landed in Scotland, and wandered the Highlands, enjoying the feel of the earth beneath my feet. It was always something I did when I needed to feel grounded. Simeon landed a few feet away and followed like a sick puppy-dog. This carried on for several weeks. Wherever I went, he followed.

Finally, on a trip to North Wales, I'd had enough. So, one night, on top of Snowdon, with no-one else around, I told him what I thought.

'Simeon, haven't you got the message yet, that our little liaison is now over? Go away and leave me alone.'

'No,' he answered. 'I want to touch you; I need to be with you.'

'Obviously that's a very unhealthy thing. I don't want to be with you any more. You bore me. You suffocate me. Please understand, I don't want to see you, and you *have* to accept it.'

'No,' he said, and that's when he resorted to force.

It was a shock to find out that Simeon was so much stronger than I was. He threw me to the ground, forcing his kisses on my mouth. My fangs burst forth and I gnashed his lips. Blue blood streamed from his mouth.

He raised his arm and hit me with the full force of his rage and frustration.

'Stop it! You will love me, and you will let me love you.'

For a moment my entire life flashed behind my eyes. The years of abuse at the hands of my family had always left their mark. Even now, centuries later, when I had well and truly rid myself of my brother Caesare, I still felt intense pain when I thought back to those days. I now saw a future that I didn't like: a future with Simeon and his jealousy and obsession. He wanted me at any price, but I couldn't be bought. I couldn't go down that road again.

The problem was, how could I rid myself of this incredible entity? He could track me anywhere, was stronger than me, and I knew that angels were alleged to have the ability to destroy the Earth if they so wanted. There was only one thing I could do to get out of this, but it might mean that this time I really was going to die.

'Okay,' I said, nursing my busted nose. 'This is silly. Let's go back to my place.'

I took his hand and we flew from Snowdon, across North Wales, and landed in Llandudno at the hotel where I'd made my temporary base.

Inside my room, I peeled off my clothes and Simeon quickly joined me as I stretched out on the bed. By then his wounds and mine had both healed, but I could see a vague scar line on his lips where my fangs had ripped into him.

'You've never asked me how I became what I am,' I said.

'It doesn't matter.'

'It does to me. I have a strange history. Once I was mortal – unlike you. When I changed, I made a promise to myself that I would never again be forced to do something I didn't want to.'

Simeon frowned. Then he began to stroke my breasts in an effort to distract me. His touch made me want to vomit, but I forced myself to stay still, to appear benign. He bent to kiss me. I met his lips; let his tongue invade my mouth, then lay as his kisses fell all over my body.

'You're not moving,' he noticed.

'You want this, then you do all the work.' I said.

Simeon chuckled. 'I'm learning that you are a … tease. You are a very difficult vampire.'

I said nothing.

As his body slid over me, I let the blood-lust surge to the fore and felt that familiar painful itch as my fangs slipped down over my lips. Simeon didn't seem to notice; he'd seen them before, and I knew he wouldn't be expecting what I did next.

The bite surprised him, and me. I didn't think his blood would be so ordinary. It was blue, and he was a different species to me, but unlike Red, he was not virtual poison. My saliva worked its usual magic and my victim was paralyzed, unable to move. He did not have a sexual response, which was interesting; rather, his cock deflated along with all of his strength. I pushed him onto his back, changing my vantage point without releasing him, and from there I drained him dry.

His body shrivelled beneath me. It was like I'd pierced an inflatable doll and the air slowly hissed from him. When he was empty, I withdrew my fangs, backing away from the bed as I stared at him from across the room. I was half-expecting a reanimation, and I knew then he'd attempt to destroy me. I stood, back against the door, ready to be destroyed.

His blood flowed through my veins, a weak, lifeless pulse. It neither strengthened nor weakened me. It was just there. It was curiously unimportant.

Simeon didn't move. As I watched, the empty body began to crumble like the special effects from an old Hammer Dracula movie, and I waited in awe as his remains dissipated to dust and then completely disappeared. It felt like something of an anticlimax. That's when I realised that Simeon was truly dead. I'd taken the life-force that sustained him – alien as it was to my veins. His blue blood had given him life, and just as with a human, the removal of it had destroyed him.

I was still alive, when I'd been sure the angel's blood would kill me. It settled in my stomach, and I could feel it there … benign and formless. And after a day or so the feeling went. But I'd certainly learnt my lesson. I wouldn't be taking any supernatural strays off to bed again anytime soon, and I'd definitely be staying away from angels.

I've seen a few more around since, and I always rapidly cloak myself and head in the opposite direction before they notice me. It may have been just Simeon who was obsessive by nature, but I don't want to test the theory that angels really do love vampires. Would you?

## Author's Notes

This one was a quirky idea from the start. I thought it would be fun to explore how the supposed goodness of an angel could be corrupted by obsession, just as humans can be. It started with the title and in this way I posed myself a problem. If angels 'love' vampires and it isn't reciprocated, then how could they be dissuaded or destroyed?

Lucrezia's nature would make her curious about Simeon, and that would be her downfall. But I also wanted to imply that vampires were perhaps like a drug to an angel as well.

I've always liked the Hammer film ending ... the

180

turning of the menace to dust always seemed to me to be a fitting end to the evil. Even if the dust could perhaps be collected and used to reanimate the vampiric fiend at some later date. You'll notice that my angel's dust vanishes completely in the story … I wanted no way for Simeon to come back to haunt my Lucrezia further.

For fans of the *Vampire Gene* series, this concludes the *Lucrezia's Stories* section of this book. I hope it has filled in a few gaps, intrigued you even more about Lucrezia, and thrown doubt on all you hoped to understand about this character. Lucrezia continues to grow and show her multi-faceted personality, and I'm certain neither you, nor I, have heard the last of her.

Now, on to the *Other* Bloody Jottings …

# Other Bloody Jottings

Within the following pages are crime, thriller, horror, dark comedy and some dark fantasy stories, followed by a section containing my mythological poetry. It is a somewhat eclectic collection, showing the variety of genres and styles that interest me as a writer. I have also used these stories as a way to challenge my own imagination and skills.

I've said many times that the thing that attracts me to the horror genre is the feeling of being 'safely' scared. Reading horror and dark fantasy can be a thrill-ride, especially when that thrill leaves you with a cold and paralysing fear that one day this could really happen. There are different forms of terror induced in these pages. I prefer psychological horror to gore, but I've experimented with both and I'm pleased with the results.

Within this section is the first story I ever had published, as well as new stories written specifically for this collection. I hope that you can see the process of evolution within my work. I'm very pleased with all of the stories, but I'm particularly proud of *Siren Song*, *Clown Addict*, *Immortal Monster* and *The Toymaker's House*, because I feel they are completely different from anything I've written before.

You might have noticed that with the exception of *Zombies in New York*, the Lucrezia tales are written in the first person, from her point of view. I like this style of storytelling and find it lends itself well to stories of all lengths. It also allows me to get inside the head of the character, effectively taking on their thoughts and feelings. It's peculiar, therefore, that my personal favourites are all written in very different ways. An example of this style and use of narrative voice comes in the form of the first story here. It is told from the perspective of a male civil servant with a clown fetish …

# Clown Addict

Bowbo the clown took it like a man whilst leaning over a Jacuzzi bath blowing up balloons for the second part of his act. We were at my niece's birthday party, and I think this is where my addiction began.

I love clowns.

Every time the circus comes to town I have to go. I sit patiently through all of the other acts, but revel in the moments when those stage-painted beauties come out and begin to throw around their buckets full of confetti and squirt water into the audience. The huge boots, always a big turn-on, as well as the baggy pants, held up precariously by brightly coloured braces, had become the strangest sexual obsession I'd ever had. Besides, most of them are pretty buff; they have to be, when you think about it. *All those acrobatic bodies, twisting and turning and falling over, arse in the air …*

But I digress. Bowbo was very hot, it has to be said,

184

and we dated for a while until he went on to bigger and better things, or rather until I met the next clown and found he was better endowed. But fortunately my sister, Susan, never found out that I had a liaison in her posh bathroom. She would, quite frankly, have killed me.

I soon learned that no two clowns are ever the same. Did you know that clowns all have exclusive make-up? I prefer the ones with the big smile, and yet there's still a hint of sadness around the eyes. I think that's what attracted me to Alejandro.

Alejandro was part of an American Circus, which was hilarious because most of the acts were Spanish or French, but when Alejandro came into the ring, I knew I had to have him. I went to see the show every night while it was in town. All for a glimpse of the sexiest clown I'd yet to see. And that night I wasn't disappointed.

'Dale!' called a voice, and I turned to find Susan and her three kids sitting a row or two behind me. 'I thought it was you! I didn't know you were coming to the circus, thought you hated this stuff.'

I was annoyed to see Susan and her irritating little brats. They were constantly whining, always demanding her attention, and their favourite cry was 'I want'. That night all three of them had popcorn, drinks and glow-sticks, and as soon as the interval arrived, they each demanded a plate-spinning kit. Little bastards.

'Just pretend you don't know me,' I told her.

She stared at me blankly for a minute, then nodded

quickly.

I'm a civil servant and I work for the security services. So I didn't have to explain anything to Susan if I pulled the official secrecy card.

Alejandro came out and threw a bucket of foam over a group of unsuspecting school kids. He tripped over his big, red shiny shoes and fell into a fake lion's cage door. Then, as the cage shook and the sound of a lion's roar came from behind the curtain, he ran away and hid inside the mouth of a huge cannon. All really cool, and very phallic. When he was shot from the cannon I got a hard-on that nearly burst my trousers, and I had to put my jacket over my lap so no-one would notice.

He was carrying a bucket of water by the end of the show, and I suddenly realised he was heading my way. He smelt of gunpowder and wood shavings by that time. I guess it must have been the cannon, but it was more seductive than any aftershave I'd ever smelt.

He pulled a face at me and made swinging motions with the bucket.

'You can soak me anytime,' I said, and by the look he gave me, I knew I was in, which was great, because usually I get more knock-backs than take-ups. Most clowns are boringly straight, you know.

After the show, carefully avoiding Susan and the brats, I went around the back of the Big Top, and as I expected, Alejandro came looking for me.

Later in his caravan he was very acrobatic, and I could barely walk straight for a week afterwards. But I guess you don't really need to know those details. Suffice to say, it was a very good night.

'You come back tomorrow,' said Alejandro. 'We be here a few more days.'

'Fuck, yes!' I said, and stumbled out of his trailer, got in my car and drove away.

I was fully satisfied and planning to return the next night for a repeat performance. Unfortunately fate had other ideas. The next day, Alejandro was found dead, stuffed into the cannon head first and with a deadly cream pie down his pants.

That is when things really started to get weird. Or perhaps it was the first time I noticed they were.

You see, on the surface, it looked as though Alejandro had been rehearsing his act alone. During which time he had tripped over his boots into the cannon, cracking open his skull. That explanation might have stuck, except for the cream pie – which contained an acid that had burnt away all of his privates. To add insult to injury, his make-up was all messed up. I recalled how finicky he'd been about his face being smeared the night before, and I was pretty certain he wouldn't have wanted to die in such a dishevelled state.

It was obvious to me that Alejandro had been murdered.

One of the perks of my job is that sometimes I can get

access to information about ongoing police investigations. I learnt that, as expected, the police had done everything they could, interviewing all of the circus troupe to establish a motive. But Alejandro was found to be well-loved by everyone. Having access to this information helped me to keep out of trouble too. After all, I didn't need anyone to find out that I had been with the clown earlier that night and we'd been having a hell of a time. Not that it matters anymore if you're gay in the security services – plenty are – it's just that it would have been frowned upon that I had casual sex with a foreign national I knew nothing about. We're supposed to sound out prospective partners *before* we get involved. But I've always found that sort of thing a bit of a passion-killer. Imagine really being attracted to someone, then finding out that they owed money on a credit card that they hadn't paid off, or took part in some protest years ago against the government or worse, what diseases they'd been cured of at the STD clinic. I'm sure you can see what I mean.

I missed Alejandro, but quickly forgot him. It wasn't love, after all, only sex. But some weeks later, another clown died. Cheerfully leaving a children's party, Pedino's car broke down catastrophically on a dual carriage way.

'It was the strangest, funniest thing, I've ever seen,' said a female eye-witness. 'His car simply fell apart.' According to her, it was like watching a Laurel and Hardy or Charlie Chaplin scene re-enacted. First the driver's door fell off into the fast-moving traffic. The driver behind swerved and loudly honked his horn. Pedino ignored this apparently comic disaster and carried on driving at 70 miles per hour. Even when the bumpers exploded off the front and back, the car made a steady and speedy progress. When the engine fell out from underneath the chassis the female witness, driving in a car not far behind, laughed in shock. And I guess that's exactly how Pedino would have wanted to go, with a bang, and especially laughter.

Of course, what the witness couldn't see was that Pedino was tied into his seat, and his braces had been used to gag him. All the time his car was falling apart, poor Pedino was drowning in his own vomit. Meanwhile his feet pressed helplessly against the useless brakes – obviously they'd been cut and the brake fluid was long since spilt out on the road. The car was being powered by the murderer by remote control. Until the engine fell out, that was. Then it swerved out of control and smashed into and through a barrier that dropped the car 50 feet down a precipice. It looked comic but in reality it was not funny and not nice.

It was fortunate that Pedino and I hadn't been seen together, although we had spent some hours cavorting that day. I'll always remember the fun we had together. Shame really.

Having said that, I'm not one to brood. So, I quickly found a new companion in Charlie.

Now Charlie really knew how to love another man.

After the death of Pedino, I felt like taking a weekend break. Brighton called, and that's where I met Charlie. He was a rough sort, which was a nice change. A broad-speaking Lancashire lad from Bolton. I'd never been there but I recognised the accent from listening to the likes of comedian Peter Kay and television and radio presenter Vernon Kay. (I always wondered if they were related.)

I spent the most fabulous three days in a hotel room in Brighton. When Charlie finally had to go to work, and I had to return to London, it was a very fond farewell indeed. I even had his work schedule, because we definitely planned to meet up again soon. All was well. That was until Charlie donned his bright blue, bulbous shoes that night and took that first fatal step that triggered a bomb carefully placed in the sole. It's safe to say that the witness, a maid working in the hotel, saw him blown clean out of his shoes. Crude. But somehow fitting.

Before this, I'd sort of dismissed the first two deaths as being a hazard of the clown's job, but when Charlie died I started to feel a little paranoid. As you've probably noticed, and I began to realise, every clown I slept with suddenly … well … died. So I think I had good reason to become concerned. At least it could be said that in each case a good sense of humour was evident!

After Charlie, I once again had to eradicate evidence that might have led the authorities to me. I was, after all, the common factor in all three deaths. All the clowns had enjoyed me – or I them, or both – almost immediately before their murder. I hacked the hotel computer system and removed my name from the guest records.

After that I decided that the best thing to do was to lay low, so I kept away from clowns and circuses for a while. This ended up as several very dry months. I got sick of visiting porn sites. They didn't have any serious clown sex at all! It was just men dressed in very dodgy clown suits and make up, getting blow-jobs from women – and it was always under the heading *Fetish*. A bit of an insult really to us genuine lovers of clownfolk.

It wasn't surprising that when I met Happy Horace, I'd fall completely in lust. By then I was desperate, and no man should have to hold out from clown companionship for that long. Horace was another, dear, sweet performer, working with a small travelling band of circus performers.

It wasn't my fault at all that time, though. I had been avoiding circuses and any chance of meeting clowns. Then work had sent a group of us away on a team-building weekend to the Cotswolds. This involved a day working with performers, learning how to juggle, spin plates and perform a few magic tricks. The idea behind it was that by learning practical skills we'd expand our minds in such a way that we'd be able to multi-task better. At least that's what I *thought* must be the point. Mostly it was just daft.

So the first day went well, Gareth, Lavinia, Daffy, Bethan and I dutifully spun plates, dropped more balls than we juggled and learnt a few card tricks in a terribly cack-handed way. The second day was another thing entirely. That's when Happy Horace donned his paint and I suddenly noticed the agility and beauty of his clownish walk.

I tried to stay away at first. Pretending I *didn't* like clowns made it far easier. Then he picked me from the group and suddenly I was completely lost in his smiling colourful eyes. I'm such a sucker for a goofy routine. It was hard to hide my complete pleasure and enjoyment from my colleagues.

'You see! Clowns aren't so bad,' said Gareth. 'My girlfriend is terrified of them for some strange reason … I keep telling her: it's all make-up.'

'The make-up is only the smallest part of it,' I answered before I could stop myself.

Gareth gave me an inquisitive look, 'You really were scared of them weren't you? What happened? Surprise party when you were a kid?'

'It was definitely a kid's party,' I agreed.

Gareth was pulled away then to practice his sleight-of-hand, and I found myself alone with Horace.

His make-up reminded me of something, or someone else, but maybe the joker's lips and tear-drop eyes were finally beginning to look alike.

'To be a clown, you must be flexible,' Horace said. 'Learning to fall without hurting yourself is the first and most important trick.'

I followed his directions, fell without tensing too much, and was only bruised a little bit by the end of the session. Horace was a good teacher.

'Here are your clown shoes,' he said, and I found myself donning those sexy bulbous boots for the first time, quickly followed by the baggy pants and braces.

It was a peculiar experience. Horace taught me to walk in the shoes.

'You have to exaggerate every step,' he said. 'Not like that. Like this, raise your leg more and stick out your bum. Then you'll get that cute little wiggle that all good clowns have.'

I walked around the huge conference room practising and wiggling as my colleagues applauded.

'You're a natural at this,' Lavinia said.

'Now it's your turn,' said Horace, pulling Bethan forward.

By the end of the second morning we were all dressed and parading around the conference room as clowns, but without the make-up.

I liked Happy Horace more and more as the weekend wore on. Plus – my gaydar was on overload. I can always spot a gay clown – for one thing, their make-up is better applied. He even managed to get us all prepared with our own unique clown make-up. As I looked into the mirror, with Horace over my shoulder, I had a vision. I would have him. It would be that simple. I wanted my legs wrapped around his ruffle-covered neck, while he pumped me in good clownish fashion. That's when I gave him my spare key.

Horace looked at it for a moment, and then slipped it into the front pocket of his dungarees. My evening of fun was assured.

Later I feigned a headache, leaving my colleagues to clock up their bar bills. Back in my room, I showered and lay in a robe on the bed waiting for Horace to appear. I felt nervous for the first time in ages. All of the old confidence was gone. That's what happens when you don't get laid for months I suppose.

'Come in,' I said in response to a 'shave and a haircut' knock on the door.

'Hi,' said Horace, and soon we were acting out my fantasy while the TV played loudly on the music channel.

I'd never done it to Eminem before, but by then any thought of clownish music was being banged, quite vigorously, from my sex-starved brain, and I didn't really care what was playing.

We curled up together. I was spooning Horace as he fell asleep quite soon after the third bout of raucous sex. But I couldn't sleep. Something was worrying me. I liked Horace, and I became acutely aware that I didn't really want anything gigglingly sinister to happen to him. That's why I got up and checked that the door was locked properly, then examined his shoes for signs of exploding gadgets. I even looked into his dungarees just in case there was a hidden acid pie, waiting to disintegrate his lovely, large member. This satisfied my phobia and that all was well, so I climbed back in bed and finally drifted off to sleep.

'You mustn't be seen leaving here,' I told him the next day.

'I'll be discrete, Dale. Chill. I know the score; your colleagues don't know you're gay.'

'Actually, no. That isn't it at all.'

Horace gave me a look that said he didn't believe me and he'd heard that one many times before.

'No, really,' I said. 'Everyone knows. Bethan is a lesbian, Gareth is straight and Daffy is Welsh. Our employer is *very* politically correct. I'm not sure about Lavinia but I think she's bi. The truth is, I'm concerned for you.'

Horace laughed. 'Everyone knows which way I swing, darlin.'

Even so, to please me, Horace left surreptitiously, with the stealth that only an experienced clown could achieve from years of practicing sneaking up on people, wearing big boots and carrying a bucket full of nastiness.

It was still early and I lay back in bed and switched the TV back on while waiting for the coffee-maker to do its stuff. I fantasised about the drilling Horace had given me, until the percolator's bubbling and hissing reminded me where I was. One more night in this hotel and the team-building course was over. We'd be off back to London and I may never see Horace again, but still, I might persuade him to sneak back later for one more round.

At that moment there was a rap on the door. I opened it to find Horace standing there, holding a cake with lit candles on it.

'How did you know it was my birthday?' he asked.

'I didn't.'

I was confused, and I stared at the cake in surprise. It was a really fancy home-made one, with delicious-looking butter cream and several fat candles rapidly melting on the top.

'Where did you find that?'

'Outside my door.'

'Oh shit!' I pushed the cake out of his hands and yanked him into my room. Slamming the door I threw us both over the bed. That's when there was a loud explosion, and something spattered all over the outside of the door.

Minutes later the hallway was buzzing, fire alarms were going off in the hotel and there was the sound of people running from their rooms in a noisy panic.

Cautiously I opened the door. The other side of it was covered with buttercream, slowly dripping down the walls and doorframe. I looked in the hallway, and that's when I saw what had been in store for Horace. The passage was covered in sponge, butter cream, jam and bits of rainbow-coloured glass. I was in a bit of a quandary after that. The hotel was in chaos, it would be hard to hide this one and Horace was now in very serious danger. How the hell was I going to tell him that? I imagined Horace's face breaking into a smile as I explained the silly ways all of the previous victims had died – but really – it wasn't funny at all, was it? I smiled. Damn straight it was! I was clearly being stalked by some crazy clown killer, and I couldn't believe how much I was *enjoying* it.

I looked back into the room at the bemused clown.

'Are you okay?' I asked.

He nodded. 'What the hell is going on?'

I picked up the phone and called my boss, Charles Mayberry. It was the rational thing to do.

'It's all beyond a joke,' I said. 'Lives are being lost and I just don't know how to stop it.'

'Why didn't you come to us before now? We could have given you protection,' Mayberry replied; he thinks he's 'M' from the James Bond films, even though he's only the office manager.

It was hard to explain. Admitting you're an addict is one thing, owning up to being a 'clown addict' was a bit fetishistic, even for me. I wasn't really sure what they could do for me, a simple clerk, anyway.

The problem was escalated *upstairs*, and before I knew it both Horace and I were being taken into protective custody, which was a bit of a surprise. New respect to the boss.

'This is very serious,' said Mayberry. 'It could be an attempt to gain access to official secrets.'

'I don't see how someone systematically killing my lovers could achieve that,' I protested.

'We know that, Dale. But obviously this criminal doesn't.'

After a week of isolation I talked Mayberry into letting me go home. There was no way of catching the crook if I was incarcerated. I thought it might be best to lay a trap instead. Besides, I was bored to death in there. Being at risk outside would be far more interesting than being locked up and safe. That's why I asked if Horace could come back with me, move into my place and be a visible part of my life.

'I'll do it,' he said.

'Even knowing the risks?'

'Yes – it sounds comically gruesome.'

It was a bit of a revelation to learn how into the macabre Horace was. Maybe this *was* a match made in clown heaven.

Horace moved in with me and, strangely, we had no trouble at all. I had always lived alone, been as promiscuous as I wanted, but I quickly got used to finding his brightly-coloured T-shirts and his stripy dungarees strewn all over the bedroom. I didn't mind having to get the Dyson out more, because he was pretty good company – and a fantastic lay.

Eventually, when the danger seemed to have passed, *upstairs* lost interest and stopped watching my apartment. Horace stayed on and we lived in something approaching domestic bliss, with just the occasional jealous catfight, or me yelling at him to clean his shit up after himself. He got a job locally in an amusement arcade, where he entertained the kids while parents poured money into machines. He didn't earn much, but he didn't need to as I earned enough to cover the bills. Occasionally I went to watch him work. Afterwards we'd have sex in the ball pool when the arcade was closed.

It all went clownish when I discovered the shoe box under the bed. I was having a cleaning frenzy – more than usual – and when I stripped the bedsheets, I spotted the box crammed under the bed.

'Bloody hell, Horace!' I yelled, even though he wasn't around to hear me. 'What the fuck? Why are you such a slob?'

I bent down, determined to shove the offending item back under with the dust and cobwebs, when the lid came off and several photographs came tumbling out.

'Shit.'

I sat down on the floor and began to tidy the mess away back into the box. That's when I saw the picture. It was of a very familiar clown. It was Bowbo. I picked out more of the prints.

'In the age of digital, why on earth would you keep a box of prints?' I sighed, but then I knew. It was obvious.

Now I realised why Horace's make-up had seemed so familiar when we first met. The clothes were different, but the make-up was essentially the same. Horace was – had been – Bowbo. My first clown sex. He'd started this addiction. Why hadn't he told me?

I picked the box up, pulling it up onto the bed beside me. Then I began to flick through the hundreds of pictures. Pictures of me visiting circuses, pictures of me going into Alejandro's trailer. Pictures of Alejandro posing with a cream pie. Pictures of Alejandro head-first down a cannon: the print was fuzzy and you could almost tell that the clown had been flapping his legs in fear and agitation. My lips twitched. It was kind of funny …

Next I found pictures of Pedino grinning insanely at the camera; Pedino wild-eyed as a hand pressed his braces forcefully down his throat. Tight leather straps were wrapped around his body, pinning him to his seat. My smile widened. Finally Charlie grinned at me, followed by a picture of him exploding from his shoes. I laughed out loud. It was too absurd!

All this time I'd been concerned that Horace would come to some harm, when in fact *he* was the stalker. It all made complete sense. I'd thrown Bowbo off for some Italian hunk and promptly forgotten him, never knowing that he hadn't forgotten me.

Obviously the exploding cake had been a ruse to take the heat off himself, or maybe he thought it would get him closer to me. And it had worked. He had me now. There was no longer any need for jealousy, which had a whole lot of different connotations. For example, what would he do if I ever got fed up with our relationship? Not that it was likely: he definitely was the best I'd ever had, and he was fun to be around mostly. But if we stayed together, I would spend the rest of my life worrying about ever looking at another man. Or not.

As I put the pictures back in the box, and carefully pushed it well under the bed, I thought things through, and made some decisions.

I dressed very carefully, knowing that Horace would be back soon.

'I'll be back late tonight, lovey,' I told him as he returned from his shift. 'I'm going to visit a sick friend.'

Horace merely looked at me and said nothing.

The clown I picked had red and black helium-filled balloons bunched together and tied on his trolley. It didn't take me long to chat him up, and soon we were getting down and dirty in the back of his van, which was conveniently parked around the corner.

When I got out, I ignored the stares of a group of teenage boys who were gawping at the van as if it had been moving all by itself. Oh. I suppose it had been. I left the van and the clown – I didn't bother to ask his name, it didn't really matter anyway – then I returned to my car and went home.

I pretended not to see the familiar bright clothing and white painted face on someone lurking behind the van as I walked away.


*Clown killed in Surrey*, read the headline as I sat on the tube train heading into my office in the centre of London the next day. *'This is a hideous crime', said a police spokesman. 'At first we thought it was an accident, but then we discovered that the helium canister was filled with mustard gas. He'd have been exposed the minute he began to blow up new balloons.'*

I laughed out loud at the newspaper report, ignoring the stares of the other passengers.

'Have you heard the news?' Mayberry asked as I sat down at my desk.

'Yes,' I nodded. 'Obviously nothing to do with me this time. But someone really has it in for clowns.'

'That's what I thought. Looks like your connection was just a coincidence.'

I smiled as he walked away.

No-one's relationship is perfect, but at least Horace was inventive. I know. My addiction – and Horace's ingenious devotion – was going to kill many more clowns before I was finished.

I'm a clown addict, and you have to admit, it is funny …

## AUTHOR'S NOTES

*Clown Addict* is a dark comedy/murder mystery and a very different type of story for me. The narrative was born from several influences. In films I'd see this as *Kind Hearts and Coronets* meets *Dr Phibes* with a dash of *Carry-On*. I'm sure you can see why.

The original inspiration came from a Whovian friend in Brighton with a robot dog and a Dyson addiction that feeds his OCD too well. He asked me, 'What does one have to do to get murdered in one of your stories?' I was happy to oblige.

At the time I was working on *The Toymaker's House* and thought I'd insert him as a victim. Then a guy started messaging me on Facebook and asked me if I would ever write about killer clowns. This is always an intriguing idea as a lot of people have clown phobias, but I didn't want to do the usual insane clown chasing kids with an axe, or zombie clown on the search for fresh brains. I certainly didn't want to explore the realms of Stephen King's *It*. And so, as these things always do, all of these events mushed around in my head.

In the end I thought that *Clown Addict* was ultimately where my friend belonged. For this reason I wanted the character of 'Dale' to behave a little like his namesake, but obviously my Dale is a completely fictional character.

I then put out a Facebook plea for information on clowns, and David also took me to an American Circus that just happened to be in town for a few weeks. It seemed that destiny smiled on this idea and wanted it to be written.

Thanks therefore go to Dale Who, Joe Young (ex-clown

and Facebook friend who gave me some great insights), David, and Otto the Clown, who recently invited me to join his Facebook friends and who is eagerly awaiting this tale.

Remember, I may have used real names, but this is *fiction* ...

# Immortal Monster

Most ghost stories begin with a house. Sometimes there's a storm, or wind beating against dusty windows and a decrepit door banging against a wall, half off its hinges. Often there is a lonely, friendless child at the heart of the terror, somehow channelling a mischievous poltergeist. At times there's been a murder and the dead reappear to warn the living. Or a deceased jealous wife plays havoc at a wedding rehearsal as her husband plans to marry another woman, his dead love almost forgotten.

But you might as well just forget everything you already know about ghosts, because this story isn't like that. There's no rain storm or locked attic or dank, dark cellar. No rattling chains to disturb the rest of a hotel's guests.

There's just me, my work and a typewriter.

The typewriter's an antique, but don't get any ideas that it is the cause or the source; this story doesn't unravel quite so easily. I bought it in a typical antique shop though, and being an original Hermes it cost me a pretty penny too. But I liked it and it was immaculate. I had my suspicions that it wasn't the real deal. It was too perfect. But the shop owner reassured me that it had been in one loving home and hadn't been used. Even the ribbons were original, and what surprised me most was how they hadn't even dried up and the ink was as fresh as the day it was made.

I brought the typewriter home and placed it on a bureau in the hallway beside the phone. I like to collect things that relate to writing, so the typewriter, along with my other knick-knacks of calligraphy pens, ancient quills and parchment, became a symbol of my success. You see, I'm a writer.

Years ago, I'd never have been able to afford it, but the fact that I could indulge myself like this felt really good.

The phone rang as I placed the typewriter down and stepped back to examine it.

'Nathaniel?'

'Yes?' I said. 'What is it Nina?'

'Ben's got sports day on Friday. Do you think you can come?'

I tried to ignore the hard edge in my ex-wife's voice as I flicked through my diary. I knew she was waiting for me to fail again as a father. I wanted to see Ben's sporting achievements, but I did have a tight schedule.

Friday flopped open and I saw meetings with my

agent and publisher in the morning, but my afternoon was clear.

'What time does it start?'

'After lunch. Around 1.40 pm.'

'No problem,' I said.

'Really?' Nina sounded disappointed.

'Yes.'

'Oh.'

That's when I knew that the call was just a courtesy. Nina didn't want me there, probably because her husband, Ryan, would be.

'Tell Ben I'm looking forward to seeing him win the race.'

I hung up; I wasn't going to give her the opportunity of stiffing me once more in her constant attempt to oust me as Ben's dad, replacing me with Ryan.

Of course Ryan was everything I wasn't. He was a good provider, with a sensible and dedicated career as an accountant. Staid, but very well paid. He was as boring as hell, but he had the money to buy Ben and Nina everything they wanted or needed. This was perfect for Nina, who'd hated that I was always working night and day to make the meagre advances for my next book.

When we'd first met I'd been something of a novelty as an aspiring writer. She'd loved the attention it brought her with friends and family, who naively believed that all published writers were making a mint. Nina soon learnt it wasn't the case, that I just about made the salary of a trainee teacher. But I won awards for my words, and so we got married: Nina was in love with the dream. She saw my future as the next Stephen King or Dean Koontz, but it never happened. After five years of not being able to buy the designer clothing she loved, or live the lifestyle she wanted – preferably jet-set – Nina moved out, taking our three-year-old son, Ben, with her.

I knew I'd failed her. So I didn't even contest the divorce papers that claimed my behaviour was 'unreasonable'. I hadn't been unreasonable, but I had definitely failed in her eyes and mine to be everything that she needed.

After that my writing changed. It became darker, somewhat depressive and definitely more gruesome. Of course, using emotion was a good thing and the horror industry began to love me. Oddly, by leaving me, Nina had done me a major favour. My career began a steady climb that soon galloped. I'd really found my voice, and all my old books were suddenly in vogue too. Royalties and advances were pouring in so fast that I didn't know what to do with the money.

By then Nina, never one to be alone, had met and married Ryan. It was a whirlwind thing that sometimes I wondered if she regretted. Surely she never seemed happy when we spoke. There was always that tone of accusation in her voice, and on some level I felt her resentment. I believed that she felt I'd been holding out on her. I didn't dare tell her the half of it. If she knew about the six figure advance I'd just banked, or the obscene royalty cheques that poured in, Nina would hate me even more. She might even go to the CSA at last and try and extract some of that money for herself in Ben's name. Although I doubted it. Ryan refused to take any money I offered for Ben's upkeep. He had this misguided notion that only he could be the breadwinner in his household. I saw it as just one more thing he took from me. He wouldn't even allow me the dignity of supporting my own son.

I looked at the typewriter again, trying to distract myself. It felt like a quiet monument to the hard years. I loved it. I straightened the inkwell beside it, and the fancy glass jar that contained an original quill, supposedly once used by William Shakespeare. Then I went back to work on my current book.


Friday came, and I sat with the other parents in their rows around the school sports field, watching Ben run. He was fast, like a little whippet! It was hard to imagine at times that he was my son; sports had never been my forte.

'Dad!' Ben said, running up to me after winning easily.

He threw his arms around me, and I looked over his head as we hugged to see the stern faces of Nina and Ryan. Ben was ten. This was his last year as a junior and he'd be off to high school in September. He was old enough to make his own mind up about things, and I knew he loved me.

'Hey buddy!' I said. 'You were great out there!'

'Dad, can we go out for a sundae after school?'

'Deffo!'

Nina and Ryan were feeling awkward as we stood together and Ben introduced me to his teachers.

'Go tell your Mom that you're coming to dinner with me,' I said. 'And give her a hug too.'

He ran off, and minutes later Nina and Ryan left. Neither of them looked happy. I waited as Ben went to change and get his school bag, then we trundled off to my car.

'Wow! Is this new?' Ben asked.

'Yep. It's a Lexus.'

'It's posh, Dad.' I laughed as he climbed in the front seat and fastened his seat belt. 'It's nicer than Ryan's car.'

I didn't reply, but it pleased me that at last I had better things than Ryan.

'Where's it to be?' I asked, and Pizza Express won the day.

Ben was really tired when I drove him home later. His face was red and he was hot despite the double helping of ice-cream for dessert.

'I think he got too much sun today,' I pointed out to Ryan as he opened the door. 'Was he wearing sun cream?'

'Of course he was!' Nina snapped walking up the hallway. 'Don't you think I'd make sure of that?'

'See you, buddy,' I said to Ben, hugging him. 'Next weekend you're with me and we'll be going to the cinema to see *Shrek 3D*'

'Cool!'

And that was the last time I saw my son alive.


At the funeral Ryan was redundant. None of my side of the family even gave him a sideways glance. Nina was sick. I'd never seen her so pale and thin. Her exterior reflected my helplessness. My son was dead, and for the last seven years I'd barely seen him. We'd never go to see *Shrek* together and there would be no more sports days. I was suffocated with the feeling that somehow I should have been there at the end. I should have been the one to find him dead, not Ryan. And I saw it in Nina's eyes – I'd failed again.

'It's so shocking,' my aunt Mary was saying. 'So sudden! Do you know what caused it?'

'Ben had a heart defect,' my sister explained as I stared empty-eyed into the distance, too flat to speak. 'It could have happened at any time. But I guess the extra exertion of the sports day didn't help.'

'That's awful. I'm so sorry.'

There were neighbours and school friends, relatives and teachers. The local church had opened its doors to the community. This was the biggest news they'd had in a long time. People came out in force to pay their respects. Parents were marginally afraid and obscenely relieved, because really they were glad: it hadn't been their child. Ben was that one chance in a million. His death was a fluke that couldn't have been foreseen, and there wasn't anyone I could blame for it.

I told you this wasn't a typical ghost story, and it isn't.

My son didn't come back from the grave with any warning for me. He wasn't in limbo with unfinished business. And no amount of wishing him back was ever going to return him to me in any form. Or so I thought.

After the funeral I locked myself away. My editor gave me an extension on my deadline, but I didn't take her up on it. Writing was all I had left, so I threw myself back in, buried myself in the fiction and began to write the new novel.

I had a strange pride in the new book, an obsessive fascination. It was the only important thing in the world. Writing stopped me thinking about my loss. And like all books, it took on a life of its own that I hadn't at first expected, nor anticipated.

So, the ghost story, *Immortal Monster*, was told.

It was the tale of a man who lost his son, who came back from the dead to tell him about the other side, which was scarier than Hell. There was a demon, an immortal monster, who posed as a human. He killed children, sacrificing them to his cultish beliefs.

The story was nothing like the synopsis I'd sold, but when I turned it over to my editor, Cynthia Fisher, she loved it.

'I never say this,' Cynthia said. 'But it's going to be a

bestseller. I can tell already. It's years since I read anything this good. I'm even going to pass it onto a producer I know. I see movie deals, large royalties and a career that's made for life.'

I stared blankly at the manuscript on her desk. Now I'd written it, the obsession had ended. I'd told that story and had already moved onto my next one. Cynthia pointed out to me that there wasn't one red mark on it.

'This will go to print as it is, Nathanial. I've never done that in my entire career. But it's perfect. The prose is faultless. Do you understand how rare that is?'

I did understand and found it hard to believe. I hadn't even edited it myself for the same reason. As the story unwound it was told perfectly and I hadn't tweaked or changed one single word or phrase from the moment I'd committed it to my Word document.

The next day I found out that Nina was pregnant.

I felt – weird.

'I'm four months,' she told me on the phone. 'I just wanted you to hear it from me.'

Four months. It was four months since Ben died. I stared at my Hermes typewriter where it had stood, unmoved, since the day I bought it. Absentmindedly, I wiped the fine layer of dust from the keys.

'Naturally Ryan is over the moon,' Nina continued.

I didn't answer.

'I know this is hard for you,' Nina added. 'I'll never get over losing Ben, but have to think of the health of my baby. Life moves on and I have this new life to care for …'

'Don't ring me again,' I said. 'I don't want to hear about it.'

I hung up.

I wrote another book. This one took only three months. It was the story of a child dying on the night his mother and stepfather took part in a strange ritual. The mother later found out she had conceived a new child and promptly forgot about the one that died.

It was an overnight success.

I went on a signing tour for *Immortal Monster*. It was the first time in my career that I'd ever had real fans. There were TV and magazine interviews. The success of the book meant that pre-orders for *The Ritual* exceeded all expectation.

At Waterstone's in London, I signed copies of my books until my arm felt like it was dropping off. The queue went out onto the street. I was an unbelievable triumph. But since writing the second book, I had no urge to write a third, no matter how much my editor nagged me. With the film deal, merchandise and the royalties from my previous books, I didn't need the money. In fact I now earned more money than I could ever spend. I had nothing and no-one to spend it on.

'Who do I sign this to?' I asked as someone handed me a copy of *Immortal Monster*.

'Me. Nina.'

I looked up. My ex-wife Nina was holding a baby in her arms. It was a little boy of about 18 months old. For a moment I was taken aback at how quickly time had gone by. The baby smiled at me. He was the image of Ben.

'I'm so pleased for you,' Nina said. 'You've made a real success of your life. Who'd have thought it?'

'Yes,' I answered dully.

I couldn't take my eyes off the little boy.

'He's cute,' I said finally. 'What did you call him?'

'Bart.'

I met Nina's eyes then. Before Ben was born we'd made a list of girls' and boys' names. Bart had been one of them. I'd been really keen on using it.

'Oh come on!' Nina had said, 'We can't call him that! He'll have the piss taken out of him at school.'

Eventually we'd opted for Benjamin.

'Bart. Nice name,' I said, and could barely suppress the cynical smile that threatened to work my lips.

It was all so ironic.

'Look, Nate. Would you like to meet for lunch sometime? I have so much I'd like to tell you.'

'I don't think that's a good idea.'

Nina moved aside as the next customer brought their book forward.

'I hate the way things ended,' she said.

'Now's not the time. I can't do this, Nina.'

'Okay. Sorry.'

I looked up once more into the eyes of Bart and saw

Ben's soul reflected back at me. I wanted to hold the little boy more than anything in the world. I wanted my son back. An uncontrollable wave of loss and sickness came over me.

'I'll go,' said Nina. 'I'm sorry. I just wanted to be friends.'

The queue was finally coming to an end.

'Look, I'm almost done. Let's go and have a coffee.'

'Really?' she said, surprised.

I nodded. I didn't know why I was doing it, but I had to spend more time with Bart.

'We've never had such a good signing,' the manager, "call me John", said.

A petite girl in a black T-shirt led me to the back entrance, where I could exit without being mobbed by the lingering fans out front.

'He's a little odd isn't he?' I heard one of the assistants say when they thought I was out of earshot.

'Yeah. He's even creepier than Stephen King. But have you read that book? It takes a sick mind to write shit like that.'

Nina smiled as I came out, and Bart was in a buggy playing with a rattle. He was grinning at the world as it went by.

We went for coffee in a little café nearby. It was nothing special, but then I got no joy at all out of my wealth and so anything more exclusive would have felt exactly the same to me.

We drank lattes and I let Nina rattle on about life, Bart and Ryan. She needed closure with me it seemed, but I felt nothing. Nina was no more interesting to me than any other woman. She was a total stranger. Bart, however, was completely fascinating.

'Is there no-one in your life?' Nina asked. 'A girlfriend?'

I thought about the one-night stands that had happened on the tour, but none of the girls was memorable. Each had been some goth teen, barely legal, who wanted to fuck a famous horror writer. I knew what the score was, always used protection, and promptly forgot names as quickly as I discarded their scribbled phone numbers.

I left the coffee house reluctantly, but not before I touched Bart's small hand.

I wrote another book.

This time it was a more traditional ghost story. I wrote about a dead child being reincarnated as his mother's new baby. The baby grew to be identical to the dead child. He also remembered that his death was anything but an accident. It was complete and perfect in two months, and Cynthia Fisher was delighted.

'You're a dark horse,' she said. 'I thought you were never going to give me another book. You've been working on this one all along, haven't you?'

I smiled.

'If you want to believe that,' I said. 'Would you like to

go out for a drink tonight?'

Cynthia was good in bed. You might think that would complicate things, but it only served to enhance our working relationship, and as before she sang my praises and sent the manuscript to her producer friend. A third film deal was cut as *Vengeful Child* was optioned.

After *The Ritual* came out, Ryan phoned me. I wasn't sure how he'd come by the number, but then remembered I hadn't changed it even after I severed contact with Nina.

'We need to talk. I don't know who told you, but it was all just a bit of fun.'

'What was?' I said.

'It was just a joke. Nina and I had been trying for a baby for ages, Nathanial. A friend of hers was into new age things. It wasn't really a ritual as such, and I don't know how you could have used it in your story like that.'

'I don't know what you're talking about, Ryan.'

'Your book, *The Ritual*! You described exactly what Nina and I did the night Ben died. But I'm telling you, it wasn't serious. And no way can you say that it caused Ben's death. That's just sick.'

I hung up on Ryan and went to my bookcase, taking down my copy of *The Ritual*. It was weird, but I couldn't even remember the main plot feature of the story. It was as if by writing it I had completely purged the memory. I opened the cover and began to read back my own story.

*Richard was determined to have his own child with Nicole. He'd always resented his stepson, even though he gave the appearance of being devoted to him. It was all part of the act of course. He'd known immediately what would attract her. The wealth and stability part was so easy to provide. But actually loving Benjamin, well that was another issue. In fact he hated him.*

*The ritual was easy. Richard didn't use it right away though; he wanted her to be completely trusting. She had to believe in everything he said, and that would take time. He spent four years proving his trustworthiness, and in all that time his hatred of Benjamin grew. The child was a constant drain on Nicola's attention. But still he gave her everything. All the designer clothing, flash cars, meals out and holidays she could possibly want. He gave her the life that her failure ex-husband had never been able to give.*

*Richard was a demon. He fed off Nicola's greed. All that he did for her would be paid for eventually, and she wouldn't see it coming.*

*'I want a child with you,' he said, knowing full well he wouldn't get her pregnant until she was completely desperate.*

*'Oh darling!' Nicola said.*

*'I'm sure Benjamin would love a brother or sister,' Richard said. 'And you know I will always treat Benjamin exactly the same. I wish he was ours, Nikki.'*

*'Me too!' Nicola said.*

*They tried of course and nothing happened. And then*

*Nicola began to worry and started to suggest they 'get checked out'. She didn't think the fault was hers – after all, she had Benjamin – but she wanted to make sure.*

*'I'd like to propose something a little less orthodox,' Richard said one evening. 'It might sound bizarre, but I think we've been a little tense about it.'*

*Richard told Nicola about the ritual. She giggled as he described how he would tie her down. It was all very fetish, but in the end it sounded kind of sexy …*

I closed the book, glancing at the phone, half expecting Ryan to call again, but the phone didn't ring. Then I re-opened the book at random points.

*The ritual was special of course. Disguised so innocently as a sex game, the power it would generate would give Richard the potency to impregnate Nikki, but the cost was high. Someone nearby had to die.*

*At the sports day, Richard felt aggrieved that Benjamin ran to his father first. That layabout musician hardly ever came near the boy. After all, it was Richard who had done everything for him over the last few years, even attending all the boring plays and parents' evenings and paying for his private tuition. Richard expected better treatment.*

*He began his preparations as the boy went out to dinner with his father. It would be a long night, and at the end of it Nicola would be all his. Besides, the little bastard deserved all he'd get.*

*At the funeral he pretended to be dejected, but the truth was he was gloating. Nicola would be even easier to control now.*

I closed my eyes and tried to shut out the image of Ryan and Nina playing the brutal game I'd described in the book. The game that had killed Benjamin. For the first time I really began to make a connection between the strangeness of my son's death and the weird way that I'd been obsessively writing. Writing a 'perfect' book had appeared to be so impossible that that I'd often been surprised by this new skill. I was even more confused that I couldn't remember the words on completion.

Ryan had appeared in Nina's life before our divorce was even finalised, but I'd let it go, knowing she would be happier with a man who could keep her in the lifestyle she wanted. Nina had always needed to be surrounded by pretty things – it made her happy, whereas I didn't care about possessions. Even Ben had been something she owned. As soon as he was born, she had proudly paraded him at mother and toddler groups as she revelled in his achievements. He always had to have the nicest things; anything less made Nina feel inferior. It was one of the reasons we had so many money worries, I just couldn't earn enough to sustain her needs.

In *The Ritual*, Benjamin dies. He is the sacrifice that gives the demon his potency, and he ends his life in agony, his heart bursting inside his chest like a rotting tomato.

I ran my hands through my hair. Horror and sickness pulled my stomach one way, then another. The thought of Ben dying like that made the bile rise to the back of my throat, but I forced the nausea away, returning once more to my bookcase.

I picked up *Immortal Monster*. The ideas that were floating through my mind were completely and utterly insane. I was beginning to believe that Ryan was the demon in both of the books.

*It is crazy! Just because he called me, and by coincidence they had done a ritual to help Nina conceive …* it seemed too improbable that I could have guessed so accurately. What was even stranger was Ryan reading my novel. It was almost as though he were looking for evidence that I had sussed him.

This isn't just a ghost story, as I've said all along.

I hadn't been haunted, as far as I knew. But being a writer, I was used to working out plots and scenarios. I didn't believe in accidents; all characters in every story had a point and purpose. My story, therefore, was no different. Maybe the plots of those novels were just something my grief-stricken brain had devised, but part of me didn't believe that. Somewhere, deep inside my heart and soul, I knew that the information was accurate and it was being *fed* to me. But by who – or what – I didn't know.

I opened *Immortal Monster*. As with *The Ritual*, I couldn't recall the story I'd written. This became an important seed in the plot that was now running through my life.

*He walked away from one life into another. Always looking for the same type. The women were always needy, always just out of a previous relationship and feeling vulnerable. Sometimes they had kids. It didn't bother him if they did; he was good at pretending to like them. He'd wangle his way into their lives until they couldn't live without him. Then he'd strike.*

*At the moment of ultimate happiness he'd kill. Then he'd feast on the misery until he grew bored and moved onto the next one.*

*He met Nancy the day he killed his wife and unborn child. But Nancy would never know that. She was taken in like everyone else. She never realised he fed on her miseries, mostly causing them, while appearing all along to be the one person she could rely on.*

*He was so unlike her ex, and at least he was always there for her son Benjamin.*

I ran to the bathroom, barely making it to the toilet, and vomited the entire contents of my stomach into the bowl until the muscles in my abdomen ached. My perfect words struck a horrible chord in my chest. Cynthia had said my writing was immaculate, that it never needed to be edited, and that was because as I wrote, the story would unfold and tell itself in a completely natural flow. The order was important and the words couldn't be changed because they rang so true.

*The demon couldn't be killed. Nigel failed in that too, as he failed in everything else in Nancy's eyes … And so he walked away from their lives, leaving his son to the mercy of the demon's whims. At least, so far, it had shown no interest in harming Benjamin.*

It wasn't possible, and was completely insane to even consider there was any such thing as a demon. I couldn't shake the nagging in my head, or the memory of the strange timbre in Ryan's voice when he said, 'That's just sick.'

A few days later, *Vengeful Child* hit the bookshops. I resisted looking once more at the text as I placed my copy on the shelf beside the other books. The film of the book was already in production. It was unlikely that I'd go to the premier; I hadn't wanted to attend the others, so this one would be no different.

When my phone rang I half expected to hear the soft threat that barely concealed the panic of Ryan's voice. Instead it was my editor, Cynthia.

'Hey! Look in the *Independent*,' she said. 'You've got a great write-up and a fantastic review. You see, I'm not the only one who loves your writing … How about dinner tonight? My treat …'

We met in an exclusive Italian that was frequented by

most of Cynthia's cronies, a few celebrities and several film-makers. It was clear she wanted to be seen with me in all of her professional glory. The books were making her look good too, especially as the named editor. No-one but she and I knew that not word had been changed on any of them. Like she said, they were perfect.

As Cynthia went to the bathroom, a woman came over and asked me to sign her copy of *Vengeful Child*.

'You won't believe it,' she told me. 'But my sister married a creep just like the demon you described in *Immortal Monster*.'

'Really?' I said, but I wasn't taking much notice.

'Yes. It was creepily similar in so many details, and I'm sure you'll think I'm some kind of stalker or weirdo for saying this …'

'Of course not,' I said indifferently.

'My sister, Marian, was pregnant, and she died under really mysterious circumstances. She didn't have any money, her husband, Ryan, had nothing to gain from her death, so …'

'Ryan?' I looked into the eyes of the woman for the first time. There was no sign of madness and I sensed complete sincerity in her words.

'Yes. The creep went and got remarried. She wasn't even in the ground for more than six months …'

I felt the colour wash from my face. Nausea rolled through my gut and I looked at the cooling veal on my plate, breaking the spell of her hypnotic, honest eyes.

'Strange, but all that stuff you described in the book … the way the demon operates, it was just like him. He comes along, Marian is all alone and destitute, he throws money at her, and the next thing you know she's dead, carrying his baby …'

I didn't answer. My mind was reeling, my heart hurting. I wanted the woman to leave. I wished I had never heard her words.

It was like being haunted, but not. Too many things just didn't add up. Fortunately at that moment Cynthia returned.

'Sorry to dump all this on you,' the woman continued. 'It just creeped me out, the similarities.'

'I understand,' I said. 'Obviously all characters have to be like real people. There's probably lots of guys like … Ryan … out there.'

She went away, thankfully.

'What was all that?' asked Cynthia. 'Your fans get everywhere, don't they?'

'Yes,' was all I could manage to answer.


I went home and read *Vengeful Child* from cover to cover. I didn't recognise the words anymore, they came out of me onto the page, became print, and suddenly the story and meaning were gone completely from my mind.

'I'm warning you!' said Ryan the next day. 'Stop writing about us. You can't really believe that my son is Benjamin reincarnated.'

226

'Why are you calling me, Ryan?' I asked. 'I write books. They are just stories. Why should it even concern you?'

'Stop it,' he said again.

'Or what?'

I glanced at the typewriter on the bureau. It was the symbol of my success. I placed a piece of paper into the back and twisted the roller.

'I don't know how you're doing it,' said Ryan in my ear. 'But I'm warning you … don't mess with me. You don't know what I'm capable of …'

'Words have power …' I answered, and I began to type.

I dropped the receiver long before the screaming ended and was unaware of the silence that followed. I was writing and the final story had to be told.

A few days later, Nina rang me to tell me Ryan was dead. She'd been making dinner when she heard him scream. She'd found him on the floor, the phone clasped in spasmed fingers.

'Bart was in the same room in his playpen. I hope he isn't traumatised by the experience,' she told me; but other than that she didn't seem to miss Ryan at all.

Bart and Nina are safe. Sometimes I go out with them to Richmond Park, and Bart's growing up to be more and more like Ben every day. Nina and I are friends. I'll never show her the typewriter though, or the piece of paper that's still in the roller. It's locked away somewhere safe from prying eyes. I shall never commit this final story to print.

*The Immortal Monster died. The truth of his evil, committed to words, destroyed his blackened soul like some perverse exposé of Dorian Gray's picture. Words have power, and truth always destroys liars.*

So this is it. This is the final chapter of my ghost story. Like I said, it isn't traditional, and on the surface I haven't been haunted. But I do believe that some power out there has been sending me a warning. Maybe it came from my son, maybe not. Though forces have definitely conspired to show me the way to end the demon's reign.

I've learnt one final truth: my words have power, and my immortality is assured through them. And in my own way, I've become an immortal monster. That's why I can never write another word.

## AUTHOR'S NOTES

The original concept for *Immortal Monster* was slightly different. When I decided to put together this collection

I wrote a short synopsis for each story. Some of the stories I already had, but I knew I'd be writing up many more of them as originals. I had thought to write this one as a Lucrezia story, but ultimately changed my mind when I was approached for a contribution to a charity anthology.

The anthology theme was ghost stories, and I wanted to write something new and original. It had to be something that hadn't been done before. I also thought long and hard about the types of stories my favourite authors had written before me.

You may not believe this is a ghost story *per se*; it isn't an obvious haunting and there are many interpretations you could devise. But that's fine, because at times it is deliberately ambiguous, and I wanted readers to bring their own ideas to the table.

So you decide. What did happen? And how did Nathanial know?

# CHILLERS AND BREATHERS

'She came in a few hours ago,' Charlie said as he opened the door of the morgue for me. 'After you.'

I floated inside. 'You don't need to do that, you know. I can pass through the bloody thing.'

'Don't keep reminding me. I'm starting to think my thermals are part of my skin. Being around you is cold work, Meg.'

I laughed at his attempt at chiller-joke. Charlie was nice, for a breather. Just to prove a point, I thinned to fog and slipped through the next door, which was unfortunate for the morgue technician standing on the other side. When I suddenly materialised in front of him he completely freaked.

'Shit. Fuck!'

His arms flailed as though I'd just tried to rip out his heart. Of course, I couldn't have done that. Well … not without some effort. But then he didn't know that I suppose.

'Shut it. I have a badge,' I hissed at the man as Charlie opened the door behind him, ghost gun at the ready.

'She … passed through me …' The tech was a dithering mess. I think his hair actually went a little whiter from the shock.

It's not like it hurts or anything. Sheesh. But breathers do have this strange idea that you're raping them in some way, or worse, taking possession. It's weird what mythology they'll make up when left to their own devices.

I folded my arms. 'You should know better than to just *stand* in front of a door. If Charlie had come through first, then that would have hurt more.'

I left Charlie apologising to the man while I floated off down the corridor. When breathers get all screamy and up tight, it has an effect on us chillers. We just feel like shutting them up. Permanently. The anger wells up like a red rage, and often it's not controllable. Even I can't hold back that sort of emotion for long. So the only answer is to get as far away from them as possible.

I reached the morgue and looked in. Lying there was a once pretty young thing. She was also standing alongside, staring at her body on the slab and clearly feeling pissed off at being dead.

'Hey. So what happened?'

She looked at me blankly. Mostly they just can't remember how they died, there's just a blank there.

However, the body looked like it had been used for target practice in a cleaver throwing contest.

'Not a pretty sight, is it? Must have hurt.' Okay, so I'm not very tactful, but I was still smarting a little from that idiot by the door.

Then I remembered the brief that Charlie and I had been given earlier. 'Er … it seems you took a nose drive off a high rise. You were found at the bottom, lying in shards of broken glass. What made you do that?'

'I … don't remember exactly,' said the girl. 'Fuck, is that me there? I wouldn't have done that to myself.' The girl shook her head. It wobbled precariously on her frame.

'I'd be careful of that for a few days. You don't want to lose it. Your form will stabilise eventually though.'

Charlie wandered in behind me. He swaggers when he walks. The girl gave him the once over, forgetting momentarily that she was dead. By any standard Charlie is pretty hot. Not that I'd noticed in any way other than a clinical one. Chillers and breathers getting it on … that was something of an anathema to me. There were rumours that some liked to cross the blur. I guess it's a fetish. But the thought of it totally creeped me out.

'Hello. Miss Sophie Johnson, isn't it? Can we do anything to make you more comfortable?' Charlie said respectfully, because he's very good at being polite, which is also something that I'm terrible at.

The former Miss Johnson beamed at him, and her

mouth went up too far at one side, like some partial attempt at 'jokerdom'. I gave her a little nudge and she began to settle again. Holding a form is the hardest thing to learn when you're dead. I glanced at Charlie to see if her variable features freaked him, but he was smiling at her kindly. Point to him.

'Well,' Sophie continued, twirling her finger through her foggy hair. 'I'm not too happy about being killed. But being dead doesn't *feel* so bad.'

'Your friends say you were a very popular girl,' Charlie said, waving the report in his hand.

'Why thank you,' Sophie flirted with another, more stable smile.

They were grinning at each other way too nicely. I moved between them, looked Charlie in the eyes, and frowned. He tried to look round me, then through me, which is really just rude. It's like having someone peek up your skirt as you climb a ladder.

'And back in the real world, breather,' I snapped.

Charlie blinked and shook his head. 'Sorry, can't believe that happened.'

The newly dead can be very attractive – something to do with an inherited glamour as they pass over – so I sympathised. Not. A police officer of his experience should have known better and been more careful.

'Sophie,' I said, turning to the girl. 'Don't look the living in the eyes for a while, okay?'

'Er … yeah. Sure.'

'So, I take it you don't remember anything?'

Sophie looked sadly at her body and reached out a hand to touch its face. The hand passed insubstantially through her ruined cheek. Her eyes shaped foggy tears that rolled down her warping face, leaving carved grooves in her cheeks.

'The last thing I remember is going to a club with my mates. On Frith Street, Soho.'

Ah. Charlie gave me a knowing look. The Karaoke Den was riddled with chillers. Breathers were known to go there for the extra thrill of chillflirt. It was mostly frequented by young girls looking for immortality crushes as the latest thrill-seek.

I guided Sophie away from the morgue slab. 'I'll take Sophie to the Transition Centre. They'll help her get over the shock of transition and keep her away from breath-… I mean living beings for the quarantine period.'

Charlie gave me a look that told me he was getting a little cross with my foul language. Breathers, you see, don't really like being called that; it's like they have some sort of disability from which we chillers don't suffer. And, frankly, they have no sense of humour about it. I took Sophie by the hand and whisked her away before he could read me the riot act. Later he'd forget and we could get on with the investigation. And that is why Charlie and I make such a good team. I'm quite tolerant of the living and he's not racist about the dead.

'Wow,' Charlie said. 'You solidify well.'

'Yeah. Whatever.'

Pretending to be a living being had many disadvantages. Walking was the main and obvious drawback. The other one was holding a form strong enough to fool the other chillers in the club. Though that was easy enough when you had my psychic ability. There were only three chillers dead that could do this to my knowledge.

'And your hair is all auburn highlights. How do you do that?'

I looked Charlie over carefully. 'Just remember what we're here for.'

Charlie nodded. 'Sophie was very popular. Was doing extremely well in college. No problems at home or with drugs that we are aware of ...'

'What about boyfriends?'

'No-one in the equation at the moment,' Charlie said.

'Hardly the typical suicide candidate,' I added. 'But her frequenting these kinds of places does make you wonder what she was into.'

Charlie shrugged. 'Each to her own. It may have been a one-off.'

'Stay close to me,' I warned as we walked down Frith Street to the club. 'These places can be a real temptation for the living.'

He took my hand, it felt all warm. I could sense his aura and it gave my solid fingers a gentle pins-and-needles sensation. I looked down at our hands; there was a purple glow around our fingers that I knew only I could see. I returned my gaze to Charlie.

'You don't feel as cold as I thought you would,' he said, surprised. 'Can you feel my hand too?'

Could I? Now that was the question.

The doorman's eyes looked at us impassively through a steel hatch in the door. I knew I looked good and solid and I'd materialised some typical clothing worn by young women when they go out. A short bum-skimming black skirt and a red halter-neck crop top. High heeled sandals completed the look, and my hair was swept up into a wavy ponytail. Charlie was wearing designer jeans and a T-shirt. His blond hair flopped down into his eyes in what can only be described as a contrived mess. He looked great.

'Entrance fee applies,' said the doorman. 'You like to sing?'

If I'd had a real lip I would have bitten it. The dead *love* to sing. It would have been an immediate give away.

'Not much. But we enjoy listening,' Charlie answered, and he waved a 50 in front of the hatch.

The bolt snapped back and the door swung open revealing the burly doorman and a flight of steps leading down. Muffled music and voices could be heard coming from below. I fought the urge to float and instead concentrated on walking confidently, still holding Charlie's hand as the doorman took the 50 from his other.

'Ouch.'

We'd reached the bottom of the stairs.

'What?'

'You don't know your own strength, lady.'

I let go of Charlie's hand and we wandered into the throng of bodies that packed the lower room, making our way across to the bar. Charlie flexed his bruised fingers and I felt a pang of guilt for not being more careful with him. I wasn't used being solid and so hadn't thought to hold back my physical strength. Physic weight was so much easier to measure.

Leaning on the rail, Charlie shouted an order for drinks. The barman, sexy and very Will Smith, put on an impressive show, throwing a cocktail shaker over his shoulder. Then he poured the mixture into two Martini glasses. Charlie handed me a glass decorated with fruit and a tiny umbrella.

I took it and looked at it wistfully. 'I can't.'

'One won't hurt.'

'No, I actually *can't*. But I'd love to be able to taste it.'

Charlie weighed me up. 'It's for appearances.'

I did my pretending-to-drink act, hoping that no-one would see the resultant splashes on the floor, and we moved further on into the club. We waded across the dance floor and I was briefly mesmerised by a hot black ghost whirling his hips like Elvis; albeit to '80s music. Then we pushed through and headed for the famed karaoke room.

'Ick!' I stopped dead just outside the room.

'What now?' Charlie looked back at me patiently. 'You look like you just tasted something really bad.'

'In a way I did. In there. The undead. And you know how I feel about those.'

It wasn't much fun being a ghost around the undead. They gloated far too much about still having a body. It was also the biggest cause of pub brawls in Soho.

'Anything else in there that you can sense?'

'Yeah. Lots of young girls.'

He moved forward, and we stepped into the room, listening to the tones of an undead Westlife fan as he screeched the notes in a perfect mimicry of the lead singer of the band. Yes. The undead have the edge on singing too. Which is very annoying for us chillers.

'I need to look at the song list,' I said, feeling a terrible compulsion to sing all night.

Charlie sighed and looked at me kindly. 'Meg, remember you're *living* tonight.'

'Aw. You're no fun at all.'

He laughed. Then pointed to a table in a corner by the karaoke stage. It looked like a great spot to scope out the entire room. We sat down and looked around. A small group of undead occupied the booth next to us. Two males and one female, accompanied by two breather females in their twenties. The undead were showing off by glowing. One of the undead men was demonstrating his party piece of making his eyes glow and then his nose, which amused the breathers a lot.

'Wow. You're so great at that,' gushed the brunette. 'Wish I was undead. It's really cool.'

'It does have its drawbacks,' smiled the undead female, deliberately flashing her white fangs.

The breather girls waited for her to elaborate, but they would wait forever. The undead rarely waste words and never explain their ambiguous comments. It 's just the way they are.

'Meg, why don't you pay a visit to the ladies room?'

'Huh?'

'The ladies room; it's over there …'

Charlie inclined his head and I followed his gaze. Across the room was Jacques. A chiller. *The* chiller. Jacques was the stuff of nightmares. In his day he had been the original bogeyman. Think Freddie Krueger and times it by as much as you like – you still wouldn't have an accurate idea of how evil this man had been. But like all long-term dead, he was apparently turning over a new leaf. Of course, these days he marketed himself as a businessman and rarely used any of his chiller powers in public. Jacques also owned the club.

I stood and left the room, heading off towards the illuminated Ladies sign, which coincidently was right behind where Jacques was standing. As I approached, I flicked my eyes towards him. He was deep in conversation with an attractive woman of about 30. Her eyes showed complete adoration as he leaned forward talking to her softly. A breather and a chiller clearly coming onto each other? If I'd had a stomach I'd have been sick for sure.

Jacques' eyes swept over me without recognition as I passed by and into the bathroom. Inside, a group of female breathers giggled together about something inconsequential while an undead powdered her nose and reapplied red lipstick.

'I love that guy,' a cute little blonde girl said, tripping a little on her high heels. She was drunk on chillflirt. 'I mean, he's like, so hot.'

'You mean cold ...' laughed her friend as she hoisted up her bra strap, which had fallen down over her shoulder.

The undead female turned and stared at them. Their laughter was getting on her nerves. I stood at the mirror and examined my solidity. It was all still in place and would take a massive disaster to shake it. I hoped. Then I went into a booth and pretended to use the toilet, flushing it as I left.

Outside again I saw Charlie talking to a chiller female who floated slightly above him. She was clearly interested in more than his words, and she wrapped her foggy arm around his waist and rubbed his bottom suggestively. But what was most annoying was that Charlie actually seemed to be enjoying it!

I stood in the middle of the room wondering what to do, until Charlie caught my eye. Then he gave me the nod that meant 'circle and investigate for God's sake'. Typical breather. He has fun. I work. Such is the lot of the dead. So I turned and gave the eye to a particularly cute chiller who had just entered the room.

'I'm Dave. How long have you been alive?' He asked looking me up and down.

'Huh? Oh … I'm 24.' Well, I was when I died anyway.

'Right. You're cute. I like living girls.'

'You do? Why?'

Dave looked at me. 'You're kidding right? You never been with a chiller? Chiller and breather sex is the best.'

I turned to look at Charlie. The chiller bitch was all over him like a rash. Something funny twitched in my brain and I began to feel murderous. Not a good sign. I returned my attention to Dave.

'But … I thought no-one did that? How's it possible?'

Dave nodded across the room at Jacques. 'He makes everything possible here. You wanna be dead for a night? Then it's a done deal. But it costs.'

Jacques freed himself from the girl he was with and glided over. I realised that Dave had given him some kind of signal. They shook hands, exchanged something, and I fought back my cop instinct to arrest them both for dealing. I had to be sure.

Jacques grinned at me and it was pervy. 'Have fun.'

'What just happened there?' I asked.

'You ever heard of blur?'

'The dimension crash or the pop group?'

'Neither,' he smiled. 'I mean this stuff.'

Dave opened his hand and showed me what appeared to be two tablets nestling in his palm. They were oval and faintly luminous. I stared down in fascination as they throbbed slightly in his foggy hand. They both held a different carved symbol on them. For some reason I shuddered.

'What does it do?'

'You won't know this, but there are two different kinds. This one,' he held up a pill that was marked with a circle with a triangle inside, 'is for the living.'

'What about the other one?' I asked, even though it was kind of obvious.

'The chiller takes it.'

I stared at the pills nestling in his palm. 'Then what?'

'The pill shifts both parties into the blur. There they can be together in the biblical sense. Chillers can then feel everything the breather does.'

'Oh yeah? What does the breather get out of it?'

'The best sex they ever had. It can blow your mind. But be warned, it's very addictive.'

'Isn't everything?'

Looking around for Charlie, I became acutely aware of the change in atmosphere. He and his new chiller friend looked like they liked each other way too much. Dave's fog was also starting to crowd me and I was a little worried that if he got too close he might realise I was a chiller.

I had an idea and shook my head. 'Come and meet

my friend,' I said.

Dave blinked, 'But I thought …'

'You thought all breathers were easy? Well, sometimes these things take time.' I smiled at him and stroked his palm gently, taking the pills. 'Come.'

I led Dave over to where Charlie and the groping chiller were entangled by the wall. As my eyes met Charlie's I realised that he was totally uncomfortable with the whole thing as well, so I took his hand and pulled him away, leaving Dave and the chiller female looking after us. It gave me the creeps that two of my own kind were so fetishy. I mean, chiller and breather sex? It was just too weird.

'You can just say "no",' I pointed out to Charlie when we were out of earshot.

'Yes. But the point is, we're supposed to be here to retrace Sophie's steps.'

I agreed. But having glamour-enhanced sex with someone you didn't like was beyond the call of duty. I told Charlie what I'd learnt about the pills and he took them from me, slipping them safely away into his zipped jeans pocket.

'What next?' I asked.

'I think we have to start asking questions.'

Charlie took out a small picture of Sophie from his wallet. She was sat outside in the sunlight looking very alive. I replicated it and we split up to go and talk to people. It took just two minutes for Jacques to appear with his bouncers.

'What're you doing? You're upsetting my customers,' he said as Charlie showed his badge.

'We're investigating a suspected murder, Mr Jacques. You don't wish to be in trouble for obstructing justice now, do you?' I was impressed. Charlie could sound very official when he wanted to.

'What do you want to know?' Jacques asked reluctantly, looking around as a few of the nearby clientele listened in on the conversation.

'We want to learn Sophie Johnson's whereabouts last night. We know she started here,' I answered.

Jacques stared at us blankly.

'We have evidence that you're dealing an unknown drug to both living beings and the dead,' Charlie said quietly. 'So we can just close you down right now. Or we can ignore that aspect, because after all, we aren't the drug squad, and we're only interested in what happened to Sophie …'

I felt a vibration in the blur, and glancing around I saw my erstwhile friend Dave and the female chiller sliding away through the wall.

'Okay. Look. I could let you see the security recordings for this room only. If she was looking for chillflirt, it would have been in here.'

We followed Jacques to his office to continue the discussion and look at the tape. I walked nicely, still faking living, and no-one questioned it when Charlie opened doors for me. You might wonder why I bothered to sustain the illusion. Well, it's like this, the least the criminal world know of my ability to solidify the better. It gives me an advantage on the other chiller cops.

Jacques' office was a typical chiller room. It had some chairs for the living to use and a desk, filing cabinet and storage for all the club's paperwork, but the lack of heating was a dead giveaway. The room was an ice box. We sat on the chairs and I mimicked Charlie's shivers to perfection.

'Hey, it's a bit cold in here,' I pointed out.

'Get 'em a heater,' Jacques ordered.

We waded through the tape on an old combined TV and video player. The night before, the club had been full of chillers and breathers having a singing competition. But of course the chillers won. Sophie didn't appear until much later in the night. We watched her walk into the bar and take up the microphone like she was the guest of honour and everyone was cheering for her. She had a great voice. It seemed as flexible as those of the undead, which could have given one of them a motive. The dead aren't very tolerant of the living at the best of times, and because breathers are in the minority, there is always some bigotry. But it seemed to us that Sophie broke down all these barriers and bonded both cultures with her voice. She later left with a group of girls and there was no obvious change in the mood or atmosphere of the club. We didn't notice anyone following after her either.

'Nothing there then,' Charlie said, reaching to pause the tape.

Something suddenly caught my eye. 'No. Wait! What was that?'

Charlie rewound the tape; the camera was slowly panning across the crowd.

'There!'

We paused it on a face. One I hadn't seen for a long time.

'I know that guy. I dated him when I was alive. Michael.'

Charlie sighed and went to press the play button.

'Wait.'

We both peered closer. A shadow lurked behind Michael. A fog so black and thick it almost had form.

'A parasite ghost!' I exclaimed.

As we watched, Sophie walked through the fog on her way out of the room, and as expected, some of it went with her.

Charlie looked at me. 'Michael is the host for a parasite ghost. They're dangerous.'

'Yes,' I agreed. 'We really need to do something about it.'

Back at the station we searched for Michael's address. I sometimes had issues remembering details from the living world. But Charlie was pissed at me for diverting the investigation.

'It's not as though that guy is a suspect. He was

just there, and now you want to go and help your ex-boyfriend 'coz he has a parasite. It's not exactly urgent though, is it?'

'Well, Sophie seemed to pick up part of the ghost. It could be a fresh lead. Michael was there, after all. He might even remember me and be a little more willing to help. And besides, it's our job to stop chillers hurting the living.'

Charlie nodded, 'Okay. I can't fault your reasoning. As usual.'

Michael's house gave me a jolt. How could I have forgotten that he owned a mansion and that the guy was loaded? A burst of memory – a room with a roaring log fire, and Michael and me cuddled up on the sofa. It was strange that I couldn't remember the end of the relationship. And it worried me that I felt a little excited at seeing him again. After all, he was a breather and we inhabited different blurs, so any future contact would be limited to friendship.

We pulled up on the drive. The house was huge. There was a blue clock built into the wall on an archway leading to the stables, and on the roof was a weathervane. Michael had very good taste, and had built this house from scratch. He'd even designed it himself. I knew that around the back there was a glass structure that held a swimming pool and a gymnasium right alongside the tennis courts.

I floated to the main door and Charlie pressed the bell.

It took a few minutes for the butler to arrive. He was typically English – with the suit and everything. I wasn't sure I remembered him though. We gave our credentials and he led us into the cavernous reception hall. Then the butler hurried off to get Michael and we waited patiently for his return.

'Wow,' Charlie whispered. 'You used to date this guy?'

I nodded.

A huge polished wooden staircase dominated the hallway, but I was never that impressed by money. Chillers didn't really need it anyway. We just liked a purpose and a job to make time pass more agreeably.

'Oh my God! Meg.' Michael sounded shocked as he walked towards us with a half-eaten apple in his hand. 'I can't believe this.'

He looked pale and sick. I should have warned him I was coming.

'It's okay. I know it's shocking. But hey, being dead has its advantages. How have you been, Michael?'

'We're here to investigate a murder,' Charlie interrupted.

Michael looked at Charlie. 'Are you?'

'Yes. I'm a detective now,' I waffled. 'Chiller Squad. We saw you on a security tape at the Karaoke Den the other night.'

'You did.' His voice was flat. It must have been the shock.

Charlie brought out Sophie's pictures, some of them stills taken from the tape. 'This girl was murdered. And we're trying to determine whether this is a living murderer or a serial chiller.'

Michael looked briefly at the pictures. 'Everyone knows Sophie. She sings well.'

'I noticed. How about that? Every bit as good as the dead …' I enthused.

Charlie gave me *the* look and I shut up. 'We'd like to ask you some questions.'

Michael glanced at his Cartier watch and then back at Charlie. 'I wish you had made an appointment. I'm expecting a business phone call any moment.'

'Michael, we drove for two hours. This really can't wait,' I said, placing a foggy hand on his arm.

Michael smiled at me, and I remembered how that felt before. 'Okay. For you. Meg, it is so good to see you … You look good, by the way. Even though you're kind of see-through.'


'Well that wasn't much use,' Charlie sighed, opening the car door. 'He didn't tell us anything new at all.'

'No. But at least we had chance to warn him about the parasite ghost that hooked up with him at the club. Strange though, I couldn't see it today at all.'

I thought about that. Maybe it had found a new host. Maybe.

'And he did say that he remembered a chiller that

she talked to a lot.' I flicked my notebook back open. 'David Cartwright. So that's a lead we should follow up. Cartwright was also on the guest list Jacques gave us.'

As Charlie drove away from the house down the drive, I gazed back wistfully. It was all no use to me now whatsoever.

David Cartwright turned out to be my wannabe sexual partner 'Dave'. His picture smiled at me from his chiller file. He'd been dead for five years. And I knew from speaking to him the night before in the club that he had ways to cross the blur. Who was to say that those sexual kinks of his didn't also lead to murder? If sex between a chiller and a breather was good, how interesting might it be if the breather crossed the blur to become a chiller *during* sex? I shuddered at the idea and perversity of it all.

Dave lived in a basement in Soho, not far from the club. So Charlie and I made that our next port of call. We took a ghost team, just in case.

'Dave?' I said as he floated through the door into the daylight. 'We need to talk to you.'

'Wow,' he said, looking me up and down. 'You're dead.'

'Yes.'

'But last night you looked ... so solid.' He was clearly impressed.

'It's a gift.'

Charlie coughed and I turned to see him standing with arms folded. 'Mr Cartwright, we need to ask you some questions about Sophie Johnson …'

That was when everything went crazy; more than usual, that is. Dave looked troubled and tried to do a disappearing act, only to find a lead cage dropped over him from above, courtesy of the ghost team. The cage narrowly missed me, and its passing caused me major disorientation for several minutes. I sort of drifted around the street a little until I felt Charlie's aura overlap my fog and, as usual, his presence stabilised me.

'We got him,' he said with a smile, and it felt as though something tenderly stroked my hair, except I don't really have hair, just an appearance of it. Charlie was looking me directly in the eyes the way he'd looked at Sophie in the morgue, like I was the first woman he'd ever seen. For the first time in many years I wished I was alive.

'Sorry,' I said, averting my gaze from his eyes. 'It must have been the close proximity to the lead. Did I turn my beam on you?'

Charlie blinked, looking confused. 'No Meg. You didn't. But we've got Dave in the van now. Trying to run, well, vanish, makes him look pretty guilty to me. Are you okay?'

I nodded.

We went around to the van where Dave was cursing and swearing in the back, banging his lead cuffs against the side in frustration.

'You have the right to remain silent,' I said. 'So shut the fuck up.'

'Tell us about Sophie.'

Charlie was sitting opposite Dave, and I floated by the door in the interview room back at the station.

'She sings,' Dave replied.

'And your relationship with her was?' I floated closer to Dave as he sat at the table, his cuffed hands supporting his head. As I approached I could feel the lead start to affect me and so backed off slightly.

'Relationship? You don't have a relationship with girls like Sophie.'

'What does that mean exactly?' Charlie asked.

'Well, we had some fun together. Did some singing. Had some chillflirt. She likes that a lot …'

'And sex,' I concluded. 'After all, you say you have the means. And we have those pills, Dave. They will be analysed.'

Dave grinned. 'Yeah. Sex too. She was great in the blur. Really, really hot. You should try it,' Dave said looking directly at Charlie. 'The pair of you should try it together …'

The rage came on me like a tide.

'Shut your dirty mouth,' I yelled. 'You freak. You're going to be snuffed for this, and you know what happens then? Nothing! Zilch! Nada!'

Dave's fog turned a greyer shade as I darted about the room.

'Okay. I told you and told you. I know Sophie, sure I know Sophie, but I didn't kill her. Why would I? I liked her. She was sexy and I wanted that to continue. I wonder if she's as good in chiller frame?'

I slapped Dave then. I couldn't help myself. I sent his cuffed fog smashing into the wall of the interview room.

'Meg,' Charlie warned. 'Calm down. Nothing will be achieved by this.'

'No? Well, beating the psychic crap out of him will make me feel a whole lot better.'

'Come outside,' Charlie ordered.

I looked daggers at him, barely controlling the rage within me. But I swallowed it down and went out reluctantly. The chillrage was on me and I wanted nothing but to smash Dave's perverted fog to wispy pulp.

Charlie sat me down in the corridor and I knew the lecture was coming.

'Meg. Although I agree one hundred percent that Dave needs to be leathered within one inch of his life, I mean death, it would look far better in the courts if we got some hard evidence on him first. Clearly he is involved in Sophie's death. But we need proof if he's to be snuffed.'

'Yeah. I know.' I breathed deeply and felt the rage subside slightly. 'But can I hit him a bit more first?' Charlie looked at me. His baby blues brooked no argument. 'You're no fun,' I continued, but the rage had fled. Charlie always had a calming effect on me.

'Charlie? Meg?' We looked around to see Elaine, the desk sergeant, standing behind us. 'Sophie Johnson is here with her transition councillor. She says she remembers what happened.'

'What?' Charlie and I said in unison.

'Yes, apparently, she's a suicide. And she's come to collect her boyfriend, a chap named Dave, because she killed herself to be with him.'

Charlie and I looked at each other dumbfounded. 'We could get him on encouraging a young girl to commit suicide?' I suggested.

'Nope,' Elaine replied. 'She's insisting it was her own idea and that Dave didn't know she was going to do it.'

'I don't fucking believe it,' I said, the rage bubbling up again.

'Okay,' sighed Charlie. 'Better get a statement.'

Shame. I so wanted to beat on Dave. Not sure what my problem with him was, but guys like him really wind me up.

'We may still have him on the use of illegal drugs,' I said hopefully. 'You put those pills in for analysis, right?'

Charlie looked at me, his eyes wide and innocent, and my heart, brain or whatever it is did that weird flip-floppy thing again.

Charlie opened his hand revealing the two little pills.

He grinned. 'Thought we might …'

As Charlie walked away, I was left gawping after him. I was confused and a little angry. Being a chiller in this world of solidity and physical sensation was hard work, and I wasn't sure whether Charlie was joking or being serious. But part of me really wanted him to be serious.

Then and there I vowed that I would not be caught beaming him in the eyes again … who knew where that might lead? I am a chiller, he's a breather. In my world, that's a definite no-no.

# AUTHOR'S NOTES

I wrote *Chillers and Breathers* in 2008, and I think this urban fantasy story would make an intriguing opening for a future book. I have been trying to think back on what influenced this story and I'm really not sure. I remember writing it – I spent two days obsessing – and eventually I had around 20,000 words.

I love the world in the story, a fascinating concept in that it is layered and multi-dimensional. There is an interesting relationship between the two cops, Charlie and Meg, which could stand further exploration as well. Having said that, I still decided to include only the first 6,000 words in this collection as I believe this stands alone as a complete story.

It is likely that this will become a book one day. I can't see when I will have the time in the immediate future, but if there are any publishers out there interested in finding out where it goes, I still have all my notes …

# BLOOD LOSS

'Caucasian female. Aged approximately 25,' Dr Showman said into the recorder.

She had been beautiful. You could tell with corpses, even when the life was drained from them. Even as they lay on the slab with blue lips, white skin, taut and frozen, cold as ice. Her eyes had been pale grey, cool and detached. They were locked half open in a face that was twisted in a parody of passion. There was a white film, which looked like a cataract, over each iris. Although that was nothing unusual.

Showman cut a 'Y' shape from her shoulders, under her breasts and down over her chest and stomach. He peeled back the skin and began to cut her breast plate with a bone saw. Within seconds his practised fingers were embedded in her body, and he ripped her open with barely a flex of his arm.

We gazed down at her near-perfect organs. No disease

256

had killed her, no virus known to man at least. There would be no cancer, no aneurysm blamed for taking this pale, young beauty. There were no wounds. She had not been shot, stabbed or beaten with a blunt instrument. There was nothing usual or definable, except that she had died of a massive loss of blood.

'Strange'

I looked up at Showman, even though I was used to his muttering during the examinations. As usual I didn't ask what he meant, merely waited for him to explain his findings.

'Will you push my glasses back, Michael?' he requested, and I reached forward and carefully placed pressure on the ridge above his nose.

Showman began to take samples from the various organs, placing them carefully in each container. Then we removed the heart and weighed it, quickly followed by all the essential organs.

It was a mystery, of course, and all the tests we had at our disposal would reveal nothing. I knew this because she wasn't the first young girl we'd had here recently.

'Tell me again about the crime scene. Omit nothing,' Showman said.

I had arrived at the scene expecting a domestic after the duty sergeant called the office requesting forensic on site to take the necessary steps before they could remove the body. The information I was given was hollow and bare, the same as the apartment they found her in. All I knew was that the estate agent, with prospective clients in tow, discovered her body lying gracefully on a clean mattress in an empty room.

Even her clothes, folded neatly and respectfully at the foot of the mattress, were pristine. She lay on her side, naked, but modestly composed, as though she were sleeping peacefully and not dead, not murdered at all. Her short dark hair was groomed, her nails, though short, were neatly manicured and painted a pale pink.

I scraped under those immaculate nails, dusted her body for prints, though I already knew that there would be no evidence of this kind. I could tell on the first examination that her veins were empty, because no blood had settled in the leg, hip and torso that rested against the mattress supporting her lifeless limbs. After they moved her, the mattress was screened and vacuumed but we found nothing. Not a fibre that didn't belong. No sign of the blood that should have soaked through to the floor below. No blood to be found at all.

Showman grunted at my description of the crime scene. He had been unavailable when the call came in. I thought he considered my style sloppy and inadequate. He called me a romancer. Maybe he was right. I did dream of these translucent beauties lying defenceless with their killer. I thought about their lives before. What had led them to this terrible end? Mostly I thought about the look on each of their faces. Had they been in the throes of passion when their killer struck?

Don't get me wrong, I'm a coroner, not a necrophile. I didn't think about having sex with them, these silent victims of an invisible plague. It was just … there had been so many of them. Dead women had been turning up all over the city: a daily occurrence it seemed. Not all died this way of course, that would be ridiculous and impossible, but a substantial number had. All of unexplainable blood loss.

Showman twitched, leaning forward over the body, pulling the mounted magnifier closer.

'What is it, doctor?' I asked.

'Here. Look.'

By now Showman had dissected the pubis, and her vagina lay open to our scrutiny.

'Sexual activity?'

'Don't be a fool, Michael. Of course sexual activity. We saw that in the others. It's not that. Look again, here …'

Showman's experienced fingers probed, parting flesh, revealing to my surprised gaze a small swelling and then another. More of them, tiny blisters or pockets of blood rippled the inner wall.

'I think we had better take a closer look at some of the others.'

Against the wishes of the families, several victims' bodies had been detained pending further investigation. Showman sent his assistants scurrying to the mortuary fridges. We examined them, finding the blisters immediately each time. Showman cursed us all for missing the obvious, yet he had performed over half of the autopsies himself. How had any of us overlooked this? What did it mean anyway?

We worked until late, when Showman finally called it a day. Tired, I wanted to file out with the rest of my colleagues and hurry home to my bath and ultimately my empty bed. I packed up my equipment and placed my surgical tools in the steriliser. The orderlies had long since wheeled away and stored the last of the victims. Showman peered into his microscope. He looked tired and aged. His hair greyer and his usually neat white coat was rumpled and smeared with gore.

'Michael,' he said without looking up, 'can you be here early tomorrow? I will need your help ...'

'Of course, doctor ...' I pushed back the fallen hair from my eyes. 'May I take a look?'

Showman stepped back, offering me his seat. Tentatively I closed one eye and looked down the microscope at the bulb of flesh the lens had enlarged. Thus enhanced, I could see for the first time a tiny scab covering a pinprick hole.

'Good Lord!'

'Yes. It's bizarre, isn't it, Michael? Perhaps some kind of perverse instrument was used to pierce the skin and drain the blood through the girl's sex organs.'

'Doctor, what are you saying? That's just ... impossible.'

'I don't know …' he sighed. 'I'm tired, Michael. Let's review it with a clear head in the morning.'

I left him still examining his discovery.

On my way home in my car, exhaustion clung to me with the smell of disinfectant. It was 11.00 pm. All I could think about was drinking a long cold beer before climbing into my bed. I parked at a bar within walking distance of my apartment and locked up my car, deciding it would remain there all night.

Inside, I perched at the end of the bar and downed the first bottle in a few swigs, quickly followed by another. It was quiet for a Thursday night. Last orders wouldn't be called for another hour, but the pub quiz was long since over, and being a week night most people had gone home. Two girls were singing a duet on the karaoke in the room next door. They sounded terrible. I glanced around the games room, then picked up my beer and wandered into the other room to watch the singers.

A pretty girl, with an urchin cut, leaned against the bar watching the karaoke. She reminded me of the girl on the slab. By that I mean she had the same colouring I would have expected the victim to have. She was a pretty girl, vibrant. And she smiled at me as I placed my empty bottle on the bar and headed off to the men's room.

When I returned, I looked for her, but the karaoke girls seemed to have flown the nest. Strangely disappointed, I returned to my stool by the bar and ordered another beer.

'Hi.'

I turned, surprised to see the dark-haired girl beside me.

'Anyone sitting here?' she asked.

'No, help yourself.'

She was wearing a cropped top and jeans. Over her bare stomach a pale pink scar ran vertically down to the waistband of her jeans. She ordered a beer and smiled at me again as the bartender placed it down in front of her.

'You wanna get this for me?' she asked.

'Sure.' I didn't know what I'd done to deserve the pleasure.

'You're cute,' she said as though she could hear my thoughts.

I paid for her drink but I was a little taken aback. I'm not usually the type of guy that women come onto. *She'll run a mile when she learns I cut up dead bodies for a living.*

'What's your name?' she asked.

'Michael.'

'I'm Anna.'


I feel the blade glide down my chest and stomach. My ribs are cracked and pulled apart. I watch through half open eyes as Showman and my replacement perform the autopsy and I find it strange that I feel no urge to rise. It doesn't hurt. It doesn't matter. There is only numbness in my bloodless skin. I am empty. Dry. I am a vessel waiting to be filled. I know that stillness will remain until they complete what must be done to ensure my continuing freedom. So I think instead of the girl in the bar. Her body was released to her family today. *My friend, we will meet again.*

'It's hard to believe,' Showman says gruffly, 'that Michael would come to this end.'

My other colleague, Dr Rick Johnson, shakes his head in sympathy, but he's glad I am out of the equation. It seems Rick has wanted my job for some time now. He thought Showman favoured me, and now I learn that he did hold me in high regard.

Anna took me to an apartment. It was empty and bare, full of echoes and hollow whispers of promises unfulfilled. We walked from room to room until we found the mattress. She loved me there, gave me everything I had ever wanted, and I gave her the nourishment she needed. The exchange happened during penetration. Tiny tendrils pierced my penis as I moved inside her. It didn't hurt, and the rhythm of our love-making aided the process, pumping the blood from my veins to hers. It was sensual, exciting. *The greatest passion a soul can endure.* Later, as I turned over, the heavy sleep took my limbs. And I thought, *this will be called* rigour mortis.

She explained it all as I lay watching her through half

open lids, aware that her skin was flushed with blood. My blood. She folded my clothes, carefully laying them on the bottom of the mattress.

'It will all be fine again soon. You'll know real freedom. No fear of sickness and disease – no pain. Nothing can touch you.'

'Why did you choose me?'

'I saw your compassion. In the apartment where they found me ... your heart was so sad. You wanted to help ... Your examination was so gentle and kind and respectful. And through all of that, I saw your isolation.'

It seems I am to be the first of many new men recruited. As she talked, the autopsy scar on her stomach – nothing more than a pencil line – was shortening by the second. While she dressed I tried to speak. I wanted to tell her to be careful, *forensics*.

She laughed, a frothing, throaty chuckle that made my heart glow with warmth and love even as my limbs and tongue turned to grey ice.

'I know all about that,' she said. 'I know everything now. And in a few hours, you will too.'

She left me then, promising me heaven again and again, but never more together.

'We are brother and sister now ...' she warned. 'It's not done ...'

I lie here in the cold, dark morgue waiting for them to

finish and release my body to my brother, Joe, who is my only remaining relative. Even though we were never close, our individual careers so consuming, I wonder if he will miss me, and I feel a momentary sadness as I realise he will. He will remember the times when he was too busy to see me, and I will remember when I was too occupied to mind.

Showman sews up my chest taking great care – his neatest stitches ever. They wheel me away. I look at my situation with clinical interest. It is a strange sensation knowing I am being stored in a coffin-shaped fridge. Seeing everything. It is unforgivable that it never occurred to me that corpses *could* feel.

Though I am alone in the dark fridge for what seems an eternity, I remember my new family awaits me and I no longer feel abandoned.

It isn't long before the door opens and my body is rolled out into the glaring lights of the mortuary.

Sally from research has come to see me. We dated once. She looks sad. Hot human tears are rolling down her blood-swollen cheeks. I am surprised to learn she misses me. That once she hoped our relationship would go further.

*Don't cry Sally. I'll visit you soon. I never knew you needed so much. But now I know everything about you just by looking in your eyes.*

Sally steps back, but her gaze never leaves my half-lidded eyes.

# BLOOD LOSS

*Don't cry, you'll never be alone again. I'll need you soon. And when I knock at your door you'll let me in. I'll show you heaven, Sally ...*

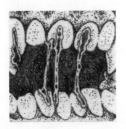

# AUTHOR'S NOTES

This story was first published in 2000 in an anthology called *Joyride*. It was the first short story I'd ever had published and I was really pleased with it. I was toying, even in those days, with the idea of creating new and original vampires. It was also something of a morbid fascination to consider the idea of corpses 'feeling' or hearing our conversations about them. My writing has changed a tremendous amount through the years and the original story didn't quite conform to my current style. Therefore *Blood Loss* has been re-edited and revised a little, but mostly it remains the same. I'm still proud of it, even though it was an early attempt and I've learnt so much about writing and editing since then.

Unfortunately I didn't learn much from the experience at the time. Although someone claimed to be the 'editor' of the collection, no actual editing was done to my story. I thought this was good. That it meant the work was 'perfect' as it was. How naive I was!

Having worked with some excellent editors in the past few years, namely David J Howe, Terry Martin, Ian Whates and Ian Watson, I've learnt that editing is very much a subjective process, but sometimes there are things you are doing *wrong* and they need to be corrected. I think it is an important experience to go through. Whether you think your work is perfect or not – again this is subjective.

I've had several editing commissions myself recently, and I'm always mindful of this one important thing. The writer is the person who puts their name to it, it's their work, it's not my job to rewrite it, but it is my job to point out areas of weakness, grammar and punctuation issues, inconsistencies etc. The writer must then choose how to act on those recommendations.

As a writer I *love* being edited. Sometimes we get too close to the story, or we're a little too ambiguous, or maybe have explained too much to the reader. It's reassuring that someone can give you constructive feedback and I will always want that. When I wrote *Blood Loss* I'd have welcomed input, because one of the wonderful things about having an editor is that they also tell you what's great about your work. It's not all negative.

Obviously you have to know yourself when something is good, or you'd follow any plot and churn out any old thing. So you have to trust your own instincts first.

Remember, no-one is perfect or infallible and we can all make mistakes. Your editor will be the person watching your back when those mistakes creep in.

# Siren Song

The apartment block is semi-empty; we've had more people leave lately and few new tenants to replace them. Strange how you appeared from nowhere to take up residence in the apartment next door. I'm running late but still I find myself standing at the door watching your movers heave in the heavy and expensive furniture. I think you must be into antiques, or perhaps you've inherited from a wealthy relation. *Why are you here, of all places?*

Questions float curiously through the back of my mind as I lock up my apartment: you can't be too careful in this neighbourhood. We've all learned the hard way to be cautious. That's why I'm so surprised that anyone is moving in.

I haven't even seen you yet, but already I'm curious about you. The manager said you were young and attractive; I imagine a tall, lithe, sophisticated female, and then you appear at the door and I realise how wrong I am.

Vulnerable is what you are. Dressed like a school teacher, with a smart skirt and loose-fitting sweater. You look too young to be out alone, and if you're even five feet tall I'll be surprised. Your hair is red. It looks natural, and your skin is as shiny and white as a newborn babe. You don't belong in this town – I should know. You should be in Malibu. Anywhere that isn't here.

'Hello,' you say, and in that one word I detect culture. 'I'm Samara. It looks like we're neighbours.'

'You're English.'

You nod but look down at the floor as though you're embarrassed that I noticed how different you are. There's a glow around your hair: I've never seen the dreary light of this hallway look so bright. You reflect it like sunshine.

'I'm Andre,' I say when the silence becomes unbearable. 'Why are you here?'

You laugh. It reminds me of the echo I once heard in a shell I found on Coney Island.

'I'm moving in, of course.'

'Yes. I know. But why *here*?'

You turn your head and look down the corridor. I try to see what you're looking at all the way down there, but there's only the dirty window at the end. I've never paid any attention to it before because the fire escape blocks out any attempt made by the sun to get in.

'I like to be near the sea …' you say.

'Well, I'd stay well away from that beach, lady. It's full of the type of men who'd eat you for breakfast and use your bones to pick their teeth with.'

'That's a little clichéd – but good.'

'What?'

'You should be a writer,' you answer.

'I am. Of sorts. I work for the local paper.'

'A reporter?'

I nod, and now I gaze down guiltily at the floor. I know what most people think of the media and it isn't pleasant.

'You should write a novel …' you tell me.

I find myself gazing into your eyes; they are as green as the moonlit water.

Evening comes and I don't remember where the day went. It passes by in a dream, I work on autopilot – but then maybe that is nothing new. I hurry back into my apartment and set to work writing that novel. Already the ideas are flowing. I want to please you, bizarre as that is, because we've only just met. Maybe you are the muse I have been waiting for.

*It is lonely and cold in the sea. The lights from the pier draw you closer and even the noise of the amusements isn't enough to scare you away. You watch the people. They walk around on what you learn are 'legs'. You want to be one, but don't know how to walk. The longer you stay, the more the need intensifies. Out of the water you have no strength. It's as though the muscles in your limbs are jelly. You don't even have the strength to crawl back in.*

*For nights you lie under the pier, waiting. But you've come in too close and the tide can't reach you.*

*You sing, just as you always have. Normally it is just to amuse yourself, but you are surprised when your call is answered. Silence is the only response you've had before.*

There is a light tapping on my door and I realise it is morning. I stare at my PC. The screen has gone on standby, so I'm sure I must have fallen asleep. I press a key and it lights up. I begin to read your story and I don't remember writing a single word.

'Andre?' I hear your call above the tapping.

For a moment I'm not sure what to do. I don't want you to see me unshaven, bedraggled, because then you'll know I have stayed up all night writing for you. I want it to be a surprise. The finished result can be something to woo you with perhaps.

'Are you there?' you call again.

I rouse myself, going over to the door, but I don't open it yet. I stand behind it imagining you on the other side. I can hear you sigh. It is like the whisper of the wind over sand dunes.

'Andre? Please let me in.'

I glance at the clock. It's 5.00 am and only the birds are awake at this time. You must be scared, or maybe something has happened. I open the door.

A breeze blows through the hallway and into the

room. You're nowhere to be seen, and now I think I must have imagined your voice outside. Maybe I'm sick. It is lack of sleep, overwork or some such thing. I haven't had a holiday in years.

'I won't be in today,' I tell my boss.

'You sick?'

'Yes.'

I don't tell him it's the job that makes me nauseous. How every time I write his untruths a part of me dies.

'Maybe I should take a holiday,' I say. 'I have days coming …'

'Take a week. Tony can fill in your pieces with some shit he can regurgitate.'

Relief or something like it floods through me, peppered with a vague uneasiness. He's not normally this helpful. I wait for the punch line, but nothing comes. He's serious. Now I can write … but write what?

The truth. There's always that.

I look back at my computer. A story has started there and I need to see it through. I barely hear the noise of your shower running next door as I sit back down to work once again on your story.

*He comes to you, stumbling like a drunk over the barnacled rocks as you lie under the pier. Part of you is still in the water, but you've lost the strength and urge to return to that freezing realm. Instead you lie still, watching and learning.*

*This world fascinates you.*

*'Fuck! You scared me!' he says. 'I thought you was a dead body.'*

*You look at him for the first time. You've never been this close to a human before. This one smells of something strong and potent. His breath is heady.*

*'Hey. You okay? Why you lying down here?'*

*You open your mouth, but the sound won't come out.*

*'You're a pretty girl,' he says. 'Hey, are you naked?'*

*He comes closer. Your eyes have him now, he won't run. He's yours for as long as you need. The strength returns to your limbs as you hold out your arms, welcoming him into your embrace.*

*Later you watch the sea swallow him.*

*Now you have movement that no longer needs the water to support it. You can sit up. You gaze at your arms. They are white and shining in the moonlight, but the air is surprisingly cold to your skin now. You wrap your arms around yourself. You shiver. You are afraid, and so you sing.*

I stand at the window looking out at the sea. It has never been more beautiful, and even the graffiti-covered walls leading to the pier don't detract from the blue. I am fascinated by it. It is as ethereal as you are and just as mysterious. Yet I know the sea is dangerous; many have died, dashed against her rocks. She is always in control. Sailors call her their mistress for a reason.

Darkness falls and the day has gone. I haven't seen

you since you moved in. But there is no need. I feel your presence through the walls. You're like the waves buffeting the shore. I feel my once-vile and incriminating words turning into a higher language that is far more satisfying. It feels as though I have been waiting for you. I must write …

*The singing always brings them, one after another. This time it's a woman. She has hair the colour of seaweed and she falls willingly into your arms. You put on her clothes as the body slips away into the mud. They are big and baggy on your tiny frame, but at least they warm your skin.*

*You start to feel stronger, attempt to raise yourself up properly onto the shore, pulling against the pier. Your legs won't move at first, but at least you can stand if you hold on tight to the blackened wood. Standing makes you dizzy; the static element is alien to your body. You are used to feeling the sea around you, making your movements buoyant, but the air is beginning to feel like the sea to you now. You breathe it in until your balance steadies and your lungs stop hurting.*

*The first step brings you tumbling down to your knees. Shards of rock pierce your sensitive skin and your blood leaks into the mud. The sea leaks from your eyes as you cry, and your mournful song echoes through the night and across the water. Out on the pier a man stops and turns, then throws himself over the barrier to be united with you.*

*Afterwards you push his carcass under the pier. Your*

*knees no longer hurt and you can now stand unaided. But walking is something you've never done. You concentrate hard …*

The phone rings but I ignore it. Your story is too important to allow interruptions and I need to finish. Time is short. The answerphone picks up, but I'm only half listening to the message.

'Andre, this is Pete. Where were you today? The boss is hitting the roof 'cos he's called your apartment and you're not answering. He says he only gave you a week off. Switch your mobile on and text me at least, buddy.'

*Your steps are as reckless as a child's and you stumble forward, out of the mud and into the world. You keep to the shadows, fumbling for stability. This is a strange and alien place. Gravity is heavy, but you are starting to get used to it. You enjoy the motion of walking, and soon you are doing it as though you always have. It's as easy as swimming once you know how.*

*Behind you the sea howls. Waves are smashing the rocks in anger, but you ignore the call and walk on, drawn by the lights and noise of the promenade.*

*'Hey, watch it lady,' says an old man as he pushes you out of the way. His touch is painful. Red welts appear on your arm and you know you need something again. The dark calls you; you're used to it, after all. The bottom of the ocean is gloomy compared with this world. You slide into it*

*and sit shivering until the main street grows quiet.*

*Most of the world sleeps, so you sing, softly until the old man returns, and this time it is you who bruises him.*

Bold bright letters glare at me on the screen as I read through the words. You're lovely and tragic and sad, just as I imagined. The deaths you cause have poetry. I cannot begrudge you them. Somehow your narrative justifies them. I want to know everything. I feel like a hero waiting to save you. You must live and grow strong.

*The body is easily disposed of: he's frailer now. The shell is an empty husk that looks like grey honeycomb. It doesn't even look like a real person any more. That's why you feel nothing as you place him carefully in the dumpster. Then, wrapping his coat around your body, you walk with more conviction.*

There is a loud knocking at the door. I try to ignore it but it pulls me back and out of your story.

'Andre?' It is Pete, my colleague and friend.

I stare at the door and then back at the screen, but the spell is momentarily broken and I feel compelled to go to the door and let him in.

'Is everything all right?' I hear you say before I can open my door.

'Oh. Hi. I was looking for Andre,' Pete says, and his usually calm voice trembles as he looks at you. This I understand. You are hypnotic. Look at me: it took only one gaze into the sea of your eyes and I was forever lost.

'Are you a friend?' you ask.

'Yes. Known him for years.'

'Can I get you a coffee while you wait for his return?'

You take him inside and the door closes. I go to the window, gaze out into the sunshine, but the sky doesn't interest me. Only the water on the distant horizon. The sea view was what sold me this place. I'd forgotten that. When did I stop looking? When did I stop seeing any beauty?

There's a disturbance in the street. I open the window and look down. A huge movers' truck is parked on a meter and a tow company is trying to hook it up. I glance at the wall connecting our apartments. I remember now: I didn't see the movers leave. But then the days have been slipping away from me since you arrived.

I need to talk to Pete. He's a nice guy and probably doesn't deserve …

I wake. It's dark and the window is still open. I've fallen asleep on the sofa, but I don't recall coming across the room and sitting down. In the distance I hear a police siren coming closer as a car rockets down the street. I close the window.

I press my ear to the wall but I can't hear you move. You must be sleeping like the rest of the building. My eyes fall on a whiskey bottle. Still where I left it days ago.

Me and old Jacky D are old friends, but I haven't even been visiting him. The bottle is still full. I think about pouring myself a glass, but the computer calls me again. Your story is unfolding and there's nothing I can do but tell it.

*At the bus stop a girl waits nervously for the late Greyhound. The depot is deserted, so you sit down on the bench next to her. She's small and blonde, your height or just a little taller. She looks at you and smiles. Your face twitches in response as you mimic her expression.*

*'Hi' she says.*

*'Hi,' you answer.*

*'I'm starting a new job,' she tells you, trying to make conversation. 'I'm a nurse. I'll be looking after this old guy. It's easy money really, because most of the time he sleeps. Plus it's by the beach and I get three days a week off.'*

*'Have you been a … nurse … long?' you ask, and your voice feels strange to your ears.*

*'Just qualified. I hope they don't expect me to give him bed baths …'*

*You note again that the girl is the same height as you. She has a large suitcase and a big purse slung over her shoulder. In her hand she clasps her bus ticket. You like her.*

*'How long?' you ask, nodding to the ticket.*

*'Half an hour,' she says. 'Glad someone else is here at this time of night. So where are you headed?'*

*'Same as you,' you say, but you have no idea where that is.*

'*Oh? Great. We could sit together; it might make us feel less vulnerable than travelling alone.*'

*But you don't feel vulnerable. You feel strong and you are ready for new adventures.*

'*Where's your luggage …?*' *the girl asks.*

*You look around, then back at the girl. Her eyes are happy, she feels safe. You take her into the shadows and take everything you need.*

*When the bus arrives you're wearing new clothes and holding a bus ticket. You look back over your shoulder, feeling a little sad. As you board the bus, you promptly forget the girl. She's not human anymore and her husk is already deteriorating in the dumpster around the corner.*

'*Tickets please,*' *says the driver, and you hold out the paper in your hand.*

The days pass into weeks. I no longer know whether it is day or night, as the blinds are always drawn to shut out the sun. The phone has stopped ringing and Pete never came back to find out why I hadn't returned to work. You are a quiet neighbour, but occasionally I hear visitors arriving but never hear them leave. Sometimes – I think it is at night – I hear a strange music in the air. At those times I feel you outside my door, but I can't pull myself away from the computer to open it and let you in. The more I learn, the more I am in love with the horror of you. The more I am afraid.

Right now, quiet fills the apartment block. The

janitor's whistle has long been silenced. The only sound is the creaking of untended pipes and the occasional rush of running water. At times it feels as though every tenant has switched on their shower at the same time and the building is filling up with enough water to top up the sea.

*'Miss Sanders?'*

*You turn to see a man in a dark suit, wearing a cap with a bronze crest on the front. He takes your bags, throwing them into the back of a long black car that has windows made of midnight. Then he holds open the door for you. You stare at the car, confused for a while.*

*'The family is waiting for you, Miss,' he says. 'Did you have a good journey?'*

*'Yes,' you say and climb into the back seat of the car.*

*Inside the car the windows are clear. You look out as the driver sits in the front and starts the engine. A tiny thrill goes through your heart as the car pulls out onto a road along the coast. You watch the sea all the way to your destination. It calls to you, speaking of duty, but the pull of this alien world is far stronger and you turn your head away and look towards the world ahead.*

*You forget the sea as the car turns into the drive. It's a long and windy track and leads to a huge house. The car comes to a halt at the front of the house and the driver jumps out to open the door for you.*

*'I'll get your bags, Miss,' he says as you look up at the house. 'Impressive, isn't it?'*

'Yes,' you say. 'I've never been inside before.'

The driver looks at you and shrugs. He thinks you're cute but a little odd.

The door is opened by a middle-aged woman in an austere uniform of black.

'You're the new nurse?' she asks.

For a moment the threshold is intimidating and you pause, afraid to enter.

'Come along, girl. Don't dawdle,' says the woman. 'I'm Mrs Anson, the housekeeper. You came highly recommended, and on that basis the family chose you. They are a nice group and they love the old man. So you'd better take good care of him.'

'I will,' you say. 'I like old people.'

'You'll be answerable to me,' Mrs Anson says.


There is a noise in the hallway. Workmen have entered the building, probably brought in by the janitor to fix the pipes.

'Mr Telser?' A voice calls outside my door. 'This is Arnold Goldstein, the landlord. I need to talk to you.'

I stare at the door and say nothing.

'I ain't seen him for weeks,' says Raoul, the janitor. 'Normally he's complaining about something.'

'Maybe he's just left,' says Goldstein. 'Owing me last month's rent …'

'I dunno,' says Raoul. 'I didn't see any movers …'

'I think we'll take a look. Try the spare key.'

'What's going on?' I hear you say.

'Oh. Miss Sanders. Nothing to concern you …' says Raoul. 'You haven't seen Mr Telser lately, have you?'

'He's out at the moment,' you say. 'I think he'll be back soon. Can I get you guys some coffee?'

*Mr Arnold is sick but he is nice to you. You like him and don't mind looking after him.*

'You're a quiet little thing,' he says. 'I like that in a nurse. The last one talked all the time, and sometimes I just needed some peace and quiet.'

*You have a nice room in the house, with your own bathroom. It's up at the top of the house and no-one bothers you on your days off. From the small window you can see the sea. It's there to remind you, but every day the pull to return lessens. Every week the housekeeper gives you an envelope containing money. You don't know what to do with it, so you keep it all in the envelopes in a drawer.*

*They call you 'Joy' now – it's the identity you've taken, and you quite enjoy having a name.*

'Joy's sweet, but a bit weird,' says Elizabeth, Mr Arnold's granddaughter. 'She barely speaks to anyone.'

'She talks to Mr Arnold,' says the housekeeper. 'He seems to like her.'

'I guess she's just shy,' says Elizabeth. 'I mean, she must be my age and she doesn't go out anywhere, does she?'

*But you do go out. Down to the ocean, but not too close. Never do you wade in, for fear that the waves will take you back. At night you need to get away from the house and be around people. You don't need much these days; the housekeeper gives you food and drink. It stays the hunger and cold that occasionally consume you. Mostly it's enough, but sometimes you need something more. Each time you take a life it brings you closer to humanity. Each time feels like the last.*

The apartment is cold and I wrap myself up in bedclothes. I've transferred your story to the laptop; it's more comfortable working in bed and my arms and legs feel less heavy lying down. These days even trips to the bathroom or kitchen are hard work. I feel dizzy and weak on my feet and have to clutch the wall even to make it across the room. I think I forget to eat, even when I order groceries in, and I can't remember the last time I did that.

I find food by the bed and know you have been here. I wish you would wake me. We can talk, but then you don't enjoy that much, do you? I stare at the meal but can't find the strength to eat. Instead I sip water; it's all I need these days.

I push aside the curtains on the window above the bed and look out. A storm is brewing somewhere out to sea. The sky fills with light but there's no sound. Singing fills the apartment. It is the only sound that penetrates these walls.

The laptop screen glares in accusation.

'All right,' I croak. 'Your story will be the death of me.

Don't you care?'

But of course you don't. You're song is all that matters. The sound of it drifts into words and images and my fingers take on a life of their own as the words tumble out of me. And with every tap, I grow weaker still.

*When the old man dies the sea pours from your eyes again. You miss him, he was kind, and now it means you are no longer needed here. Two years you've been here. You've learnt a lot about people and things in that time. Money is important in order to live and you know you'll need another job.*

*The family asks you to stay until after the funeral.*

*'Don't see why you've been invited,' says Mrs Anson as they gather round in the study while Mr Arnold's lawyer reads his will. You don't know why you're there either. It seems too personal and you're not family.*

*'Joy,' says the lawyer. 'Mr Arnold grew very fond of you. He was worried that you wouldn't find employment anytime soon.'*

*You look at the lawyer. He has kind eyes that make you feel hungry. You look away as his words falter.*

*'He left you some money to tide you over. One hundred thousand dollars. It won't be enough to live off forever but it should make life easier for you.'*

*The family make a collective gasping sound. You look around the room, bemused and surprised.*

*'He was a nice man,' you say. 'That was just too kind.'*

*The lawyer helps you set up a bank account, and all of your unused salary goes in. You now have a lot of money and a legal identity.*

The tide is coming in. It feels like it will reach my apartment block and will wash me from my bed into the sea. You're kind. You like caring for the sick, and I let you feed me and help me sit up.

'How did you get in here?' I ask.

You smile at me and it's tender. 'I've always been here.'

Later you prop up my pillows as I return to the story.

'Do you want to see it?' I ask, but you shake your head and a long strand of red falls down onto the bedclothes. I don't push it away and I don't insist you read the story. No-one knows what happened better than you.

*You travel. At times you take a short lease on an apartment, but the building always ends up feeling solitary and not everywhere has the sea view that you crave. Men are attracted to you, but you don't want the attention; you're looking for something else, but it always seems to elude you. Then, one day you see it.*

*Written on a page. Words.*

'I'm dying,' I say.

'No.'

'What are you?'

'You know the answer. You just have to write it and you'll remember.'

I look at the laptop. I can't lift my hand. I shake my head.

'I can't. There's nothing left.'

You place my hands on the keys.


*You've been looking everywhere. But then you see him in the pages of a newspaper. His words are calling you. They are sensitive, solitary and all lies. You know it's him. And then you remember why you left the water, why you've been alone for so long.*

*As you move into his apartment building you know that everything will be fine again. But he doesn't recognise you, his eyes are empty. This alien world has swallowed all of his essence. He's forgotten the sea, and so did you for a time. You need to remind him who he is.*

*You sing. The music is heard and it draws them in. Embracing them makes you stronger in this world, but it doesn't dull the pain, because he still resists you. He's the only one who can. The sea pours from you and your song is mournful as your story unravels. You want him to know the truth.*


Hidden memories seep back out from the blackness. They crowd and suffocate all that I believed was reality.

'I am drowning,' I say. 'The air is poison and I need the water. I see you in the distance as they haul me out. I'm tangled in one of their nets. As they cut me loose, one of them shouts. They know I live, but I'm struggling to breathe. My lungs scream. I do what must be done in order to survive.'

It is easy after that. They are willing when I sing our song. They drown in our ocean so that we can breathe and survive in their world. It's a trade. My memory of the sea fades, and worse, I have already forgotten *you*. The shadows swallow me and I take up an identity, become involved in their words and their world.

And now I realise our stories are different but the same. You came to find me, and this world almost swallowed you too.

'The sea calls us yet,' you say. 'It is not too late.'

I eat the food you give me, drink the salty water: it sits like poison in my gut. Then I take your hand as you lead me out towards the beach.

The sea is fierce. It rages as we reach the pier. It is almost as though it claws the earth, looking to take us back where we belong. I gaze down into the foam.

'I'll drown,' I say. 'I've been gone too long.'

You pull me to you. Your kiss fills my lungs with salty tears and I breathe in despite the pain. I choke, but force my chest to accept the living water.

We fall forward into the sea. I'm sinking, drowning, but you won't let go and I pull you down as your limbs and gills remember how to work. Mine don't. My eyes are blurred; the water seems thick and muddy. Panic absorbs the remainder of my mind and I kick and thrash, pushing you away.

*You have to want to return,* you say.

I force it, but I don't believe. I *know* I'm drowning.

*Please*, you say.

But my rebellious body refuses to work. I splash towards the shore, staggering onto the beach, and fall forward, vomiting out the cold dark poison that once sustained me. When I feel better, oxygen re-inflates my lungs and the pain is slipping away once more. I turn to see you still in the water.

'Come back with me,' I call. 'You can live here with me. We can still be together.'

You shake your head. Already you're changing, and you love being home.

'I've been so alone,' I say. 'Don't go back. Stay with me.'

But I know it is impossible now. The moment has passed and you can't return without more pain. The sea bursts from my eyes as you swim away, revelling in the weightless love given by the ocean. And suddenly I want it. I want to go home, but, with every passing moment, you are swimming farther away. I stumble forward once more down into the water, but the waves throw me back towards land. I call your name, but my cry goes unanswered.

I struggle back onto the beach, weak and drained. The living water no longer recognises me. I sob on the sand, hoping you'll hear my call.

'Don't give up on me,' I cry to you, but I know it's too late.

I look up to see a woman, then a man, then many people. They stare blankly as I sing, shambling towards me like asylum patients on lithium. The siren song pours from my lips. It is the song of loneliness, and no matter how many come to answer the call, I will never feel full again.

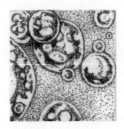

# AUTHOR'S NOTES

The voice of the character came to me first and this story wrote itself after that. My initial idea was to create a mystery that the reporter would solve: people would be disappearing from the apartment and he would eventually come to the conclusion that the new tenant was responsible. All of these ideas had to be formed in some way, and for a while I didn't know what shape they would take.

The first line floated across my mind as I was trying to fall asleep. Quickly followed by the shape and direction of the story. This is usually a bad thing, because I'm incredibly lazy once I'm drifting off and I don't like to rouse myself to take notes. Having said that, I do most of my plotting just in my mind, often working out all the problems and characterisation before I commit a word to the page. This is a method that mostly works best for me because I find once I've plotted on paper it almost feels like I've written the story, and the compulsion to write in full lessens.

Fortunately I remembered that first line the next morning, and by then I'd already established all of the characters. That same day another Whovian friend contacted me and reminded me that I'd promised to use him as a character sometime. I thought – Oh. That's brilliant! Of course! The reporter is called 'Andre' after my friend, Andre Tessier.

After that, Samara's story was as hypnotic as her song and the flow of this story occurred as though it was being washed in from the sea.

# THE TOYMAKER'S HOUSE

'Come back to work,' Simon said. 'I don't want to demean what you've been through, but it might help take your mind off things.'

Caron always found it hard to resist Simon Marshall. His enthusiasm had been the driving force that kept her in the film industry.

'It's a great script,' Simon pointed out. 'And I found this terrific SFX guy. I need you Caron. No one is as organised as you, and the temp Assistant Director is driving me mad with her total stupidity.'

'Say it like it is, Si, don't hold back,' Caron laughed.

'I mean it. I'm beginning to think I employed her to be on her back. She's been through most of the crew and is working her way over to the cast … Tell me what I want to hear. Come back in tomorrow and save me from strangling the little bitch.'

'Okay. When you put it that way … Anyway, I think

292

Stuart would prefer it if I kept busy.'

Caron's doctor had advised against an early return to work. It was only a month after her pregnancy had ended in a still-birth. Seven months in, stretch-marks and extra pounds, and Caron had unexpectedly given birth to a dead son. The pain of the labour, coupled with the months of excitement and waiting for their child, had all left a mark on her that would not be easily erased.

'It'll do you good,' Stuart said as he poured over a contract for one of his clients. He was one of the best agents in the business and people clamoured to be on his books. Caron had met him when one of his clients was hired to co-star in a movie she was working on. She'd only been Assistant Director 3 at that time, but Stuart didn't care about what job she did, because it was obvious they hit it off straight from the start.

'Simon will keep me so busy. I won't have time to think,' Caron said.

Stuart nodded, but was sensitive enough to look up to see if she was okay. 'We'll try again, babe. As soon as the doc says it's okay.'

Caron sat on his knee and cuddled up to him. She'd dropped so much weight since the funeral, Stuart and her mother had both been concerned that she'd become ill. She was little more than seven and a half stone, which was smaller than she had been when she'd first conceived. Although she'd tried to hide it, Caron had been suffering from a quiet depression.

'Just promise me you won't forget to eat,' Stuart said.

Caron kissed him, and he was distracted from the contract for a while as she curled up in his arms.

'You bet,' she said. 'I'm actually looking forward to going back to work.'

'I really think it will do you good,' Stuart said. 'You know, darling, I'm actually relieved. I was a bit worried that you might be home alone too much, secretly brooding.'

Later that evening, Caron's mother had been less than enthusiastic about it.

'Sweetheart! Whatever are you thinking? It is way too soon for that.'

'Oh come on, Mom. You know I'm a workaholic. The film sounds really exciting and Simon is having trouble with the new AD,' Caron said.

'I really don't think it's a good idea …'

Caron wouldn't be put off, she needed to go back. Brooding over the loss of her child would be even more unhealthy than returning to work, but she couldn't make her mother understand that all she wanted was to take her mind off things.

'Hey!' said Simon as Caron turned up on set, clipboard in hand and a full schedule for the day's filming already organised. 'This is amazing. It's great to have you back. How are you feeling?'

'Let's get to work,' Caron said, changing the subject.

'Yeah. About that. I have to keep the bimbo, she's on contract, but I've put her under you. Get her making coffee for everyone and keep her out of my hair, will you?

Caron smiled and shook her head. 'You are so politically correct, Si …'

'Yeah, I know … so sue me.'

'One day, someone will. But until then, where's the girl?' she asked.

'Trish!' Simon shouted.

Trish appeared a few minutes later from one of the trailers. She looked ruffled and disorientated. As she drew nearer, Caron could smell the stale odour of alcohol on her breath.

'I'll leave you to it,' Simon said, and he ducked away as quickly as possible.

'Right. For a start, you're going home,' said Caron. 'Get yourself straightened up, and if I learn of you shagging around on set again you'll be off this picture faster than you can drop your knickers.'

'You can't talk to me like that!' Trish said. 'I'm under contract.'

'If you want respect, and indeed to gain another contract as an AD in any format again, then you'll damn well sort yourself out. Dress professionally. Start doing the job you've been hired to do. This is not a club 18-30, Trish. This is a business. Now go home. I want you back in here tomorrow at 6.00 am, ready to work.'

'You can't do this to me …' Trish protested. 'I'm not a child; you can't just send me home.'

'Yes I can. I'm first AD here and I'm not happy with you. You could always resign if you don't agree?'

Trish shook her head. 'No.'

She knew resigning would be a bad idea mid-shoot, as it would be unlikely anyone would hire her again. Rumours spread quickly in the business.

'Think about what I've said,' Caron said before she left. 'I want improvement, or Si will want you out of here. You may not realise this now, but this is for your own good.'

Trish was furious that Caron had turned up and been given so much power over her. *No way will I make it easy for them to shove me out,* she thought. As she drove home, she pondered the problem. *I don't want to lose this job. I love it!* She'd been having too much of a good time, and now she'd been pulled up for it. She had to admit, even to herself, that it was something of a fair cop.

There were two ways this could go. Trish weighed up the pros and cons. She could ignore Caron's instructions, which meant she would lose this job, leaving with no reference. That would mean she was guaranteed to be blacklisted from every production company that any of the team worked for. Rumours spread quickly in this business – she would probably never work again. Or she could knuckle down and prove to them that she was capable of working in this environment and behaving, as Caron had put it, 'professionally'. She didn't like being told it by someone she'd just met, but Trish knew Caron was right. She hadn't been very discreet and had lost the respect that an AD deserved.

By the time she reached her apartment, Trish had talked herself round. 'Stupid!' she told herself. 'I've been really stupid. Now they think I'm some kind of bimbo.'

Caron had given her options though, so it wasn't all over yet. If she proved her worth, she could still salvage things, and she'd get that good reference to take away to the next job. There was one small problem with this though. She really fancied the SFX guy, Mark. As soon as she met him she knew he'd be a bit of a challenge. He wasn't like the other guys in the crew. He was shy, reserved and something of a mystery man.

*Okay,* Trish thought. *This could actually work to my advantage. Playing coy might not be such a bad thing under the circumstances.*

Trish set her sights on Mark. It would give her a reason to stay focused, because the thought of being ordered around by Caron and Simon, all for their stupid reference, just wasn't enough of an incentive.

From that first day Caron took over as Assistant Director, the schedule quickly got back on track and Simon was happy.

'I've chosen this place because the house is truly warped. I couldn't replicate it if I tried,' Simon told Caron a few days later when they changed location. They were moving from the studio to a house 50 miles away.

'This is the house of the SFX guy?'

'Yes. It's perfect for *The Toymaker's House*. Wait till you see it.'

As Caron drove up to the location, a weird feeling prickled over the back of her neck. If she were superstitious, which she wasn't, she would have thought that someone had walked over her grave. Instead she shook the feeling off. She was tired, the gruelling schedule of the shoot was taking its toll on her barely recovered body, but she was determined to get back into the demanding routine she'd been used to.

The house appeared to be on a normal street. Caron followed the sat-nav's directions, turned into the road and carried on down to the end.

'In 400 yards, turn right ...'

Caron turned the car into a surprisingly sudden country lane that led off from the road and down a wide, bumpy, gravelled track. About 500 yards down, the track curved left and Caron briefly wondered if she'd gone wrong when she found herself circling a huge old barn. Around the back, out on an unkempt field, she saw the crew trailers and food wagon and pulled in next to Simon Marshall's car, which was parked behind the barn.

Through her windscreen she saw that the barn was

converted. There was a large, impressive doorway that stood open and numerous extra windows that looked down on the courtyard with a gleaming malevolence.

*Okay, so the house is creepy. Now I know what Simon meant,* she thought.

She got out of the car and reached for her bag and folder. Trish had been designated AD for the morning session and Caron would now relieve her and send her home for the rest of the day. But first she would have to find her and get the rundown on how the schedule had gone so far. Fortunately Trish had taken on board the threat of dismissal and had begun to behave a little more dignified. Even Simon hadn't complained about her the last few days, so Caron wasn't expecting any problems.

She walked up to the house. A weird sensation, like a tingling in her arms and legs, made her halt and look up at the windows on the second floor. It felt like she was being watched by a thousand hateful eyes. Above the door was a pane of glass that stretched up almost to the roof. This close, Caron could see through the glass the staircase that spiralled up the other side of the window, and under normal circumstances she would have thought it a nice feature, but standing at the top, faces turned towards her, were four statues.

'What the …?'

'Grotesque, aren't they?' said Simon as he came out of the front door. 'Thought I heard your car. We've just stopped for a tea-break.'

'What are they?' Caron asked.

'Dolls. Toys. Go in and climb the stairs. Get a better look.'

Caron shuddered, feeling an overwhelming urge to back away and run to her car, but she forced her feet to move and stepped over the threshold.

Inside, there was an absence of sound. It was as though all noise was sucked out of the front door and into the field, or worse still, that the house itself was consuming any sound that might be made. Caron paused at the foot of the stairs, and then, helplessly drawn, she began to climb. The staircase wound inwards and then back to the window, where a large balcony held the dolls. From outside, Caron had been sure they were looking over the courtyard, but as she reached the balcony she found the figures facing the stairs as though waiting for her.

The first one at the top was child size and was stood on a plinth that put its horrible face at eye level with her. It had the cheeks and rosy complexion of a sweet, plump girl of six. Little hands were half reaching out as if to be hugged by a parent. She was wearing a Little Red Riding Hood dress and cape. At first glance it appeared to be a pretty, sweet, life-size porcelain doll. Its eyes, though, were terrible. Tiny spikes pierced the eyelids, pushing them back and wide open to stare, dry eyed and horrified, out onto the staircase. The expression of the doll – and for a moment Caron almost thought 'child' – was one of abject terror and pain.

Caron took a step back, only to find Simon behind her.

'That … is hideous,' she said.

'Yeah,' said Simon. 'He's got a thing about stakes in the eyes. Look at the next one.'

An adult male doll was pierced through the head and body and spun vertically on a large skewer as though he were a pig roasting over a fire. The spike emerged from its groin and was embedded in the display plinth. Again the eyelids were pierced, but this time the doll looked as though it had tried to force its eyes shut, and the spikes had dragged half out of the brow above, piercing the lower part of the eye instead. A brown, rancid-looking pus was painted around the wounds. The male doll's arms were rigid at its sides, but Caron was shocked when the hands clenched and opened in a reflexive gesture. The doll was dressed as a woodcutter and an axe rested against the wall, just out of reach of his twitching hands.

'Oh my God!' said Caron. 'It looks as though he's been captured in the moment of being skewered alive.'

'Yes,' Simon replied. 'And the hands are moving, a bit like when you cut a chicken's head off and it's body still runs around for a while.'

Caron peered closer. 'How has he done that? Maybe electrics running through the body and down the spike?'

Simon shrugged. 'The two at the window are the worst.'

And indeed they were. Caron had never seen anything like the two dwarves and hoped she never would again.

The eyes of the female dwarf flickered over a pair of thick safety pins that penetrated the lids and were fastened to the skin below each eye. Caron could see dark brown irises painted in the gap as though the dwarf had been caught trying to open its eyes. The dummy's hands were outstretched and had sharp titanium poles rammed through the backs, exiting the downturned palms only to be buried in the wooden plinth below. The model was wearing normal clothing: jeans and a sweater; which made the overall effect infinitely worse. Caron could see that the dwarf-doll was mounted on the plinth by a spike inserted in its anus that seemed to pass all the way through its tiny body, exiting via the back of its neck. This made the doll's head appear lopsided. Spikes penetrated the dwarf's bare feet, and Caron saw the tiny, misshapen toes twitch and spasm.

Swallowing dryly, Caron turned her attention to the other model. The male dwarf was naked and had been crucified. A black spike was driven through its forehead, holding the small body against a solid wood beam, while its hands were stretched out and nailed into the wall. A rusty spike had been inserted into the doll's penis and through the body into the wall. One foot only was secured, the other, in a macabre touch, still in a child-size trainer, hung lifelessly over the stand. The eye sockets were empty, cavernous holes and the mouth was wide open in a silent scream. Caron gagged and stepped back.

'I've seen enough,' said Caron, turning back to the stairs.

She hurried down and out into the courtyard, to stare at the crew as they congregated at the food wagon. She took in a lungful of air, realising she'd been holding her breath until she got outside. The sounds of normality were welcome. The air inside the barn was tainted by something, but she couldn't put her finger on what. There was a subtle smell of spices, or maybe it was incense that permeated the hallway and now drifted outside.

She took a tissue from her pocket and blew her nose, but the smell only intensified.

Simon put a hand on her shoulder.

'You okay? They are just dolls.'

Caron nodded. 'So this is your SFX man's home. Pretty sick place to live …'

'I suppose when you've created something like that then it doesn't gross you out. Anyway, we're using the staircase and dolls as part of the shoot.'

'You're right, you couldn't have recreated that. It seems beyond human imagination. It will be a terrifying sequence. They look so real.'

At that moment, Trish came around the side of the house and Caron greeted her. For a time her mind was taken away from the bizarre dolls as she went over the day's schedule. Filming had gone well, the props had been primed and the atmosphere of the house leant itself to the mood that Simon wanted the actors to create. Simon was pleased, especially as everything was on schedule.

'I'm clocking off then,' said Trish. 'See you tomorrow.'

'Thanks. You've done good, girl,' Caron said, and Trish smiled.

As Trish headed towards her car, she stopped and turned back to Caron. 'Thanks for ragging my ass that first day – did me some good.'

'It's easy to get carried away in our business,' Caron said. 'Where's the SFX guy anyway, I'd like to speak to him?'

'He's in his studio, and Simon says he's not to be disturbed.'

The afternoon stretched to early evening and Caron made sure everything ran smoothly as Simon directed the actors.

'It's not hard to be scared,' said the lead actress, Gina Bellom, during one of the breaks. 'This place gives me the creeps.'

At six o'clock the crew were preparing for their final scene, which was taking place on the stairs.

'Caron, this is Mark,' Simon said, approaching with someone else behind him. 'The Toymaker, I mean SFX guy. He owns the house.'

Caron shook Mark's hand and pulled back quickly. Mark looked normal. He was actually quite attractive in a geeky kind of way. He wore glasses, had floppy dark hair, cut in a fashionable style. He wore shirt and jeans that were smart, but casual. There was nothing unique or strange about him at all. *If you passed him in the street you would never guess the level of sick imagination he has*, Caron thought. But when Simon and Mark weren't looking, she couldn't resist the urge to wipe her hand down her skirt in a subconscious gesture.

'Where on earth do your ideas come from?' she asked. 'I've never seen anything like this place.'

'That's a few successes,' Mark said. 'You should see the failures …'

A tingling, unreasonable sense of fear rippled down Caron's spine as her imagination filled in the blanks. She saw in her mind's eye a studio full of half skewered and tortured bodies, still alive, still in pain, but unable to scream their agony through their paralysed lips.

Everything went black.

'Caron? Caron? You okay?'

'Jesus, what happened?'

'She's fainted.'

A flurry of blurred figures bustled around her.

Caron came round to find herself back inside the house and lying on a chaise longue in the Toymaker's lounge.

'Are you okay?' asked Mark, a genuine look of concern on his face.

Caron nodded. 'What happened?'

'You collapsed,' he said.

Caron looked around the room in alarm: she was

alone with Mark, and the thought terrified her. She tried to sit up but Mark placed a hand on her shoulder.

'Hey! Don't rush. Simon has gone to fetch you some water. You're safe, there's nothing to fear here.'

*I bet he told the dwarves that*, Caron thought as she lay back down. She was afraid to show the turmoil that raged inside her head. The insane thoughts she had about Mark and his 'art', and how she couldn't shake the terrible notion that the dolls weren't dolls at all. Her eyes cast around the Toymaker's lounge. It was full of unusual ornaments, jars and bottles. All with Chinese symbols and designs painted on them.

Mark saw her eyes fall on a huge Ming vase that stood in the corner of the room.

'I collect Chinese artefacts. Some of the jars and bottles still contain the original ointments and liquors that would have been used by their doctors.'

'Medicine jars?' Caron asked.

'Yes. Some of them, anyway. It's supposed to be potent stuff … but you wouldn't try it of course; after all these years, there's no telling how poisonous the stuff could be.'

'Why not empty them?' Caron asked.

'Because the contents are what make these jars so valuable.'

At that moment Simon came back, and Caron felt an overwhelming surge of relief. Mark's intensity and fanaticism seemed to go even as far as having these potentially poisonous potions in his living room. Caron knew then she didn't want to investigate any other rooms in the house, and fortunately they weren't scheduled to use any others.

'Here you are,' Simon said, bringing in a glass of water. 'Drink this.'

Caron took the glass and sipped slowly. She was overwhelmingly relieved to see Simon and even more relieved when Mark left the room to go and prepare the props for the final shoot. Her head started to return to normal.

'Sorry,' she said to Simon. 'I don't know what happened.'

'I do. I've been working you too hard, and under the circumstances …'

Caron shook her head. 'I think maybe I was too busy to eat today.'

After that, the days of the shoot at the house passed quickly. Caron made sure she ate regularly, even if it was a small snack here and there, and the conclusion of the filming rapidly approached.

'What are you going to do after this job finishes?' Trish asked her as they prepared the schedule for the last week.

'Simon has me lined up for his next project,' Caron said, 'but a week off first before that starts. What about you?'

'Well, thanks to that great reference you gave me, I'm starting work almost straight away on a new horror film. The SFX guy, Mark, is also working on it.'

Caron nodded. 'He's never out of work from what I

can gather.'

'Yeah. He's very unique. I'm going out with him for a drink later – to talk over the schedule.'

Caron grinned at Trish. 'Well, I guess there's no harm in that.'

Later Caron saw Trish and Mark leave for their drink, but she couldn't understand what she saw in the man. Self-consciously she gazed back at Mark's house. Caron had learnt to ignore the grotesque figures on the balcony once she got over the initial shock of them, but still whenever she passed the front of the house, she couldn't shake that overwhelming feeling of being watched. In her mind's eye, she imagined the dwarves, swivelling on their plinths to stare down at her through the large window. She never looked up; she didn't want to find those half-closed eyes, screaming with silent malevolence as they stared down at her. Still, it all came down to Mark and his warped mind, and Caron tried her hardest not to let it affect her professional judgement. She just didn't like the man and spent as little time in his company as she could.

Unlike Caron, Trish's approach to work was based more around the emotional attachments she could make with the male members of the cast and crew, and what benefits they might bring her in the future. Simply put, she was a slut. But she loved it. She'd toned it down a lot, though, learning to be more discreet. This worked to her benefit, and Caron had already sent her reference on to the next job. That's why she felt safe to let her new-found halo slip a little.

She'd been through most of the crew before they'd reached the *Toymaker's House* location. Mark was a fascination and this kept her on track, despite the urge to have a little fun. She realised she wanted him to like her, really like her, not just sleep with her. They'd chatted a little each day at the food wagon, or on set when he uncovered his latest monstrosity.

True to her initial promise, Trish had played shy and coy to Mark's reserved friendship. That's why she was so was pleased when Mark invited her out for a drink and then back to the house later that evening.

Unlike Caron, Trish didn't feel strange about the dolls – they were just special effects, after all. She saw it as 'art', and it made Mark all the more intriguing.

She watched him pour her drink from a fancy jar on a Chinese-style bureau in the lounge. She'd not been in that room before and she found it fascinating.

'What's this?' she asked as he handed her the drink.

'A kind of brandy liqueur,' he answered. 'It's rather strong though, so I hope you can hold your drink.'

Trish laughed, leaning back on the chaise. She draped herself lasciviously and turned her pale blue eyes up to Mark as she brought the shot glass to her lips.

'Well, I'm sure you wouldn't take advantage of me if I wasn't.'

Mark smiled, then pushed his glasses back up his nose.

Trish sipped the drink and crossed her legs. 'Why not sit down beside me?' she suggested.

'Do you like the drink?' Mark asked.

'Yes – it's warming.' She sipped some more. 'Aren't you having any?'

'It's made from an ancient recipe,' Mark said, turning and gently repositioning some of the vases on a nearby table. 'Chinese physicians used it to numb their patients during minor surgeries. It had surprising effects. Basically it paralysed the nervous system, creating a state of unconsciousness in the patient. The idea was that they then couldn't feel the surgery; their minds and bodies would shut down completely. It's not unlike suspended animation.'

Trish frowned and looked at the final dribble of liqueur in the glass.

'Yeah. Right. Next you'll be telling me all your dolls are real people you gave this to.'

'Precisely,' said Mark, turning to look at her. 'I don't think they can feel a thing either. But they are all very much alive.'

'Show … whaz your shaying …' Trish tried to lift her hand to her mouth. Her tongue felt swollen, her limbs suddenly weak. Blackness floated behind her eyes as she slumped back onto the chaise.

'Of course, you'll still be able to hear me for a while longer I should think. And don't worry; you won't feel a thing when the real work starts.'

Trish's eyes twitched, her fingers and toes spasmed and her body began to jerk as though she were having a seizure.

'That's perfectly normal,' Mark told her gently. 'The paralysis is reaching into every nerve ending, every muscle and every synapse in your brain. You will completely stop functioning. It's like turning off a switch on a computer. It all still works when you re-boot, but when off, it simply stops functioning. Clever, isn't it? There is so much that people don't understand about Chinese medicine. They think it is all acupuncture and hokey pokey. But actually they are among the most informed on age manipulation. The ancients had a cure for cancer too. The art of it was lost long ago. Or at least, it was hidden away in these jars and others like them. I'm still learning what the contents do and how to reproduce them.'

Mark bent over Trish; she could see him in a blurry haze now. A claustrophobic terror was clutching her heart even as Mark began to strip off the bottom half of her clothing. She felt the stockings she'd worn being ripped away, along with the thong. She was bare from the waist down as he pulled her roughly onto the floor. She tried to talk again, tell him she didn't mind, she'd been more than willing – he hadn't needed to resort to this. But her body continued to twitch, even while her mouth clamped shut and froze.

'I came across the jars by accident. You see, before I

was in the movie business I studied medicine. Chinese medicine.'

Mark removed his glasses. Trish wondered why she hadn't noticed that slight curve to the eyes before. He was tall too, so it hadn't occurred to her he was of mixed race, with his westernised dress and ways. But she should have seen it; there was a certain Gok Wan look about him, after all.

'My mother was from China. I adopted her beliefs after my father died and we went to live there with her parents. I was five at the time.'

Trish was aware that Mark was unzipping himself. She felt him spread her legs, but nothing happened. He stood, removed all of his clothes. She couldn't see it, but was aware that he was folding them neatly onto the chaise. Then she felt and heard the plastic sheeting being put under her. Mark raised her bottom and slid the cold material under her naked skin.

'I think I know the kind of piercing you wanted this evening my dear, and I'm very happy to oblige,' Mark said. 'I always try to give what is deserved.'

At first she felt nothing. The rod was thicker than those used on the dwarves, the man and the child. Mark moved it inside her gently as first, as though he were trying to arouse her, and then he pulled his arm back and rammed it as deep and sharp as he could, right into her vagina.

Trish would have screamed if she could. Her whole

body exploded with pain as the rod pierced her cervix and entered her womb. Her body continued to twitch and spasm in some parody of orgasm. But it was agony, not pleasure that flooded her body. Her mind blanked, switched off, as something snapped inside her skull. She didn't feel the second rod enter her temple. Mark prised open her mouth, feeding in the penis-shaped, barbed rod of another thick skewer.

'I think you will appreciate the irony,' said Mark. 'I heard all about you before you arrived on set. I make it my business to know who I'm working with. The roadies were keen to talk about you and your exploits.'

Trish's mouth clamped over the rod, the muscles inside tightened and released in a sucking motion even as the barb cut up her tongue and burrowed into the back of her throat. Her teeth ground hard against the metal over and over again until there was nothing left but a crumpled mass of stumps.

'There's a cure for the paralysis, in case you're wondering. Obviously the doctors had to be able to bring their patients around again. The only trouble is, after this, you'd beg me to put you back under. I like to create a half-state sometimes. It makes the subject more artistically interesting. When I've finished, you'll have some awareness again, but not enough to feel the pain. I'm an artist, not a sadist.'

But Trish did feel pain. It was the worst agony she'd ever experienced; so much so that her mind was completely lost. She didn't even have enough remaining intellect to wonder on what basis Mark had made his assumption that his ministrations didn't hurt.

Caron woke in a cold sweat.

'What's wrong?' asked Stuart pulling her into his arms even as she trembled and shook, her ragged breath tearing painfully with every palpitating beat of her heart. The images floated behind her eyes as she hugged him closely.

'Awful dream. I think the content of this film is playing on my mind too much.'

'Maybe it was too soon to return,' Stuart said gently.

Caron nuzzled him. Her heart rate was slowly returning to normal but she needed his closeness to reassure her that she had only been dreaming.

'Only a few more days and I'll be off for a week. I don't mind saying I'm ready for a rest.'

Stuart went back to sleep quickly, but Caron lay awake. The horrible dream still lingered. She'd be glad to be finished with *The Toymaker's House*. And she hoped she never saw Mark again.

'Trish has done a runner,' Simon said. 'I'm livid. I got in this morning to find her trailer space cleared of all of her crap. She waited till we gave her that reference and now she's done a bunk.'

Caron stared at Simon. 'I don't believe it. She only

had a few days left. I can't imagine why she would …'

'She was telling me she has a new man in her life,' Mark said, coming into the trailer. 'We went out for a drink last night. Then she said she had to pick up a few things from here. She wasn't long. I had no idea she was cleaning out all of her stuff.'

'What new man?' Caron asked. Something about the shift of Mark's eyes made her feel uneasy enough to suspect him of lying.

'I didn't ask his name. But someone she's on the new shoot with, I guess.'

'She told me you were on her next picture.'

'Me?' Mark said. 'That's not right. Simon's already booked me for his next one. I guess we'll be working together again, Caron.'

Caron felt a sickening ripple of fear curl up into her stomach.

'I don't believe Trish has quit,' Caron said to Simon once they were alone again. 'I think something has happened to her.'

'What are you saying?'

'I had this awful dream last night, Si. It was about Trish and Mark … In my dream he …' Caron stopped.

'Caron, dreams don't mean anything. You and I both know that. Let's face it, the content of this film is pretty sick, and we've been working intensely for months …'

'He killed her, Si. He killed her and he turned her into one of those … *things*.'

Simon sighed. He wasn't in the mood for female hysterics today; there was still too much to do.

'Maybe you should call it a day here today. I can manage, and I know you've been through a lot.'

'Don't patronise me, Si. I'm fine. But there's just … something wrong here. Can't you feel it?'

Simon shook his head.

'Go home. Get some sleep. I'll see you tomorrow for the final shoot. It will all feel better when the final take is in the can.'

Caron went home. She knew there was no point in arguing with Simon, but she was deeply concerned about Trish. Before she left, she retrieved Trish's contact details and tried to call her.

'*This is Trish. I'm hot and ready to trot … leave me a message or miss out.*'

'Trish. It's Caron. I'm just ringing to see if you're okay. Can you call or text me? Just let me know you're fine.'

Caron hung up and left the trailer.

Mark watched Caron open her car door as he stood in the window above. His hand rested on the head of the female dwarf. Behind him a new mannequin was placed at the top of the stairs, still wrapped in brown paper. The doll twitched and jerked, the paper rustling, as though it was trying to fight free from the bonds and spikes that pinned it to a wooden plinth. The female dwarf's eyes tried to blink, but Mark didn't notice, even though he absentmindedly stroked her hair. He watched Caron

316

drive away.

'Hey Mark?' Simon shouted from below. 'Where's that new doll you promised me for the last scene?'

Mark looked at the wrapped figure and headed for the stairs.

'It's in my studio.'

Simon went with him; he hadn't ventured up the stairs and hadn't seen the new addition. But Mark had no intention of unwrapping his latest artwork until after the crew left for good.

Mark glanced back towards the window as he heard Caron leave. Instinct told him that Caron could be a problem. Shrugging, he walked slowly downstairs.

'This way,' he said, leading Simon from the house.

The studio was as horrible as Caron's imagination had determined, but Simon barely noticed the half-dissected figures or the hideous remains of animals. He believed these were all the artistic creations of Mark.

The new figure stood in the corner, a sheet draped over it.

'Let's see then,' Simon said, and as Mark removed the cover, he couldn't help gasping at the horror of the doll. 'Oh my God!'

Behind him, Mark smiled. 'I'm particularly proud of this one.'

The next day, Caron drove into work with a heavy heart. Trish hadn't replied to her many phone messages and she'd had another terrible night's sleep. Even so, she was determined just to get through the last day. She could barely wait to be off the project and take a much-deserved week's rest. As she drove into the courtyard of what she now thought of as the *Toymaker's House*, anxiety squeezed the air from her lungs. For a moment she thought she saw Trish's shape silhouetted in the window, and then it was gone.

*I'm going nuts,* she thought. *Maybe I did return to work too soon.*

Simon was in the doorway as Caron parked.

'All set?' she asked, trying to appear calm and professional.

'Yes. Last day, but lots to do. Mark's latest creation is as sick as it could possibly be. Just thought I ought to warn you …'

Caron made some excuse about checking on the actors and crew and went off instead to the make-up trailer. She decided to keep off set as much as possible that day.

'Mark's made that final doll to look like me,' said Gina Bellom as Caron entered.

'Oh?'

'Yeah! It's gross. But fortunately I won't be in the scene with it. By then I'll be murdered.'

'Is it me or is it cold in here?' Caron said quickly to disguise the shudder that wracked her body at Gina's words. It felt so possible that Gina could be killed, that she didn't know what else to say. 'Have you got everything you need, Gina?'

'Yes. My final scene this morning, then I'm out of here. Flying out to the Caribbean tomorrow for a fortnight – I'm hoping to shift this trailer pallor before the next job.'

Caron left the trailer and went to check on the crew. All seemed well and everyone was aware of the schedule they had to follow. They were all ready for the final scene.

Caron arrived on set and checked that everyone and everything was in place.

'Action!' she called, and as filming began she and Simon watched through the monitor connected to the cameras.

The evil Toymaker chased Gina across the set. As directed, she stumbled and fell. The Toymaker was on her and Simon shouted, 'Cut!', as Gina let loose an ear-splitting scream.

They reviewed the footage.

'That's in the can!' said Simon, which was unusual, because he rarely accepted a first take.

'Okay, set up for the next scene,' Caron shouted, and the crew burst into action.

'It's a shame you can't make the end-of-shoot party, Gina,' Simon told the actress as he kissed both of her cheeks. 'But have a great trip.'

Mark wheeled in his latest doll, still covered in a sheet,

on a low trolley.

'Okay, guys. Let's get this off and in position for the final scene.'

'Careful,' said Mark. 'Don't damage her …'

The doll was set up in the middle of the second set, which was of the Toymaker's studio.

'Jesus,' said the cameraman. 'That's … awful.'

Caron couldn't resist looking, even though she knew she didn't want the image of any more of Mark's macabre dolls in her head.

For a moment she wasn't sure what she was seeing. Only the head and shoulders were visible from where she was sitting. The doll was blonde and similar in height and build to Gina Bellom, but Caron felt an overwhelming certainty that it wasn't a doll, but someone carefully chosen because she looked like Gina. The face of the doll had been severely mutilated; there were spikes like tribal piercings in the skin of its cheek bones. One eye was pinned completely open while the other was sewn shut. The mouth was all wrong. The lower lip was pulled down on one side and stapled to the chin, the skin stretched almost to ripping point.

Despite herself, Caron had to see more. She stood up and moved closer, and as she did so, the real horror of the creation was revealed. The doll was naked. The stomach was cut open – revealing the internal organs, as the flesh was stretched wide and pinned to two pieces of wood on either side of the slender body. Inside the now-exposed womb was a small foetus, no more than 20 weeks judging by the size and development.

Caron raised her hands to her mouth in horror. 'Oh my God!' she murmured, and then she turned and ran.

Simon was waiting outside the bathroom when Caron emerged. She'd only just made it in time before she threw up the entire contents of the breakfast Stuart had made her eat that morning.

'Sorry,' Simon said. 'I should have thought. It was so insensitive to have you on set just then. I'll understand if you don't want to come back in.'

Caron's face was blotchy and pale. Nausea still curled around her insides.

'Yeah. Bad timing for this movie, I think,' she said, and gave him a half-hearted smile. 'It's okay, go back in and finish up. I have other things I can do, and I'll take you up on that offer. I've had more than enough of the Toymaker's dolls to last me a lifetime.'

The day and the shoot drew to a close, and as the crew packed up, Caron gave a sigh of relief that it was finally over. She saw Mark briefly removing his new doll back to the studio, covered once more, but chose to ignore him. She didn't want to get into any casual conversations with him; the man gave her the creeps and she just couldn't shake the insane feeling that he really was a psycho.

'Caron, come on in. We're having a drink here with

Mark then we're all moving onto the restaurant I've booked. All expenses are on the production today, as the producer is delighted at how well we've kept on budget.'

'Thanks, Si. But I think I need to get home now.'

'Okay. But I'll call you in a day or two to talk about the next picture.'

Caron nodded, but she wasn't at all sure she could stomach another set with Mark on it.

As she packed her briefcase and private documents up into her car, Caron's phone vibrated in her pocket. She stared at the screen for a moment, reading the words over and over, before she could believe what she read.

*'Upstairs. Help me.'*

The message was from Trish.

Caron looked up at Mark's house, the Toymaker's house, and saw another shape now positioned between the two dwarves. All three dolls stared down at her. Caron slammed the car boot down and went to the driver's door.

*This is insane. She's not there. She's not dead. It's some sick game she's playing with Mark.*

As Caron turned on the engine her phone vibrated again.

*'Please!'*

She sat for a moment in the car looking at her phone, and then up at the shadowy figures watching her from the upper landing. She reached out and switched off the engine. If Trish really was in trouble, she couldn't just leave her.

At the door to the house, Caron could hear the sounds of chatting and revelry coming from Mark's lounge.

'Here's to the next great movie,' shouted Mark, and Caron heard a champagne cork pop.

'Hear, hear,' Simon said. 'Great champers, Mark!'

These were all familiar sounds after weeks of intensive shooting and Caron found nothing odd in their celebrations. She debated going in and asking Simon to come upstairs with her, but was afraid to because Mark was there. Instead she stared at the staircase. She had thought from the first day that something was severely wrong here. Sweat trickled down her back, an icy finger tracing her spine.

Her phone vibrated again but she ignored it this time. Caron's feet took on a will of their own and she found herself at the bottom of the stairs, foot on the first step. She began to climb, slowly as first, and then she hurried. *He could come out of the party at any time!*

The balcony was in shadow as she reached the top step. She looked for the light switch but once again considered the possibility of discovery if she used it. Instead she moved forward, heading towards the window. *A quick look, then I'm out of here!*

The figure was partially wrapped in brown paper. Caron was afraid to touch it, but she had to see inside. In the gloom, Caron could see that one hand had broken free from the wrapping and was clutching a mobile phone, the fingers sped over the keyboard and once again, her own phone buzzed in her pocket. She reached out, yanked at the paper, ripping it downwards and away from the face.

Trish stared back at her, her eyes half closed but glowing with a fierce, primal intelligence.

'Fuck!'

Caron stepped back, her mind refusing to take in what she was seeing. She felt a movement by her hand, and tiny fingers reached out and stroked her palm. She looked down and saw that one of the dwarves had taken her hand in its own and was holding it. She pulled away and looked again at the pitiful creatures pinioned on their wooden bases. Now their mouths were opening and closing silently. Caron looked back at Trish, and saw the terror and pain in her hooded eyes. She realised she had to go down and tell Simon and the crew.

'I'm sorry,' she said. 'I'll get help!'

She turned, and as she did so, she saw the slight movement of the woodcutter as his hands and body twisted and turned, always reaching for his axe but never quite close enough to grasp the handle. Beside him the Little Red Riding Hood girl cried tears of blood.

Caron backed away, hands waving in front of her. She blinked back tears and turned and raced down the stairs, her feet clattering as she went.

She ran across the lobby and burst into the lounge.

'Si!'

Simon was sitting on the chaise. His eyes were blank and frozen, and the other crew members were collapsed around him on the floor. Mark stood by his Chinese bureau.

'Caron,' he turned and smiled, holding out a small shot glass. 'I've been waiting for you.'

## AUTHOR'S NOTES

Well this was a strange one. I had been watching some *Doctor Who* episodes with David and we'd being talking about 'The Celestial Toymaker', a '60s story that starred Michael Gough as the Toymaker, dressed in an oriental Mandarin outfit. That night I dreamt about my Toymaker. In the dream he was wearing Chinese Imperial clothing. I remember going to use his bathroom and discovering these hideous toys that everyone thought were just dolls, however I realised that they were in fact real people. When I tried to expose the 'Toymaker' he'd already poisoned everyone, and I ran from the house terrified. End of dream.

I woke shaken and upset and couldn't sleep again for

a while that night as the horror of the story played in my mind.

My imagination has filled in the details since then, and I think this is the most horrific story I've written to date. I particularly wanted to challenge myself on describing the most nightmarish scenes and tortures that I could. It's a pet hate of mine that female horror writers are sometimes categorised as horror/romance. Although this genre is perfectly valid it annoys me because there is the implication tagged on to it that women can't write 'real' horror. It's a discussion that's come up many times during panels at different conventions and during conversations I've had with various authors. It's also something that David and I have talked about at length, and I'm of the mind-set that it is the intention *behind* the writing that counts. If I intend to write horror then that is what I write.

I intended to write a horror story here. Something that wasn't supernatural but was more a psychological thriller. I also intended to provide graphic descriptions of the dolls and of Trish's murder. In this way I hoped to create that sense of fear and tension I'd experienced when I had the dream that gave me this scenario in the first place.

I could have finished *The Toymaker's House* in a variety of different ways, maybe let Caron out to call the police … Or maybe the dolls could have turned on their maker. But then that wouldn't have given you enough leeway to make up your own nightmares – would it?

# Poems

This is a short section featuring six of my favourite poems. I've chosen each of these for reasons that are somewhat private but I will briefly talk about the influences behind each poem. All of the poems in this section were written between 2006 and 2009. I haven't written many since and now see myself as a prose writer more than a poet. At the time these were experiments that I was proud of, and you'll notice that they are all performance poetry. They were written with the idea of reading them aloud in mind.

I was greatly influenced by Carol Anne Duffy. One of my favourite poetry collections, even to this day, is *The World's Wife*. Carol Anne was an honorary fellow of the University of Bolton where I studied, and I was privileged to see her read many times. Over the years I've dabbled with various types of poetry. I love the ambiguity of poetry and the tightly described imagery.

Poetic imagery is one of the things I strive to include in my prose, which is why my descriptions tend to be concise and fast-paced. It's a deliberate style that I worked hard to develop and I hope you will enjoy the story behind each one.

# Not All Vampires Drink Blood

It is the touch of my body, firm against yours
That rips your soul from this universe.
I drink from your lips, deeper than vein
Take you to heaven, drive you insane

It is only the way of one of my kind
To make you suffer, losing your mind.
I drain your energy, without using tooth
Make myself glow with your glorious youth.

I am the succubus who enters your dreams
Taking your vigour through your ecstasy screams
You can't turn me away: I'm in your blood.
I pull on your potency like a woman should.

And though you are emptied you come back for more
Down on your knees you knock on my door
I love you, my beauty, at least for now
Till all that you are has fed me somehow.

And then I can walk out into the rain,
Lovely, young, beautiful again.

# AUTHOR'S NOTES

I love the idea of the succubus, which I've also explored in the first story in this book, *Ameline*. When I wrote this poem towards the end of 2006, I was completing my MA in Creative Writing. As with all of the poems here, I was looking to write something in the first person, from the perspective of the succubus, and it is a short dramatic monologue.

# DEMON LOVER

The smokescreen of youth hides a wizened frame;
Hooked claws, scraping the floor,
Penetrate an aura with a single curl.

You will pay for the service, orgasm guaranteed.
Pain of my length, a sharpened sword,
Disguised as pleasure.

This is how I feed.

Five years of life – given so easily – Your
Female energy – pours from the mouth in
A moist aging rush.

My talons hold fast, feeding, growing,
Phallic vigour becoming my glamour;
A facade that the lonely see.

I am a demon lover.

I know climax, I know ecstasy. I am the
Ultimate extreme sport. Giving me your
Passion is selling a piece of your soul.

But I never take too much, am never greedy.
And though it will never be the same again
I'll leave some of your life intact …

I am a demon lover
Open to me at your peril.

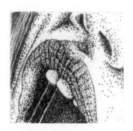

## AUTHOR'S NOTES

This is the incubus, which is the male version of the succubus.
But it could be read in many ways. I almost don't want to
write the next line as it would be nice if future generations
decide for themselves what this poem is about … Could I
have meant, for example, that casual sex is dangerous, 'an
extreme sport'? Or was I just telling the story of this particular
supernatural being? I'll let you analyse it. But I will say this:
at university I always saw Freud in everything …

# WEREWOLF

As we race together under the full moon
Your hunger call to me.
Like the first mortals we are unique
Original, the parents of a new race.
And yet – we look like them in the daytime.

In the dark we stalk our prey.
I am the swiftest,
And will feed our young while you
Stand by to protect us.

When you bite the back of my neck I submit,
Like a good bitch, to your superior strength.
But know this; I am the one who brings home
The food that you eat,
I am the one that follows, but leads.

I hold your paws as they change to fingers.
Transition crackles through our remoulding flesh
Painfully forced with the coming dawn.

In the morning, I guard you when you sleep.
We are exhausted but I cannot rest.
Our love has swollen my belly,
And I wait, wondering, will this
Baby be man, or wolf?

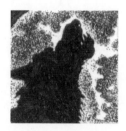

## AUTHOR'S NOTES

Ah. The male/female tussle. Who really is in charge when it comes to wolves? Or humans? I was going through a lot of life changes when I wrote this … read it how you will.

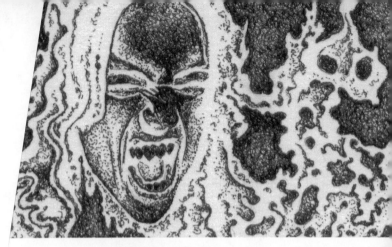

# PHOENIX

urn me at the stake and I elevate again;
Phoenix. An immortal. Wrapping my
eathered arms around the air.

Ashes reform into limbs, torso, face, eyes, hair.
My senses return as I suck in the feathers,
Disguise myself as human.

Renewed, reborn – I learn from previous mistakes;
I'll keep the shine from bursting forth,
Hide behind this dull exterior.

Humans dread what they do not understand;
My strong light stings their fragile eyes,
And they destroy what they fear.

But one day there will be a humanity that will accept

The Phoenix Super Nova. And then,
I will spread my wings and take on the world.

## AUTHOR'S NOTES

The idea of being immolated and then rising like a Phoenix from the ashes – a common metaphor that has been used repeatedly. If the shoe fits though, you wear it. This poem is about renewal. There are many times through our lives when we reinvent ourselves, or when people knock us down we get back up again and brush ourselves down.

# VAMPYRE

told me it was just a story –
arasitical being exists to suck the life
the living.

I knew, deep down, something inside me
ed for you to be real.

ey told me it was insanity –
truth in my nightmare world when you
me to me at night.

ut I felt you – you sucked me down, tore
my soul inside out.

They told me you were a figmentation –
But my imagination didn't believe you
Weren't real.

When you penetrated me – your fangs tore
away my inhibitions.

They told me the scars weren't real –
I'd hurt myself in some cry for help;
There were no Vampyres.

When I rose from my grave – the doctor cried
as I bled him.

He welcomes me tonight.

# AUTHOR'S NOTES

I've been asked many times if I believe in vampires. My usual response is 'No, they are fictional'. I do believe in vampires though, and I don't mean the kind that flash fangs. This poem is as much about human parasites as it is about vampires. Negativity sucks the life out of the living just as surely as any vampire ever did. Those who know me will understand what I mean about that.

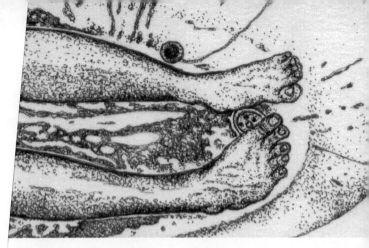

# I Wish I Was Dead
## (The cry of the unloved)

h I was dead;
rpse lying with open vein
ding into grey grouting

tiles absorb my pain;
ey are the sponge for my fury,
e well that fills with my blood tears

es would glare an empty accusation;
ul ripped from me,
t the ceiling of this mortal prison

wish I was dead;

Bone china skin hardening
Without the heat of kiln
Expression frozen;
The concluding moments recorded
On my face for all time

And my red – the closing blight;
The third dimension on greyscale
Giving ultimate colour to the finish

I wish I was dead;
And then the world would remember
The fragile child

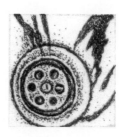

# AUTHOR'S NOTES

This is one of my favourite poems and I think it is because it is so delightfully morbid. I wanted to be in the head of someone wishing to commit suicide, but not necessarily because they were depressed or suffering from some other form of mental illness. This character is selfish about his/her urge to die. They romanticise it; seeing only that they would be remembered for having killed themselves.

# I WISH I WAS DEAD

It will probably surprise you to know that I suffered from depression for years. Hard to imagine now as I am a very positive, upbeat person. Depression can be selfish; you are obsessed with your own darkness and unhappiness. My life has changed a lot since I wrote this poem, and in some ways so has the meaning for me. At the time, I may well have been in the place where I wanted to die … or maybe I was just imagining that abyss. I have many philosophies about life. The one I live by, that keeps me focused, is that I truly believe negativity breeds negativity. Therefore I choose now to be happy and rarely get maudlin. But I can still appreciate, perhaps more than most, how bad things have to be before you look down into the darkness of the grave and so wish you could just lie down and close your eyes.

So concludes my collection, *Zombies In New York and Other Bloody Jottings.*

I hope the poems lulled away the horror of *The Toymaker's House* and you sleep well with the dreams that you want to have. Come back soon and stroll through the Moulin Rouge, or take a peek from the safety of these pages at the streets of New York as it fills with dissolving zombies. You never know, there might well be an Immortal Monster living in your neighbourhood (forewarned is forearmed) or a civil servant with a deadly clown addiction – be wary of those red and black balloons! I for one will remain curious about the remains extracted from the tar pits of La Brea and will enjoy the addiction of a certain sexy wolf.

For now though I recommend you avoid areas where there is an excess of fool's gold on the ground and, if you're a vampire, keep well away from angels.

Finally, I leave you with this … turn and run if you ever hear the haunting melody of the Siren's song …

*Sam Stone*

# Afterword

## Frazer Hines

As an actor often associated with the weird and the strange, mainly due to my travelling in the TARDIS in *Doctor Who* for several years in the Sixties, I was delighted to be asked by Sam to pen a few words to close her collection of unsettling tales.

I don't normally read fantastic fiction, preferring factual biographic fare, but I read Sam's first novel, *Killing Kiss*, while touring on a cruise ship a year or so back, and her work is gripping, unsettling and poetic. I therefore decided to pen something of my own as a tribute to her collection. I have dabbled with poetry off and on over the years, and so I leave you with my own contribution to this book, and hope that Sam's work gives you many sleepless nights:

# Zombies in New York

Walking the streets at night,
Zombies in New York,
Looking for you to scare and bite.
Zombies in New York.
All of them undead:
Zombies in New York.

Have you looked underneath your bed?
Zombies in New York.
Like bees around a hive,
Zombies in New York.
Looks like you're still alive!
Zombies in New York.
Batten the hatches down,
Zombies in New York.
Better still, try leaving town.
Zombies in New York.
You're now frightened like a mouse.
Zombies in New York.
Too late! They're in your house!

# Copyright Information

# About the Author

Dark Fantasy author Sam Stone began writing aged 11 after reading her first adult fiction book, *The Collector* by John Fowles. 'I'd never read anything like it. It was terrifying – but so exciting … That's when I realised I liked to be scared,' she admits.

Her love of horror fiction began soon afterwards when she stayed up late one night with her sister to watch Christopher Lee in the classic Hammer film *Dracula*. Since then she's been a huge fan of vampire movies and novels old and new.

The youngest of seven children, Sam struggled to find her own space and is a self-confessed bookworm. 'I always have a book on the go,' says Sam. 'It's my time. Life wouldn't be the same if I couldn't chill sometimes with a good book. It's where I learnt about life, long before I lived it.'

Sam's writing has appeared in seven anthologies for poetry and prose. Her first novel was the fulfilment of a lifelong dream. Like all good authors she drew on her own knowledge and passions to write it. The novel won the Silver Award for Best Horror Novel in *ForeWord* magazine's book of the year awards in 2007.

In September 2008 the novel was re-edited and republished by The House of Murky Depths as *Killing Kiss*. The sequel, *Futile Flame*, went on to become a finalist in the same awards for 2009. *Futile Flame* was later shortlisted for the British Fantasy Society Award for Best Novel 2010.

An eclectic and skilled prose writer, Sam also has a BA (Hons) in English and Writing for Performance and an MA in Creative Writing, which means that she is frequently invited to talk about writing in schools, colleges and universities in the UK. She is said to be an inspirational speaker.

# Other Telos Titles Available

URBAN GOTHIC: LACUNA AND OTHER TRIPS edited by DAVID J HOWE
Tales of horror from and inspired by the *Urban Gothic* televison series. Contributors: Graham Masterton, Christopher Fowler, Simon Clark, Steve Lockley & Paul Lewis, Paul Finch and Debbie Bennett.
£8.00 (+ £2.50 UK p&p) Standard p/b ISBN: 1-903889-00-6

KING OF ALL THE DEAD by STEVE LOCKLEY & PAUL LEWIS
The king of all the dead will have what is his.
£8.00 (+ £2.50 UK p&p) Standard p/b ISBN: 1-903889-61-8

THE HUMAN ABSTRACT by GEORGE MANN
A future tale of private detectives, AIs, Nanobots, love and death.
£7.99 (+ £2.50 UK p&p) Standard p/b ISBN: 1-903889-65-0

BREATHE by CHRISTOPHER FOWLER
*The Office* meets *Night of the Living Dead.*
£20.00 (+ £2.50 UK p&p) Deluxe signed and
numbered h/b ISBN: 1-903889-68-5

HOUDINI'S LAST ILLUSION by STEVE
SAVILE
Can the master illusionist Harry Houdini outwit
the dead shades of his past?
£7.99 (+ £2.50 UK p&p) Standard p/b ISBN: 1-
903889-66-9

ALICE'S JOURNEY BEYOND THE MOON by
R J CARTER
A sequel to the classic Lewis Carroll tales.
£6.99 (+ £2.50 UK p&p) Standard p/b ISBN: 1-
903889-76-6
£20.00 (+ £2.50 UK p&p) Deluxe signed and
numbered h/b ISBN: 1-903889-77-4

APPROACHING OMEGA by ERIC BROWN
A colonisation mission to Earth runs into
problems.
£7.99 (+ £2.50 UK p&p) Standard p/b ISBN: 1-
903889-98-7
£20.00 (+ £2.50 UK p&p) Deluxe signed and
numbered h/b ISBN: 1-903889-99-5

VALLEY OF LIGHTS by STEPHEN GALLAGHER
A cop comes up against a body-hopping murderer.
£9.99 (+ £3.00 UK p&p) Standard p/b ISBN: 1-903889-74-X
£20.00 (+ £3.00 UK p&p) Deluxe signed and numbered h/b ISBN: 1-903889-75-8

PRETTY YOUNG THINGS by DOMINIC MCDONAGH
A nest of lesbian rave bunny vampires is at large in Manchester. When Chelsey's ex-boyfriend is taken as food, Chelsey has to get out fast.
£7.99 (+ £2.50 UK p&p) Standard p/b ISBN: 1-84583-045-8

A MANHATTAN GHOST STORY by T M WRIGHT
Do you see ghosts? A classic tale of love and the supernatural.
£9.99 (+ £3.00 UK p&p) Standard p/b ISBN: 1-84583-048-2

SHROUDED BY DARKNESS: TALES OF TERROR edited by ALISON L R DAVIES
An anthology of tales guaranteed to bring a chill to the spine. This collection has been published to raise money for DebRA, a national charity working on behalf of people with the genetic skin blistering condition, Epidermolysis Bullosa (EB). Featuring stories by: Debbie Bennett, Poppy Z Brite, Simon Clark, Storm Constantine, Peter Crowther, Alison L R Davies, Paul Finch, Christopher Fowler, Neil Gaiman, Gary Greenwood, David J Howe, Dawn Knox, Tim Lebbon, Charles de Lint, Steven Lockley & Paul Lewis, James Lovegrove, Graham Masterton, Richard Christian Matheson, Justina Robson, Mark Samuels, Darren Shan and Michael Marshall Smith. With a frontispiece by Clive Barker and a foreword by Stephen Jones. Deluxe hardback cover by Simon Marsden.
£12.99 (+ £3.00 UK p&p) Standard p/b ISBN: 1-84583-046-6
£30.00 (+ £3.00 UK p&p) Deluxe signed and numbered h/b ISBN: 978-1-84583-047-2

BLACK TIDE by DEL STONE JR
A college professor and his students find themselves trapped by an encroaching horde of zombies following a waste spillage.
£7.99 (+ £2.50 UK p&p) Standard p/b ISBN: 978-1-84583-043-4

FORCE MAJEURE by DANIEL O'MAHONY
An incredible fantasy novel. Kay finds herself trapped in a strange city in the Andes … a place where dreams can become reality, and where dragons may reside.
£7.99 (+ £2.50 UK p&p) Standard p/b ISBN: 978-1-84583-050-2

HUMPTY'S BONES by SIMON CLARK
Something nasty is found in a village garden … but what happens when the bones are removed and Humpty once more stalks the Earth?
£9.99 (+ £2.50 UK p&p) Standard p/b ISBN: 978-1-84583-051-9

RULES OF DUEL by GRAHAM MASTERTON
with WILLIAM S BURROUGHS
A clever and pervasive novel, which turns
literature on its head, and makes the reader
work to be part of the evolving plot.
£9.99 (+ £2.50 UK p&p) Standard p/b ISBN:
978-1-84583-054-0

THE DJINN by GRAHAM MASTERTON
Graham Masterton's terrifying 1977 novel is
republished by Telos in a brand new edition,
complete with an exclusive introduction by the
author
£9.99 (+ £2.50 UK p&p) Standard p/b ISBN:
978-1-84583-052-6